Emigrants

Emigrants

a novel by
Ferreira de Castro

translated from the Portuguese by
Dorothy Ball

THE MACMILLAN COMPANY   NEW YORK
MACMILLAN NEW YORK, LONDON

First Printing

The Macmillan Company, New York
Collier-Macmillan Canada, Ltd., Galt, Ontario
Divisions of The Crowell-Collier Publishing Company

Printed in the United States of America

Library of Congress catalog card number: 62-18375

DESIGNED BY CHRISTIAN OHSER

Part One

BLACK and white, black and white, the black smooth and shining and the white really snow-white, was a magpie with its tail nervously twitching, moving about among the pine needles and heather, in and out of sight, and from time to time it would rise in flight to the very top of the pine tree, carrying in its beak some small sprig or dry twig.

The pinewood—thick trunks and rough creviced bark—drowsed austerely in the limpid silence of a spring afternoon. All its cones seemed to be sterile or nullified by Malthusian antidote, because down on the uneven and chestnut-colored ground no young pine tree lifted its little green branches to the sky. The bare boles, almost black, asymmetrical, were like pillars in a barbaric temple, and in its transparent dome the sun was weaving a fantastic silver tracery. At times the airy fabric thinned out into capricious liquid lights that flickered in the branches like bracelets, or flashed down to the ground, condensing into a treasure of exotic jewelry.

Farther down, and cutting off the slope, stretched the reddish line of the ditch that fenced in the serried crowd of lusty saplings —progeny the ancestor pines had felt no wish to keep under the shelter of their ancient wings.

To the left, beyond the lower slope of the hill, the houses of the village glittered white between the trance-still branches. And from that side too, surely on its way back from pecking the crimson trinkets on the cherry trees, a jackdaw came along from time to time to hide its particolored plumage in the pine-wood. "Shooah, shooah!" was the only sound that disturbed the airy silence of the old trance-still trees.

The magpie went on tirelessly poking about, searching, and then, rising up into the chosen treetop, it would go on building its nest—a big patch already, a thick mass of twigs set in the topmost fork of the pine tree.

Stretched out where he had thought the shade was most pleasant, Manuel da Bouça was watching the bird at work and thinking over his distant childhood days, when he used to ransack plains and hills in search of nests, just for the fun of finding them and boasting about it afterward to the other village lads. In those days he wouldn't have hesitated a minute. *Clip-clap,* he would have gone up the tree to see what state the new nest was in, and then he would go back later for the eggs or the featherless chicks with their eyes still unsealed and their small greedy beaks opening at the slightest sound. But today it would have to be a low tree to tempt him, and a jackdaw or wood pigeon, good with rice!

Yes, those were happy times when he used to take the goat to browse in the ravines, and steal apples from the Almeida farm, and in the springtime watch the birds fly from branch to branch.

He set his dark calloused hand on the pine needles and, flexing his muscles, heaved himself up, but a sharp pain made him sit down again. Bending his left leg over the right one, he examined the sole of the foot, eyes watchful and index finger feeling for the place.

He drew his clasp knife from his waistcoat pocket, opened it, and began to remove bits of hard cracked skin. So there the damned thing was! A black point hardly bigger than a pinhead, but as painful as a barbed nail. Slowly, and with extreme care so that the blade should not cut him, he worked out the treacherous thorn, and a drop of blood welled up in the small hole left behind.

From the bell tower down in the village the clock struck three. Making up his mind again, Manuel da Bouça got up once more and crossed the pinewood, limping along on his sore foot. But at the point where the hill, with its soft feminine curves, linked up with the winding lane that led to the village, he stopped to look meditatively at his little house almost hanging over the Caima. And automatically his gnarled fingers began to roll another cigarette, and his left shoulder reached for the support of the rough trunk of a cork tree.

There was a little plume of smoke rising from his house, smoke from the evening meal that was being prepared inside. It was like cotton, floating, thinning out to transparency, almost blue. It drifted away in spirals from the blackened roof to the stately fig tree, at times blowing down into the branches as though it wanted to kiss the youthful clusters.

Beyond the four white walls of the house was the fowl pen, and the garden, well looked after and very green. The beans were twining round their stakes, and the peas were very dainty with their violetlike flowers. There were enough lush tender lettuces to regale all the grasshoppers in the neighborhood— that one-noted orchestra that played ceaselessly on warm summer afternoons and starry nights. Farther up was the well-filled cabbage patch: big round cabbages very stocky and squat, and tall-stemmed prolific ones, some solemn, others gay, and all of them the daily reserve for Amélia to draw on for her soups.

After that, standing like sentinels over the little fertile garden, were the two cherry trees, their freshness and rich leafage contrasting with the dry fig tree—though this one had a happier fate than the biblical one, because, instead of Judas, there was only a big yellow pumpkin hanging from the first fork.

Round these lush gifts of nature, and serving as a canopy to many of them, ran the vine trellised on oak and wire, and fastened with spikes in the white wall. And he had built that wall himself on Sundays, without any help, from the foundations to the top layer of broken glass—that indispensable "no" to the enterprise of pilferers.

But Manuel da Bouça's eyes didn't rest with the same satisfaction on the fields outside the wall, stretching out level and well watered almost as far as the old church. To possess them, be their owner, sow and harvest the maize that ripened at the first hot weather, and in winter have meadow grass in a dewy carpet: that was his only dream, the great ambition of his life. And on its realization depended all the projects he had formed, from Deolinda's marriage (not to some good-for-nothing with neither hearth nor home, but to some decent man of property) up to their own tranquil old age in a big house, solidly roofed, up there in the Salgueiros district—a house with two Alentejo pigs embalmed in its salting room!

But unless he got out of this place, unless he went off to other lands in search of squint-eyed fortune, never would he be able to realize his ambition. A laborer's wages were low, and the little garden and strips of land provided just enough to eke out a living, but you couldn't save. And wasn't it something like injustice on God's part that those wide, fertile fields should be left almost neglected because Senhor Esteves was rich and lived in town, and never came here, and the tenant was old and miserly, preferring to leave the land uncultivated rather than pay anyone to help him. Whereas, yes, in his own case, those fields were just what he wanted: close at hand, and he'd only have to prolong the wall up to the line of pine trees, because on the lower side the Caima made a natural boundary. And Senhor Esteves, if the matter were put to him in the right way and with a nice present of trout, would be certain to agree to the arrangement, because, when all's said and done, it's always better to get ten in a lump than five spread over a lifetime.

The cigarette had burned right down to Manuel da Bouça's lips, but his eyes went on drinking in the scene: the riverbank where the coveted fields lay and where his own little house was, with the smoke rising lazily from it in the quietness of the afternoon.

Then gradually other images formed and blotted out the scene in front of him: a tin trunk being closed with shirts and pants inside it; a slow train crawling over the miles to Lisbon; then the ship and the sea . . . the sea . . . These images were followed by vague notions such as: "You never know your luck till you try," "Who wants more must travel far," and "Hard work ne'er brought starvation." Why were his womenfolk afraid? He'd send them money, and after four or five years he'd come back with quite a sum in his pocket. There was no doubt about it; he'd come back with money, God willing and granting him health! He'd a strong pair of arms, and he who seeks shall find. . . .

While imagining this future success, his expression had become grave: his brown eyes, which were small and restless normally, took on a fixed look; his dry cheeks were less taut over his long black moustache, and his mouth—with its clear-cut lips and tobacco-darkened teeth—had a quiet air above the strong, sharp, common-looking chin. In this still attitude, he was like a rugged caryatid supporting the cork tree: medium height, but tight-knit and with vigorous lines, not an ounce of superfluous fat anywhere, and everything about him indicating perseverance and country health—the health of those who get up when the last stars fade and go to bed when the first stars appear in the sky.

Then he pictured his homecoming: he would have one of Santiago's carriages, or perhaps Carrelhas' car to bring him from town to the village and carry his two traveling trunks full of good clothes, and good hats such as never had been made in São João da Madeira.

In the meantime the landscape in front of him had undergone enormous changes: the little house had expanded upward and outward; it had even changed its position and moved over to Salgueiros, and its wall stretched away as far as the bridge; higher up, where the sun lasted longest, were the threshing floor and the baskets for drying the maize, and, at plowing time, he himself and as many men as were necessary (for he wouldn't be miserly like old Domingos) worked the whole of this fine land. There were two, three, four yoke of oxen patiently pulling the plow or the harrow; for the maize stripping he'd have to get all the village girls together; and the grapes gathered only from the trellis vines on the riverbank would fill half-a-dozen presses. And it would all be his! Everything earned by his own effort and sweat, day after day, hour by hour.

Yes, he'd certainly go!

It was a pity he hadn't made his mind up long ago, before he married, and when his blood was lively.

Then he would have had plenty of time to slog away and make good, and, if everything had turned out all right, he would even have been able to go one better than those Moradais people, because it wouldn't just have been a school he would have offered to the village, but the new bridge too that his reverence the priest talked about.

But with his forty-one years all told—and if it hadn't been for that plaguey notary who had obliged him to find out his exact age, to make out the mortgage, he'd still be thinking he was younger—and with a daughter already old enough to marry, he wouldn't be able to stay over there very long. He'd stay just long enough to be able to scrape enough money together for the fields, with a bit over for Amélia to have at hand in case of sickness. And even though nowadays a handbreadth of land cost as much as a league years ago, Senhor Esteves would let him have it all, if nobody went dinning anything to the contrary into his ears, for some fifty contos or thereabouts. And the devil! Fifty contos! If he went about it the right way, he'd be able to get them together in two brace of years. When five réis had been worth something, then perhaps the job would have been more difficult; but now with Brazilian money the good hard currency it is . . .

He spat out the stub of his cigarette and, because of his sore foot, got down the few feet of bank that separated him from the rough lane with the care and awkwardness of a townsman. And never had the hamlet appeared such a wretched place in his eyes, deserving only pity and a haughty look. Neighboring villages prospered, sprouted new houses, fountains, and big estates with iron gateways, because the young men of those places went off, once free of military service—goodbye, for I'm off to seek my fortune—and only came back once they had made their pile.

But in this hole, not counting Moradais, which was an exception, men left the shelter of their mothers' skirts only to go and get tied to their wives' apron strings—and that was the reason why the village would always be the same dull, ugly place. They all wanted nothing more than their soup in the morning, their sardines at night, and half a liter of wine on Sundays at the Nove fair or at Lopes' wineshop.

The people of Sandiães, Lordelo, and Vila Chã hit the mark when they said that the men of Frágua were as soft and slack as slugs!

The sea seemed to frighten them, and yet some of them got themselves crushed like bugs in the mines at Nogueira do Cravo.

But he was going to show them that he was no fainthearted funk like the others and that he was capable of carrying out everything he had talked about at Valseves' door after mass on Sunday!

In spite of this feeling of confidence, Manuel da Bouça began to look worried when he got to the field path that led from the village to his own house standing by itself in the fields. His absorption in his fixed idea, the effort of will he had been making, and the projects seething about in his head made him sullen and preoccupied.

When Amélia saw him come limping through the gate, she asked anxiously: "What's the matter? What's happened?"

"Nothing." Then because she was looking at his leg he added, "Oh, only a thorn. Nothing serious."

"But what a face you've got on!" And then, with a rapid shift of thought, she continued, "I'm surprised Soares was at home today. Isn't it his day to go to the glass factory?"

"I haven't been to see him. I've been to town."

"Ah, I thought so! Then why did you say you were going over for a talk with Soares?"

Manuel da Bouça didn't reply. He pulled the bench over to the window and sat down to look out at the fields, his expression becoming more and more sullen and morose.

"What's the matter, man? Come on, out with it! You can't be feeling up to the mark. . . ."

And as she stood there perplexed, arms akimbo, hands on her hips, looking at him questioningly, he turned and mumbled through his teeth, "I've made up my mind. . . . I'm going . . . I'm going to Brazil. . . ."

"You . . . ?" His heavy tragic silence upset her still more. She began to cry. Then she called out, "Deolinda! Deolinda! Come here, my girl!"

At her mother's cries, the girl showed a startled face at the kitchen door. As soon as Amélia saw her, she ran to her and threw her arms round her, covering her face, hands, and neck with tears. "He's going," she said. "He's still set on going!"

"Oh!" And Deolinda began to cry too.

For some moments there was nothing but weeping, the mother noisily, the daughter in silence. Then suddenly Manuel da Bouça stood up in a temper. He kicked the bench away and shouted, "Now that's enough of your women's weeping! You'd think the world were coming to an end. . . . Did you ever see anything like it!"

Amélia obeyed, and her tears began to roll down silently. He threw her a haughty look, and then went on: "That's it! That's exactly it! Frágua women have all got the habit of keeping their menfolk tied to their skirts. . . . As though it were something altogether unheard-of for anyone to go to Brazil! Yet one can't make a living here."

Amélia let her daughter go and dried her eyes on a corner of her apron. "It's such a long way!" she said. "It breaks my heart only to think of it. . . ."

"Well, you'll have to get used to it, that's all."

He was trying to carry it off with a high hand, thinking the scene would be less painful, but it cost him an effort to get each word through the lump in his throat. He had leaned his hard countryman's hand on the windowsill, and a ray of sunlight was shining on it.

Plucking up courage, Deolinda came up closer to give her opinion. "If I were you, Dad, I wouldn't go. . . ."

"What do you know about it!"

"Other places, other people . . . Here at least we know what it's like. But over there . . ." He shrugged his shoulders, but she went on gently: "If we can't have more, we can do with less. And we've always managed till now. . . ."

"That's what makes this village what it is! Nobody ever wants to get on."

"But, Dad, some people have even less than we have, yet they don't go and leave their homes."

"It's a fine lot we've got! Three little strips of land that drain all the blood from my body before they yield anything worth gathering, and a garden plot here too small to hold a yoke of oxen. . . ."

"Well, we don't go hungry. Much or little, we always have enough to eat, and many a poor soul would be only too glad to live like us."

"And I'm the one who knows what it costs! Work from morning till night like a nigger, on my own land and on other people's land, and all there is to show for it is what you see!"

"We ought to be thankful you've got your health," put in Amélia, "whereas over there, who knows?"

"That was in the old days. Nowadays when people come back, they bring more flesh back with them. Look at the Marquis of Sinfães."

Deolinda went on again, "I'm sure that our dad, even without leaving home, could always manage to make a decent living."

"How?"

"I don't know. I've just got a feeling."

"Just silliness. At your age, that's what they all think; then later on they have to change their tune. But that's enough of this chatter! Everything's decided. So instead of standing there like a couple of weeping-women, just see about getting something ready to eat."

"It's all ready," said Amélia submissively.

He walked to the kitchen and down the three steps. At the far end, under the mantelpiece blackened with soot, a fire was smoldering weakly, for only one log, resinous at the still untouched end, was burning stubbornly. At some distance from the embers the old stewpot, with one foot broken, was steaming, weaving a veil of vapor in the black mouth of the fireplace. Through the door that opened onto the garden, along with the dying sunlight, which shone white on the ocher of the water pitcher, came the gruntings of the pig they were fattening.

Manuel da Bouça sat down at the pinewood table that was already pitted and worm-eaten. He bent hungrily over the bowl of soup his wife placed before him and, after the first few mouthfuls, began to break up a hunk of maize bread.

At his side, tall and dark, her face lined with wrinkles and her great earrings almost brushing against her cheeks, Amélia stood lost in thought with her eyes fixed on the table, and when he finished the bowl she asked him suddenly, "And how are you getting the money for the passage and the papers?"

He hesitated; then, mumbling the words as though he were confessing a crime, he answered, "With the strips of land . . ."

"The strips of land? Have you sold them?"

"No, I've taken out a mortgage or something. . . ."

"A mortgage? What's that?"

"I don't quite know. Soares told me about it. They advance me the money, which I have to pay back six years later, and the strips of land stand as security. . . ."

"But then, man, what do we live on?"

"Just like a silly woman to get everything wrong! The strips stay just as they have been up to now. We go on working on them, and the crops are ours. . . ."

"So that's it! And who advanced the money?"

Deolinda, who had been outside to empty the bucket of meal and water into the pig trough, came back and leaned against the doorpost to listen.

"Carrazedas, in town."

"Carrazedas! But the man's got a bad name!"

"Well, everything was put down on paper in black and white. And Soares, he's a steady chap. If it weren't shipshape he'd never have advised me to do it. . . . You'll have the strips of land and the garden, and I'll send you money for extras."

"But are you really going haphazard like that?"

"Haphazard, what nonsense! Isn't Cipriano there already?"

"Which Cipriano?"

"Why, Cipriano from Lordelo."

"Oh."

"Tomorrow, Deolinda will have to write a nice letter to him. He's a good chap, and he's getting on well. Wouldn't I like to be doing the same! Why, his mother told me only the other day that he can earn as much as he likes."

"And when are you going, Dad?" asked Deolinda, coming into the middle of the kitchen.

"As soon as the papers are in order. Next month, very likely."

And the two women began to cry again.

2

*L*IKE a restless dragonfly darting about in the stagnant atmosphere, the unchanging world round a well, the tidings flew from mouth to mouth and, passing beyond the village, spread as far as the neighboring parishes.

"Manuel da Bouça's going to Brazil. . . ."

Children heard their parents commenting on the news, and they thought it as exciting as a death. The menfolk, even the most timorous of them, approved of his decision—and in almost all of them was the secret wish to imitate his enterprise. There was no future in the village, and the examples they quoted of men who had grown rich in Brazil were more numerous than mullet in the seabed after a charge of dynamite.

The women were always finding reasons for passing near Manuel da Bouça's house, for confidential talks with Amélia about the great event. All of them tried to cheer her up by foretelling the life of plenty and leisure she would have thanks to the money from Brazil. And on their lips the remark that they would willingly accept the same bid for wealth was a constant refrain.

"Well now, if my man decided to go too, I don't say I shouldn't feel it, but I shouldn't do anything to stop him, not I! Other lands, Senhora Amélia, other opportunities!"

There very soon grew up round Manuel da Bouça an atmosphere of respect and interest. From the moment he had made up his mind to go, he became another man in the estimation of the village. They looked at him with other eyes, and even his stature seemed different from what it was before. He had taken on an air of pride: his lips had more of a curl, his moustache was more upturned, the lines of his body were more assured and his gestures more restrained.

From Lordelo, Vila Chã, and Castelões came inquiries about the date of departure and promises to go with him.

In all the neighboring villages and surrounding parishes was the same eagerness to emigrate, to go to a distant continent in search of wealth. It was a deep-rooted dream, a deep-seated ambition eating into people's hearts from childhood to old age. The wealth of Brazil was part of the general tradition and had the prestige of a legend among these rude, simple people. They saw it come to fruition in the churches, mansions, schools, bridges, and new roads donated by men who had grown rich on the other shore of the Atlantic. They imagined it blossoming, glittering and dazzling in coins the size of the sun when it dropped to the horizon just in the direction where that wonderful country lay. No hope of great prosperity existed that was not based on the wealth that sprang up unceasingly in profusion over there. On the other hand, they felt hopeless, and put no heart into work in their own land, because not a single one believed that work at home would yield sufficient return for the trouble and effort put into it.

The magic word "Brazil" always worked like a charm, and the mere sound of it was enough to call up visions of splendor, dazzling opulence, and lives freed from drudgery. Bound to the struggle for daily bread, living a hard and limited life, all these country places dreamed of coming into their own, from the fertile land of the plain up to the ridges of the mountains, through gold gained in that distant land. This urge was lodged in the breast of every man, even gnawing relentlessly into the feelings of those who clung most to their native soil. They in- herited it from their great-grandfathers, and from farther back still; they inherited it and passed it on to their descendants, a restless compulsion that harassed them all their lives. All genera- tions were born with this innate ambition, and it made a nuisance of itself when not satisfied. It always lurked round a corner in the mind, to be brought out like a talisman in moments of chal- lenge to fate, or used as a prop in times when desperate remedies were needed.

But like any other charm, it was a source of fear as well as attraction. From that faraway time, when ships sailed across oceans for months at a stretch, came a legacy, a gust of fear and superstition that chilled the hearts of the strongest. They themselves didn't really know why, but the idea of going to Brazil was always accompanied by a presentiment of danger. Fever? Shipwreck? All this, and on top of it the untutored imagination at grips with the unknown. Always when they accepted the idea of going over there, it took their breath away and they felt a tremor of apprehension. As though they were wrestling with death till one of them came out victorious.

The overcoming of this fear demanded a real heroism equal to throwing off old terrors and all the evil reports ever heard. Yet few there were who gave up the pursuit of the mirage through lack of courage. They were dominated by ambition, which was their invulnerable cuirass against all vicissitudes. And with ambi- tion went the love of adventure, latent in the blood like a taint.

And so their number made up an exodus, poor in everything else, but rich in golden visions, and they went streaming to the sea, leaving behind them land covered with furze that could have yielded bread, in order to go and make the land of promise fruitful.

For Lordelo, Castelões, and Vila Chã, Manuel da Bouça became the signal for departure. Message bearers and men who were interested came to Frágua to see him, and all of them, handicapped by their ignorance, sat on trying to figure out the facts so that they shouldn't finally find themselves leaving by different boats. But he couldn't give them the information they wanted; all he could say was that he would be very glad, very glad indeed, if they could all leave together. But they had better come back the following Friday, because on Thursday he would be going to town again, and then he could give them the proper information.

The men drained the last drop from their mugs, wiped their lips on the back of their hands, and took leave, thanking him. Manuel da Bouça went with them as far as the gate, and then stood watching them as they walked away: Zé do Aido, a lanky chap, red-cheeked and indomitable; Anacleto and Rosalino, not so tall, swarthy and a bit hump-shouldered from working with the mattock.

When he got back to the house, Amélia was standing near the table with the handles of the mugs threaded on the fingers of her right hand to carry them away, and she suddenly said to him, "Look here, have you thought about the girl?"

"Which girl?"

"Why, ours of course. What other girl could it be?"

"Well, what's the matter with her?"

Amélia stood looking at him in astonishment because the same line of thought had not occurred to him. Then she set the mugs down, and went up to him. "It's time the girl got married."

"I know that. What about it?"

"I don't want to have to decide anything in your absence and without your consent. . . ."

Manuel da Bouça gave her a quick look of surprise. "What do you mean?"

"I thought you knew. . . ."

"I don't know anything! Come on, out with it!"

"Don't make a fuss, man. It's nothing bad. It's Zefa da Portela's son who's courting her. But didn't you know?"

"How should I know?" he answered angrily. "Did you ever tell me anything about it? Now, answer me that! Why didn't you warn me? Here I've been going about all unsuspecting, and not knowing what's been going on in my own house! It was your place to tell me!"

"What was there to tell you? I thought you knew, and things like that should be talked about only when there are proper grounds. Now, it was only yesterday, after hearing that you were really going to Brazil, that the lad spoke seriously to Deolinda. . . ."

Manuel da Bouça bit his lips; he went to the window, came back to the middle of the room, moved the reel of thread about that was on the sewing machine, and then, restraining his anger, he brought out with a sneer, "So that brazen-faced Afonso has had the nerve to go after my daughter? That's about the limit. . . . We really only needed something like that! A lump of an ass who hasn't even got a place to fall dead on!" And at last, giving full vent to his indignation, he went on, "Never! Do you hear? Never! What he wants is some good thwacks from a cudgel on his behind!"

"Man, you always get into a boil about nothing! Afonso's an honest, hard-working lad. . . ."

"Good luck to him from it!"

"And he's got something of his own. When old Zefa dies . . ."

"He's got something of his own, indeed! Two handbreadths of land even maize won't look at, and an old hut. . . . Yes, that place is nothing but an old hut, and one day when there's a breath of wind it'll get blown to bits!"

"He told the girl he's got a bit of money put by. . . ."

"I don't approve, and that's enough! Deolinda's got to marry . . . she's got to marry someone who suits me!"

"You know very well we can't give her a marriage portion; she's got nothing—"

"She's got nothing? Just listen to that! When I—"

He broke off because it suddenly struck him that his argument was based on conjecture only, and with a quick change he went on: "Well, she has nothing now, but, God willing, she will have something in time to come! So that good-for-nothing had better keep out of my sight, or he'll feel my stick!"

And he went on shifting the reel about, irritated and angry. There was a moment's silence, then Amélia quietly and gently tried to make a suggestion. "But if they like each other . . . If Deolinda likes him . . ."

"What! Likes him? Are you sure?" He stood digesting the unpleasant surprise in silence; then he went on: "She'll get over it! Tell her I don't approve, do you hear? I don't want it. And it's for her own good! The wench isn't twenty yet, and already thinking about marriage. . . . She'll get over it! You were five-and-twenty when you got married, and you still had a lot to learn about running a house. Now they've no sooner left their mothers' apron strings . . . She's got plenty of time! A nice thing it's all been!"

Amélia didn't insist anymore; she picked the mugs up again and went off to the kitchen, sighing.

Still in a bad temper, he began putting the stools in place, to soothe his nerves. Then he took his broad-brimmed hat from its peg and went out.

A few minutes later he was striding along the riverbank, mattock on shoulder, making for his strips of land.

His heart bled to see so much water here, while up there, where his bits of land were, everything died of thirst except rye. Ah, when he came back, he would have to open a deep well or install a machine pump, like those he'd seen near Gandra!

Evening was coming on, and from far away, from the direction of Mosteiro, came the sound of a sad, plaintive song.

When he reached his strips of land, Manuel da Bouça began to hack out the weeds between the rows of green maize. But he no longer felt the enthusiasm of earlier days, when the urge had often driven him to try and slake the thirst of the soil by carrying buckets of water from the river right up there. Now, it all seemed small and provisional. The maize plot, when it grew ripe, would turn out just the same as in other years, scanty and anemic.

He let his attention wander off in a riotous stream of thoughts and images. What would it be like? Would there be a lot of people working and a lot of money? But what kind of work would they do? Zé do Aido, Rosalino, and Anacleto, would they know anything about what they were going to do? And that baggage of a girl! Here he was thinking of her future, and she was just set on spoiling everything. Would Amélia cry a lot when the time came to say goodbye?

His mind jumped backward and forward, mixing up all the questions he was asking himself in an attempt to catch a glimpse of his future life. He'd certainly have to buy the land from Esteves, wouldn't he just! And for Amélia, he'd bring back a chain thicker than those the baker's women wore at Vilar!

When he had finished hacking out the weeds, he set the mattock upright and leaned his elbow on it, and gave himself up to his obsession again. His eyes, lingering here and there, glanced fondly over the nearby fields washed by the Caima—the fields that would be his! The sun was moving over from Mount Crasto to the Felgueira Range. And everywhere within sight people were still toiling. They had been working from the time the cocks began to crow, and so they went on, bent-backed, here disappearing in the grass, there scratching away at the hungry earth, till night fell. It was one continual effort in a rain of sweat, between scanty meals: a bowl of soup and a glass of wine when the farmer was generous, because there were some who spent the whole day with nothing but their bread soup in the morning.

And all to what purpose, if, on a holiday or at a village fair, they had to dress up ever afterward in the same clothes they got married in? To what purpose, if they couldn't save anything, but always had to go on working, or do like old Leonardo who, when he grew old, went out onto the road with his knapsack on his shoulder, begging five réis for the love of Christ, from passers-by? And those who did possess two fingerbreadths of land had to give everything up for tithes, which were so heavy that either you had to have a lot of land or it was better to have none at all.

Manuel da Bouça now turned back to Frágua and Cimo de Vila, his eyes taking Barreiro and Salgueiros in at the same time, which were already losing their clear outlines in the half-light. Old houses everywhere, and land measured out by the hand-breadth—people who worked with no promise for the future, who worked till they died, deprived of all comfort, as though their fate were solely to live in poverty. And the few roofs that rose higher than the common level either belonged to cloth merchants or to people back from Brazil who had gone away in early youth.

Night was falling, but a liquid tenderness still lay over the valley, a soft pearl light breaking slowly away from its embrace with earth.

In the last life throb of day, everything became aureoled in grace, everything became humble before the arches of newborn night. There was a feeling of mildness, universal peace, intangible velvet wrapping everything in ecstasy.

For one moment, the green of the meadows took on a more vivid green, then faded into pool-green, sea-green, till the transparency of light remained only over the tranced oakwood.

On the riverbank, the twittering of birds was dying down; the melancholy rumbling of an oxcart far away could be heard with greater clearness; the movements of men still at work became more indistinct; the pine trees climbing the sides of Mount Crasto had turned into a jet-black stain as the light gradually failed. Sadness seemed to be scattering petals of withered roses over the earth.

Then the roads and vineyards darkened—and to complete the eeriness of the scene, certain oak trees seemed only to require the corpse of a man hanging from one of their branches.

The bramble hedges lost their clean contours and became big wedges of shadow winding along the edges of the fields. The blue of the Caima was turning black, water hardly distinguishable from land, merged under the same dark veil. The black alders with their foliage blurred, like figures of dream, muffled forms, stood scrutinizing the mystery of night.

Only on a hillock here and there some rock unstained by moss still caught the light. The old tower stood out from Mosteiro, too. But the last light weakly wandering in space was powerless to survive.

From the plinths of the Felgueira Range, creeping from the chestnut trees already covered in shadow, the darkness moved stealthily up toward the ridge of the mountain chain. And the huge wave, gray at the crest and black at its winding base, rose, loomed, took everything softly into its embrace. So dark it was, it seemed that if some devil-disguised shape had made a megaphone with its hands and uttered a great shout over the mountainside, the whole world would have started with fear.

On the narrow roads passing between trees and maize fields, the people walking homeward seemed unreal. Some were whistling, and up toward Gândara a woman's voice began to sing an old sad song, as though to charm the spirit of night.

Old Mother Rita dos Anjos noisily made her presence known by shouting, "Get along there, you old rogue of a goat!" And then came the irritating jingle of the bell hanging round the goat's neck.

In the valley, only the doors of houses, where light showed, seemed to be alive. Living doors, then emptiness lapped in deep, dark, mysterious frightening night.

When Manuel da Bouça got home, Deolinda shouted from the kitchen, "Wait a minute, and I'll bring the lamp."

"There's no need."

But she was already at the inside door, carrying the light.

"It wasn't necessary," Manuel da Bouça said again. "And now I want my supper." And he walked toward the kitchen.

"Dad . . ."

It was a tearful supplicating voice that called him. He stopped, first surprised, then stern, guessing what was in his daughter's mind. "What is it?"

"Our mother's told me everything. . . ."

"Well, what about it?"

"I can't, Dad!" And choking, getting the words out with difficulty, she went on, "I can't . . . I like Afonso a lot. . . ."

"What do you mean by talking to me like that, eh? Now be quiet!" he answered angrily. And, turning his back, he left her and made for the kitchen.

She had hoped to touch his heart by speaking of her love, and now she felt powerless in the face of this rough reception. Pain and resentment welled like black froth rising from a boiling vessel, up to her throat, nostrils, and ears. She couldn't breathe; noises lost their separate meaning and became fused in a single sound—like the monotonous murmur, broken only here and there, of a field of insects. She let herself fall onto one of the stools, leaned on the table, and sat in a daze, eyes very wide open, seeing nothing.

ᴅᴀʏ was breaking when Manuel da Bouça reached the
top of the forest. There were faint flushes of color in
patches of sky glimpsed through trees, and the secret union of
night and day was clothed in fantastic draperies that changed
tint from moment to moment, changing so subtly that only the
eye of an artist could determine the sudden merging. The dawn
of light, which made one blotch of the pine boughs, forcing the
darkness to take refuge where the furze was highest and the pines
lower and more serried, was followed by a thin wash of purple—
whether soft stroke of brush or wake of light wind traced under
the still dark sky was hard to determine. It was an undefined
purple, without uniformity, more accentuated here, more at-
tenuated there, and with the dark silk train of retreating night
visible through it. Then it seemed as though an exhalation from
the earth breathed rose color on some parts of the purple drapery,
which began to break up, scattering the huge dome of the sky
with rags and tatters—some ash-colored, others ocher, others re-

maining purple, but all wavering, formless, torn in capricious rents against a blue-colored bar.

Then the black outline of the pines became visible as light descended to earth, making its way among the trunks, lighting up the scars from which resin was oozing, spreading everywhere slowly, slowly, like a veil sinking softly and languidly down. Only the compact, mysterious whortleberry trees resisted the invasion of light and formed dark shapes among the pines.

The blue bar, which had been like a flounce on a huge canopy, lost its outline and stretched out in great arabesques of deeper blue. Now there were traces of *gouache* on the concave canvas, and in the forest, glints of old ivory on the roots that crossed the path, worn down by the tread of passersby. It was as though a gigantic lazy eyelid were being opened, revealing an eye still drowsed with sleep and void of curiosity.

But when Manuel da Bouça reached the lower slope of the hill, a more extensive panorama opened up before him, beyond the young eucalyptus trees that formed a flock in the wake of the old pines. Now everything seemed poised, in suspense, waiting for the rehearsal of the great transformation scene. There was a cool silence that isolated the cry of each bird and made it distinct. And both the base of the mountain chain girdled by river sounds, as well as the forested peaks, from the palace of the Counts of Covo whitening among the cork trees, up to the blur of houses of the village of Vilar, everything lay in strange expectancy.

In this atmosphere of miracle, everything seemed to be waiting for a marvel. Tree that did not ask what was going to happen wrapped itself in ecstasy, not of evening trance and languor, but morning freshness and exhilaration. A wood pigeon skimmed across the clearing and then hid itself among the eucalyptus trees, so that the whir of its wings should not trouble the dominant expectancy.

Little by little, from the top of the mountain chain that held

Pinhao as within walls, the mystery began to reveal itself. A huge projector, hidden far away, began to sweep the sky clear of all the ocher, purple, and ash-colored wisps. Before this fan of white radiant light the skin-smooth surface of the vast vault of the sky turned limpid blue in a mystic ceremony of purification. Only over the distant coast, great crags of cloud added yellow to the rose, and finished by taking on all the rarest colors of the rainbow.

And the fan continued to open, spreading its diaphanous ribs over more than half the dome of the sky. Drops of dew glittered on the spines of the young pine trees, like silver beads on Christmas trees. And in delight, the woods drank in the newborn light.

In the distance, Vilar became clearer, with the outline of its grouped houses more and more distinct, and a dunghill smoking beside them.

Manuel da Bouça continued down the hill. Below him, the stream was a leaden track winding between gilded osiers and willow clusters where blackbirds were darting about. The roof-tiles of a mill glittered too, and its wheel had begun to churn the water slowly on one of the corners of the old moss-covered house.

Finally, the great countenance of the sun showed above the ridge of the mountains. The white radiant fan had moved lower down, and the pure blue sky, virginal skin fine-textured, could be seen through it. There were subtle vibrations in the light, as though invisible strings up there were sending out waves of light instead of sound.

And the expectancy finished in a burst of joy.

Birds and insects, no longer isolated musicians, formed a single orchestra.

The whole earth was an immense corolla opening beneath the spell of morning. Everything shone. Everything, even the trunks of the young oak trees planted singly up the slope Manuel da Bouça was now climbing, to reach the road to town.

The stream had changed from lead to silver. The forest, now viewed from the other side, lay stretched under a snowy, im-

stairs, the inner door opened, and Nunes came through—tall, lean, one eyelid half closed over an empty socket.

He went to his desk, sat down, moved various papers, placed his cigarette on the edge of the ashtray, and exchanged a few words with the clerk that Manuel da Bouça didn't understand, but he gathered they were about himself. At last Nunes turned to him. "What do you want?"

And Manuel da Bouça came forward, respectful, hesitating in step and gesture. "It's about a passage to Brazil . . . and to look after the papers. . . . Senhor Carrazedas told me that he'd spoken to you. . . ."

"Yes, yes, I remember something of the sort. But that was some days ago."

"It was last week."

"All right, sit down."

"Thank you, with your permission, sir."

"So you want to take ship to Brazil, is that it?"

Manuel da Bouça nodded his head in agreement, and Nunes, relighting his cigarette, went on: "So you're going to try your luck? You're right, you're certainly right. Brazil's the place, and they know how to appreciate a man's work there. For ten years now I've been helping a lot of people to get there, and up to now, as far as I know, nobody's had cause to regret it."

"But I've always been a bit afraid of catching some fever."

"What fever, man? What a story! That's all an old tale. Today the guarantees of good health are so great over there that even a man who isn't sound in health can stand it. Why, take my own case! I'd go and try my luck myself if I weren't close on fifty, because frankly this job here yields nothing at all."

Manuel da Bouça gave a timid, almost loutish smile. These words, spoken by a townsman who inspired respect, reassured him and gave him new courage, dispelling the cloud that had darkened his spirits a short time before in front of the signboard. If Senhor Nunes said he was ready to go too, it was because he meant it; men like that didn't think one thing and say another.

Nunes, having delivered these encouraging phrases, came to the real point. "Now let's see what we can do. Where do you want to go? North or South?"

Manuel da Bouça looked at him, perplexed.

"I asked where do you want to go: Manaus, Pará, or Rio . . ."

"I want to go to Santos—"

"Ah, Santos. That's a good spot. Lots of Portuguese people go there and they almost all make money. Have you got relations there?"

"Only a friend—Cipriano de Lordelo."

"Ah, and did he write and tell you to go?"

"No, I sent him a letter to say I was going."

"Very good. Have you got your birth certificate?"

"Yes."

"And your service certificate?"

"Yes."

"Good, good. And you know what it's going to cost, don't you?"

"No, senhor, that I don't know."

"Well, it all costs a lot nowadays; passage, papers, everything costs a lot." And while he was talking, Nunes was eyeing Manuel da Bouça from head to foot. "What with the exchange rate going up and the government not doing anything about it . . . The cost of the passage and papers is something round three contos . . . three thousand escudos."

The clerk bent lower over his desk, pretending to give closer attention to the work he was doing. Manuel da Bouça didn't speak.

"Yes, senhor."

"Is that all right?" asked Nunes.

"You have to leave one conto as a deposit, for the first expenses."

"Yes, senhor." And he drew a big flower-patterned handkerchief from his pocket, untied the knot at one of the corners, and counted out some crumpled notes onto the desk.

"That's right. It'll take about a fortnight, more or less. But you'd better call here again next week to see how things are." And with superb indifference he opened one of the drawers of his desk and dropped the notes into it. Then he turned to the clerk. "Now, you go with him to get his identity card."

The little man got up and, without troubling to get his hat, made for the street muttering "Come along" between his teeth.

"Yes, you just go along with him."

The two men crossed the square and went into the municipal offices, where Manuel da Bouça meekly went through all the formalities and answered all the questions asked. And when Nunes' clerk finally left him at the door of the building saying, "Well, that's all; come again next week," he felt suddenly relieved from the feeling of oppression that contact with townspeople never failed to cast over him.

When he got back into the square he saw a crowd of people—children pushing between the women's skirts, and men closely watching what was going on in the center. It wasn't Sunday, which would be a holiday, nor would people from the fair be there without their stalls. It couldn't be anyone killed or hurt either, because in that case there wouldn't be that pleased surprise; everybody would crowd up and make a stir, like a flock coming out of the fold. Then what was it?

He went nearer, and the sound of a tambourine that met him halfway told him what it was all about. When he reached the crowd, he craned his neck and saw the bear that had passed by earlier in the morning now dancing on its hind legs. The showman, holding a heavy stick under his arm, was beating time on the tambourine, and the two monkeys were sitting at his feet looking at the crowd with mocking eyes.

The black bear, its long snout lifted up, went on with the lumbering, disjointed steps of the dance and then, at a shout from its master, stretched out its arms and the monkeys leaped up on them, skipping and capering as though on a circus trapeze. Standing still to give firmness to its body, the bear looked like some great solemn nightmare creature that, after motion, had suddenly become petrified into a block of shadow or a tree stump standing on a riverbank.

Through the forest of adult legs street urchins with radiant faces watched the spectacle. Then the program came to an end, the monkeys climbed down, and the weary bear, driven without reason or pity, went round with the tambourine to collect the coppers necessary to support their wandering life.

Manuel da Bouça was among those who slipped quietly away so as not to have to pay for the entertainment. . . .

4

ACCORDING to his custom, as soon as midday had struck at the mother church Nunes got up, tidied his papers a bit and, bending his lanky form, passed through the inside door. Then, from the darkness beyond, he called out, "Francisco, did you manage to tell Borges that I wanted a talk with him?"

"Yes, yes, I've told him, yesterday it was. He promised to come here today, before you left."

"If he comes, tell him to come up." And Nunes' footsteps began to sound again on the dark stairs.

Upstairs, with a sunray glittering on the glass in the center of the table, lunch was waiting for him, piping hot and savory. Rubbing his hands, he sat down in a satisfied frame of mind and said to his wife, "Let's get on with it; I'm in a hurry."

She sat down too; then, glancing over the table: "Maria! Maria! Bring the wine. You always have to go and forget something!"

The servant, fifty peasant years poorly dressed in wide brown-colored skirts, came in and placed a round decanter near Nunes, full of good red wine so transparent that sun-spots could be seen through it.

And then the lunch began. Nunes' expression was so bright that Dona Clementina remarked in surprise, "You're very pleased with things today."

"Well, there's no cause to be downhearted, thank God. Things are beginning to look up again."

"Were there many people today?"

"Only one. But, counting him, that makes eight this week."

"Are your plans beginning to yield results, then?"

"No, woman, not yet! My plans are for the new agency. This spate of people wanting passports here, it's all due to Carrazedas. It suits him to get hold of mortgages, so he goes stirring these blockheads up about Brazil and America. I pretend I don't see through it, but he can't take me in. My plans go beyond that. . . ."

There was a knock at the door. Someone answered the servant's question, and Nunes recognized the voice and called out: "Ah, it's Borges! Come in, Borges, come in!"

A small fat man came through the little hall into the dining room, his bald head shining, and glasses over a round red smiling face. "I hope you'll enjoy your lunch!" he said, and with an open smile greeted Nunes and his wife ceremoniously.

"Sit down, man, and join us!"

"No, no, thanks. I've already had lunch. I always lunch at eleven, so as to get back to the Department in good time."

"At least, try a leg of rabbit."

"No, thanks, really I'm not hungry."

"Oh, but you can manage a glass of wine and a bit of plum preserve," put in Dona Clementina.

"Thanks, if you like . . ."

"Maria! Bring me the jar of plum preserve!"

"So there's a big do at Cambra today?" said Borges while the compote was being served.

"Yes, and it ought to turn out all right. That's why I asked you to come. I want you to go over there with me."

"Me?"

"Yes, you."

"But . . ."

"Now, there's no but about it. At one o'clock sharp, Carrelhas' car will be here to take us. I want you to be present. The provincial press ought to receive the same treatment as the city press. In Lisbon and Oporto, for instance, whenever any new establishment is opened the journalists are invited. And are city reporters by any chance more competent than provincial ones? Than you, for example, my friend?"

"Oh, Senhor Nunes!"

"Now, don't be modest. Their big advantage is that they write for big newspapers. But it's my private conviction that there are a lot of journalists in the provinces who could teach them a thing or two if one fine day they got to Lisbon or Oporto. Wouldn't they just! Now, I don't pretend to be a man of letters, but only the other day I came across a mistake in *O Século* that would have got a schoolboy the cane. I can't call to mind at the moment just what it was, but I do know that whoever wrote it ought to be ashamed. Whereas I've never found anything of the sort in our *Liberal*, even though I always read it from beginning to end. You've got the gift, my dear Borges, you've certainly got it!"

"One does one's best," replied Borges, feeling rather awkward with a trickle of syrup running inopportunely down his chin.

"So that's that. You're going to be present at the opening of my new agency. There'll be champagne and cakes, and all the local authorities of Cambra will be there."

"I'm sorry, I can't," said Borges. "I'd like to very much; it would make quite a nice outing too, but I can't manage it. I'm really sorry, believe me! But today of all days Senhor Eugénio had to go off to Santiago de Riba-Ul, and he's left me in charge of the Department. So you see: what would he say if he didn't find me there when he got back? And then again, it would put me in a false position with regard to the others—they've already got a grudge against me because I'm already head clerk. Just imagine, only yesterday Almeida said to Macedo the hotelkeeper that I should be a nobody if I hadn't come into the newspaper through my father-in-law's death."

"Well, if that's the case, I won't insist. It'll be for some other time." Then, changing his tone, "Have another glass?"

"No, thanks."

"Just one more."

"No, thanks, I've had all I can manage."

"Then a little more dessert?"

"No, no, Dona Clementina, thanks all the same."

There was a short silence, just long enough for Nunes to turn round in his chair and settle in his own mind the line to take in order to persuade Borges.

"You know, Borges," he went on, "I'm your friend. I subscribe to your paper, advertise in every issue, and never tire of saying that it's the best organ our party possesses in the whole district. If our side comes into power again, we shall have to try and arrange a little subsidy for you from the committee. . . . Apart from that, with the opening of my new agency in Cambra, you can count on another regular advertisement."

"Thank you very much. Believe me that I really appreciate this."

"No need for thanks, man! We go through this life in order to help one another. All I ask is that, before the notice about the opening of my agency—you are going to put an account in the *Liberal*, aren't you?"

"Certainly, certainly!"

"Good. Then, since you can't go with me, I'll tell you what happened, when I come back. But, as I was saying, what I would really like would be for you to write an article on emigration to North America, before the notice about the inauguration. Something like this: We know that there's great lack of manpower in North America, and that all those who emigrate there easily find work and earn heaps of money. As the dollar is good currency, a number of Portuguese emigrants have made fortunes in a short time. For this reason, Italians and Spaniards are emigrating in masses to that country, even though our own people are in a better position to get rich quickly. . . . Anyway, you'll treat it as you think best, and you'll excuse me for 'teaching Our Father to the priest.' What I really want is for this article to go directly under the one about the opening of the agency. That is, one above and the other below. Have you got the idea, Borges?"

"To be frank, I can't say that I do quite understand."

"Well, if you like, I'll scribble out the article and then you can arrange it your own way afterward."

"That isn't what I meant. What I don't understand is the subject of the article . . . because, if I'm not mistaken, I read a short time ago in the Lisbon papers that there's a great lack of work in America and that emigrants are having a shocking time. . . ."

"What? You've read that?" Then, changing his tone, Nunes went on in great indignation. "You see! You see! That's false information propagated by . . . by—now who could it be!—by the farmers of Alentejo who exploit the poor devils shamefully who go down there to find work. They are the people who put such things in the Lisbon papers. But, Borges, you don't believe it's true, do you?"

"Really, if we were to believe everything we saw, even in the big newspapers . . ."

"You see! The whole thing's a lie!"

"Well, I wouldn't say the whole thing, but—"

Nunes didn't allow him to finish. "Of course, of course. Don't attach any importance to it! And you'll publish the article won't you?"

"Oh, yes, senhor, you can rely on that."

"To the effect that there's a lot of work to be had in America, good money to be earned, and fortunes to be made in a short time . . . You'll read it over to me before publishing."

"All right."

"Ah, and in the notice about the inauguration of my agency, don't forget to mention that it's qualified to handle passages and passports for America. That's an important point, you understand?"

"Perfectly."

Changing his tone again and speaking in a familiar manner as he gave a friendly tap on Borges' arm, Nunes added: "And now good news for you! Get in enough paper, because I want three thousand copies of this issue of the *Liberal*. Three thousand at two tostões, that makes six hundred milréis. Six hundred escudos, friend Borges, apart from the advertisement! This time, your paper will print off more copies than the *Século* or the *Janeiro*. Come now, have another glass, eh?"

"No, thank you very much. Will you be back today?"

"Yes, tonight, why?"

"For the details to put in the notice about the inauguration."

"Ah, yes."

"You see, the paper comes out on Saturday, and it's already Wednesday."

"Well, as soon as I get back I'll just come over to your house . . ."

"Oh, that isn't necessary. I'll come here. And if I have time at the office to rough out the note on America, I'll bring it along for you to see."

"Good, good! We shall have to see about making the *Liberal* a daily, with our municipality developing as it is—"

"Difficult . . . very difficult . . ." Borges interrupted in a sad and skeptical tone. "Scarcely anyone reads. This country is illiterate. If it weren't for subscribers from Brazil . . ."

"Let time do its work, and you'll see!"

From time to time Borges had been glancing stealthily at the big dining-room clock, and he now thought it opportune to remark on the hour. "Oh, a quarter to one! I must be getting back to the Department. . . ."

"Stay a bit longer. I've got to go down too. I'm just waiting to hear the car outside."

"Thanks, but I'd rather go now, if you don't mind. I'm late as it is. I usually go back soon after midday, and I don't want Senhor Eugénio to imagine that I'm taking advantage of his being away, the more so as I'm deputizing for him."

"Oh, in that case, I understand. . . . See you later?"

"Yes, see you later."

Borges took his leave very cordially and went off bowing to Dona Clementina. As soon as his footsteps could no longer be heard on the stairs, Nunes exclaimed, "However much you talk to that fellow, you can never find out whether he's a fool or a knave!"

"It seems to me he's a smart one," was Dona Clementina's opinion.

Nunes was silent for a moment, and then he remarked, as though answering his own queries, "The main thing is for him to publish the articles."

"Are you very set on it?"

"I certainly am. It's necessary to attract people to the Cambra agency who want to go to North America. It's more remunerative than Brazil. It isn't easy to get the passports, and so you can charge more. Well, it's time to go, so give me my hat."

Dona Clementina got up. A motor horn honked outside.

"There it is! Quick!"

From the stairs Francisco shouted, "Senhor Nunes, Senhor Nunes, the car's there!"

"I know." He put his hat on quickly, felt in his pockets to make sure he hadn't forgotten anything, and went out in a merry mood, feeling as though he'd like to race down the steps two at a time, as he had when he was a boy.

He settled himself very comfortably in the car, in one of the corners, with his walking stick between his legs and the gold knob rubbing against his stomach.

"I've got to get there early, Albino, so make haste. . . ."

The vehicle, an out-of-date model Carrelhas had bought secondhand from a doctor at Albergaria, set off in a tremor, traversed the town and, frightening dogs and hens, coursed along the main road. In a twinkling it seemed to connect Cidacos with Covo, and even up the Vermoim rise it made breakaway pines run quickly one after the other. When it passed through Sobradelo, it overtook Manuel da Bouça who was tramping along the road on his way home. He recognized Nunes and politely whipped off his hat, but Nunes didn't see him, and the car passed on, whirling a cloud of dust in his face.

Nunes, who knew the road well, wasn't looking at anything. He was lost in his own reflections, thinking about the coming event and the stream of money the new agency ought to bring him. At Baralhas he glanced at his watch. Half-past one . . . Serafim must have got everything ready. . . . Then he relapsed into his own reflections again.

When at last the car turned into the square of Macieira de Cambra, Nunes ran his eyes anxiously over the facade of his new agency. The rapid photograph they took left him satisfied. On the wall, newly painted in ocher, was the signboard:

NUNES & COSTA

PASSAGE AND PASSPORT AGENCY

And overhead, now falling into folds, now streaming in the air, flew the national flag. As soon as the car stopped, Serafim Costa came running out to greet his partner. Nunes got out, shook the hand the other man stretched out to him, and, casting a scrutinizing glance over the inside of the shop, asked, "So? Is everything ready?"

"Everything! It was no end of a job, but we managed all right."

The new agency was much more showy than the one where Nunes had laid the foundations of his fortune. Taking advantage of the length of the building, he had given orders to have the counter placed in the foreground, running from one side to the other, and along the counter, to make the office look even more important, was a wire netting with various wickets in it. Inside the counter, to left and right, were two kneehole desks flanked by tall American-style filing cabinets, and between them were three highly polished, shining tables for the clerks. On the walls were a series of shipping-company posters—great liners sailing on glaucous seas—which made the inside of the agency bright with color.

Nunes had planned with shrewdness and, hoping to attract not only the inhabitants of the Cambra Valley but also people from the Arouca mountains, he had ordered all this pretentious fitting up to be done, knowing that countryfolk would be impressed by the show and would place their fate in his hands without hesitation.

After looking at the final touches that had been carried out in his absence under Serafim Costa's orders, Nunes passed on to the next room where, set out on a white cloth, were mountains of sweet things and platoons of champagne glasses placed round a big vase of flowers.

Serafim Costa had placed only a little capital in the business, and so, respecting Nunes as if he were an employer, he was carefully following his glance round, anxious to see the effect of the *mise en scène* that was his handiwork. But Nunes uttered only a curt "It's all right," while he helped himself to a coconut cake. But then he had to change the leisurely tempo of his proceedings, because a rocket went off outside, followed by another, and another.

"They're there! They're there!" Serafim exclaimed.

"What time is it?"

And Nunes looked at his watch, but Serafim was quicker, and informed him, "It's five past three. It's time—"

"Come along."

And they turned back into the office. Several municipal officials had already assembled behind the counter, and Nunes went up to them with outstretched hand. "Why didn't you send some-

one to say you had arrived? I was inside there, and didn't know.
. . ." Then they all moved toward the door.

To the accompaniment of exploding rockets, the governor of
the council and the sergeant commanding the station of the
Republican Guard had crossed the square, and now Nunes was
the first to go forward and greet them effusively.

"How is your Excellency?" he said to the governor, and to
the sergeant, "How are you?"

They entered the agency and cast a glance round the interior.
Nunes gave explanations; then they all exclaimed together, "It's
fine! It's really fine! The best to be found in Cambra!" Then they
stood in groups round the desks, spinning out small talk, waiting
for the arrival of the chairman of the Municipal Chamber.

It was almost four o'clock when Dr. Arruda got down from
his sorrel horse at the door of the agency. Would they please
excuse him for not coming earlier? He had to go to Gandra
unexpectedly.

To the accompaniment of compliments and more rockets he
was conducted inside the office and there confirmed the approval
already expressed by the others. Yes, the agency was really well
fitted up. He already knew it, because he had passed by some
days before, and Serafim had invited him to go in.

Huddling between the tables and the counter, they made
their way to the inner room where the refreshments were to
be served. Nunes showed them their places. "Dr. Arruda here,"
and he pointed to the head of the table, "and here at your side,
the governor . . . Here, the officer of the Guard." And then
turning to the other guests, "Gentlemen, please sit down where
you like."

Serafim Costa, with the help of an old woman who didn't
seem used to the job, was opening champagne. As soon as he
heard the first cork pop, Nunes said, "Hand me that bottle, so
that I can be serving these gentlemen." And he filled their
glasses.

"Enough, thanks."

"That's fine."

"Thanks."

Then there was a short silence, a pause of thinly disguised expectation. They were waiting for Serafim to serve the other guests. Arruda, who had been the delegate of the public prosecutor in Aveiro and who prided himself on being a man of breeding, didn't think this pause was very satisfactory, and took the initiative to end it.

"What do you think of this weather? Hot, eh? Just as though we were in July!"

"That's right," agreed the sergeant.

"My horse got into the devil of a sweat coming from Gandra to here," Arruda went on.

"Since you mention it, Doctor . . . what about the road . . . the Gandra road? You know, only a short time back I was almost shot out of the car. There are such holes, room for an ox in some of them!" said Nunes.

"The matter's being looked into, it's being looked into."

"With your influence in Aveiro, Doctor, you could, if you wanted . . ."

"My influence, now, it's not as much as all that," answered Arruda, trying to look modest.

Nunes turned to the other end of the table and exclaimed, "Come, gentlemen, what are we waiting for?" and picking up a dish of sweetmeats he offered it to Arruda. "Help yourself, Doctor." When the chairman of the Chamber, having helped himself, was passing the delicacies on to the governor of the council, Nunes again gave a general invitation to fall to. "No ceremony, gentlemen, I beg of you!" Then greedy teeth began to bite into sugary pastries, and champagne glasses were lifted up, unsteady in some hands not used to the ritual.

Arruda was the first to give a slight cough, signal to make ready for the toast. He turned round in his chair, looked steadily at Nunes and, letting the light fall full on his face, which was white, still young-looking, on the long side, with well-developed forehead, haughty monocle and impertinent pointed chin, he ejaculated, "My friend . . ."

Nunes hastily put on a modest countenance, and the sergeant, hearing a murmur of voices still coming from the other end of the table where the pose just taken up by Arruda had not been noticed, warned them in a very friendly way, "Sh . . . sh . . . sh . . ."

The chairman of the Chamber was moderate with the moderation of one who knows his position, who knows he's superior, and doesn't doubt the rightness of his opinions. So he was sparing in words. Nunes had unquestionably effected an improvement, so he merited congratulations. He, as chairman of the municipality and as a patriot, was interested in everything that signified progress. And that was the reason for his being there on the present occasion, by his presence to give encouragement to new undertakings. He drank to the success of the agency.

They had not all had time to gulp down the customary mouthful of champagne the toast required before the governor of the council was off and saying, "Worthy gentlemen, Evaristo Nunes and Serafim Costa, my illustrious friends and great patriots . . ." and then all the old threadbare phrases from *The Art of Speaking in Public,* which seemed to apply to the present purpose, began to unroll.

In this solemn moment, the inauguration of the new agency was an occasion for congratulation. As Dr. Arruda had well said, it represented a great improvement for Macieira de Cambra. When this region should one day be given its due, and tourists from home and abroad came there to satisfy their curiosity, upon seeing such an up-to-date office they would realize that they were not in a district indifferent to the gigantic work of civilization. He knew all the principal towns of the land, and he did not hesitate to state that, even if there were bigger offices than this one, there did not exist one that could surpass it for good taste and up-to-dateness. With four or five other business houses equipped up to the same level, Macieira would take on the appearance of a great commercial center. For this reason, he desired the example set by Nunes to bear fruit. Nunes was a great patriot, in the purest meaning of the word. Even though belonging to another district, he had not hesitated to endow Macieira de Cambra with an organization of this nature. It is true, a big campaign was being set in motion against emigration, principally in the cities. He must confess that this campaign was in part well founded and worthy of his support. He thought it was necessary to put a stop to the abuses of dishonest agents and recruiters, but at the same time it was necessary to encourage men of the moral stature of Evaristo Nunes. Because the truth is that only emigration carried out conscientiously and intelligently could be of use to the country. Everything of mark that the provinces of Portugal possessed—and he knew them all well—was due to those emigrants who had made fortunes overseas. Hospitals, road extensions, churches, public fountains, public improvements of all kinds that were being put into service every day, who were responsible for them? Without question, those emigrants who had gone away poor and come back rich. If such men had never left their home towns, never would they have been able to come back and confer on them those benefits of which they might well be proud!

The governor's concluding words were received with enthusiastic applause.

Nunes, still keeping up his attitude of unassuming modesty, made his reply holding his champagne glass between long dark fingers lightly resting on the table.

He did not merit such praise. He had only done his duty as a patriot and a republican. If he drew attention here to his political opinions, it was because he found himself in the presence of two other republicans of high repute—Dr. Arruda and their respected governor—and also because he thought that every good republican should work for the improvement of his own province under republican auspices, because that was tantamount to enriching the Republic itself. His affection for Macieira was of long standing. There were people who looked upon this district as a rival of his own district; but he was not of that opinion. He looked upon them as two brothers, and in his own mind they were mingled in such a way that, though he was born in Oliveira, he would like to die or at least be buried in Cambra. He was touched by the fact that the governor had referred to his affection for Macieira; and indeed it was so deep that, owing to it, he had not hesitated to open an agency here with the up-to-date accessories that all present had seen and been kind enough to praise, while the head office he had been running for many years in his home town was nothing more than a very modest office.

Nunes spoke with long pauses, sometimes dragging out the phrases of his harangue with difficulty, but when he found the words he wanted and was carried away by his own enthusiasm, then his pale face seemed to expand and under the wide-open lid the blind eye dilated, white with a tragic whiteness.

Replying to the last part of the governor's speech, he declared that all of them could be easy in mind. He defended emigration because it was the biggest source of gold entering the country. But never could he condone those who exploited the emigrant. He had been agent for passages and passports for many years past, and he could boast that his hands were clean. And his past was the guarantee of his future. The only pride of his life was to be an honest man and—why not say it—a sincere and disinterested patriot!

5

THE *Liberal,* with the two articles marked round with red pencil—patient labor of Francisco during a whole afternoon—was distributed gratis at the Nove market. Drilled by Nunes, Serafim had gone to Gandra with two strapping youths to hand out Borges' paper to vendors and passersby. The two youths carrying the papers under their arms moved on from the strip of ground where earthenware was sold—ocher glaze glittering among packing straw—to the eucalyptus trees where the animals were tied: resigned indifferent oxen chewing the cud; male and female calves restless on the short rope and because of the presence of so many strangers; mares and mules flipping the flies away with a flick of their tails. They made their way among groups gathered round grunting young pigs—some lead-colored, others speckled black and white, and all with the rosy little snout of youth. Handing out papers, they had even penetrated into the dark, dirty booths where men and women were eating skate and fried plaice with a great deal of noise and shouting, and calling for great tankards of wine. Coming out again, they pushed by a cripple selling holy medals and chapbooks, "The Almanac" and "The Story of Jack Soldier," who stood looking at them with misgiving, fearing competitors; and away they went —Take it, take it; it costs you nothing—along the row of country-men and their women who were either eyeing or trafficking the knickknacks and cheap jewelry on stalls piled high with articles of fanciful form and nature. Then they took a turn among the cloth sellers' section—Covilhã cheviots repeatedly fingered by knowing rustic hands, and printed calicoes that were a fancy fair of color tantalizing the eager eyes of marriageable girls—and finally gave out the last few copies among the people who were buying strings of onions, all spread out on the ground like braids of hair with golden fruits caught in them.

Throughout the whole market full of awnings, dust, and sun the *Liberal* was unfolded amid the dark crowd of men, and for a moment its pages sometimes covered the multicolored bosoms of girls wandering about from stall to stall.

Some of those who had been to the elementary school and learned to write a letter and the four rules of arithmetic settled down and read the paper, astounded that it should be given out in that out-of-the-way place where even publicity leaflets hadn't yet penetrated.

Those who couldn't read stared for a moment at the red lines Francisco had drawn, and kept the paper for domestic use or for some neighbor to read who was better acquainted with letters.

And at night, when the market ground was as dusty and empty as an old battlefield, silent groups gathered in cottage yards in all the surrounding villages—as Nunes had foreseen—to listen attentively while a neighbor (called in for the purpose) read the *Liberal* aloud.

And listening, those who had some small property felt pleased surprise at the thought of the wealth that was said to exist in America, and they let their fancy wander over a number of things, imagining the possibility of perhaps deciding to go—but all vague, smoke without fire, the beginning of a revery that went on to include the names of Dr. Leal, the new minister, or the notary Sampaio who was taking a cure at Gerez, and others mentioned in other parts of the paper that the reader had also read out on request.

But in the minds of poor men who sweated all day long in someone else's fields, the mirage was fascinating; it was even painful, as though there were arms winding round their throats. The great difficulty that chafed them most was the lack of money for the passage. Old longings and repressed desires surged up from an old whirlpool that had simmered inside for years—just a little surface swirl on days when the larder was full, a vortex when other people killed pigs and there wasn't even black pudding for them. So much money, and they couldn't get hold of it, couldn't even stretch their hands out to it! And plans began to form, the same old plans, but now taking on new shapes: greater ambition entailing greater sacrifice; those who had nothing at all once again nourishing the hope of raising a loan; those who had some strips of land turning over the idea of mortgaging or selling them—and all fascinated by the same mirage, all of them hanging giddy over the same abyss. Even old Domingos who loved his sheep as though they were daughters, who cried brokenheartedly if one got lost or hidden while dragging a few green leaves from tree stumps, even he mentally totted up their value and considered the bitter sacrifice of selling them and going off—an old man who limped along, the stick with which he stumped over hill and dale his sole support.

Next day, the impulse faded in the minds of many of them, withdrawing again into the secret places of the soul; but in some it remained latent, on the alert for any excuse to burst forth anew.

It was something they talked about on the roads, ax on shoulder, or elbow resting on the haft of their mattock; in the fields while they were digging side by side; at the pump and at the dam where the women did their washing. Vague, more vague and transparent than a May cloud, the dream of America had already come that way before in remarks passed by someone or other. But now it had taken on consistency, printed and backed up by the newspaper—a reliable opinion you could really believe, because the gentlemen who directed it wouldn't go and tell lies.

Even Zé do Aido was influenced by the new train of thought; his imagination took the new direction and he changed his plans, persuading Anacleto and Rosalino to go along with him too. They were the first clients to call at the Nunes & Costa Agency, and they were warmly received by Serafim. He agreed to arrange an early date of departure for them—though not so early as might be wished. There was more money to be made in America, therefore more competition to get there; it was necessary to select, and so it wasn't as easy to set foot in America as in Brazil.

When the news of Zé's decision reached Frágua, Manuel da Bouça felt his own courage weaken, and he muttered smothered imprecations about that fickle fellow who changed his mind oftener than his shirt. He had grown used to the idea of setting out with companions, and now, without that support, it cost him something to face the harsh truth. And to make matters worse, another man who had talked of going, António do Pico, sent word from Ponte Nova that he couldn't get away before winter.

Manuel da Bouça turned the disappointment over and over in his mind; it wasn't the thought of the new country that disturbed him; there was plenty of time to think about that, and it was something vague on the other side of the Atlantic. What worried him was the train to Lisbon, and Lisbon itself, a place he always imagined as a hectic confusion in which you got lost in an amazing way. Then, there was going on board, and the boat . . . It would all have been pleasant if Zé do Aido and the others had been with him; but by himself, he felt really bewildered.

But his face didn't show the worm that was gnawing him inside. It had become even more reserved, determined, and proud.

And one night when Amélia was bewailing this lack of companions—you'd feel better about it, man—he exclaimed with angry
contempt: "They're a lot of cowards! They just run like dogs
after the first bone!" And he made up his mind to go on with the
final preparations, but sometimes in the evil temper of a man
going out to kill.

Nunes wanted more money; because of the army discharge,
it would be necessary to grease the palms of the officials in Aveiro
who attended to the passports. He would certainly understand
that cases like his gave a lot of trouble, because he was still fit
for service.

As down an inclined plane and into a vortex went rolling all
the money that Manuel da Bouça had received from Carrazedas.
He could do nothing but agree, because he was helpless against
that kind of thing . . . and he still had very unpleasant memories of his stay in the Barracks of the Twenty-fourth. But he
didn't tell his wife that the money was gone, so that she wouldn't
bother him with worries and wailings.

At last the document came with a lot of rubber stamps, stamps,
and scrawls on it. Nunes handed it to him with the words: "The
ship will be in Lisbon next Thursday. You'd better get there
three days earlier, so that they can put the visa on your passport
at the Brazilian Consultate." Manuel da Bouça didn't seem to
have understood, so he added: "They'll tell you there what you
have to do. Ask for the Brazilian Consulate, and they'll tell you.
. . . They've got to put another rubber stamp on yet."

Manuel da Bouça thanked him with great politeness, and
went out memorizing the instructions—Brazilian Consulate . . .
another rubber stamp . . . Brazilian Consulate. Out in the
street, facing the future, totting up accounts, a thought struck
him that made him turn back. He went timidly into the agency
again, and found Nunes smoking a cigar, legs crossed, chair
pushed away from the desk, and reading the *Janeiro,* while Francisco, head down, was scribbling on papers.

"If you please, sir . . ."

Nunes put his newspaper down and turned round coldly. "Have you forgotten something?"

"I just thought . . . I'd like to know whether it'll be necessary to pay anything more at the consulate. It's so as to go prepared. . . ."

"Yes, there's something, but not much. Less than a hundred escudos," answered Nunes with a lavish air.

"Thank you, sir. That's all I wanted to know. Good day." And his voice died away in his throat.

Back in the village, he said to his wife and daughter, "It's next Thursday, but I've got to get to Lisbon three days earlier."

They began to cry, as though the fixing of the date intensified the distress they had been living in for weeks. He, gentler than usual, tried to console them. "Now, now, what are you crying about? While there's life there's hope! And it had to be . . ." And a little later, as though the idea that would be a help to him in the big city would also be a comfort to the women, he added: "Well, now, when I get to Lisbon, I shall have to look up Custódio de São Martinho, and he'll show me what to do. You'll have to ask old Ana for his address. Did you hear?" Amélia answered with a nod and went on wiping her eyes on her apron, so he said again, "It's not worth crying about! What's the use?"

But that same evening, down by the river near the rotting trunk of an oak in which woodpeckers had made their nest, he said to himself, "I shan't be able to come and see this again." And the thought made him feel as sad as though someone had died.

6

A MÉLIA, crying and struggling to get free, kept on repeating, "Let me go, let me go with him as far as Oliveira!" and the neighbors—close friends, all the women of Frágua, and many of the men and youths who had crowded into the yard—listened with compassion to the pitiful entreaty.

"But why, why, Senhora Amélia? Trouble should be kept at home. . . ."

Curiosity showed on the faces of the young, and distress on the faces of the adults—old women with deeper wrinkles and wisps of whitish hair showing like tow from under their flowered kerchiefs.

"Manuel, let me go with you as far as Oliveira! Oh, my heart will break!"

"Calm yourself, Senhora Amélia; don't take on so. . . ."

Followed by his brother-in-law Joaquim, Manuel da Bouça passed through the gate in the wall and put on a brave face so as not to give way to his wife's entreaties. Then old Domingos came limping up, panting from his long walk, and blocked the path. He held out a bottle and said with forced cheeriness, "Take this! It's for the journey, because it's cold at sea. . . . And it's good, drawn from the São Martinho still."

"Thank you, thank you, Father Domingos! Here's health to you and many years yet! I'll see you when I come back. . . ."

And the old man, sensing the stress of the moment, stood there very serious with his lips open and two solitary teeth showing.

Manuel da Bouça, without turning round so as not to show any weakening of spirit, said again in a louder voice, "Till I come back, then!" But Amélia, breaking loose from friends and spectators, ran after him. "My Manuel, my Manuel!" Unable to hold out, he came back, opened his arms and silently pressed the sobbing woman to his breast. The bottle slipped from his hands, rolled down Amélia's skirt, and fell to the ground. Deolinda came up and joined them, followed by all the little throng that had gathered in the yard. "My dad!"

He took her in his arms once more. "Now, don't cry. You must be brave . . . and one fine day I'll be back."

"We shall miss the bus," said brother-in-law Joaquim, bending down and picking up the bottle.

"I'm coming, I'm coming."

"Let me go with you as far as Oliveira!" Amélia begged again.

"No, wife; that's not possible; it would be still worse for you."

He pulled free at last, and *click-clack* along the road tramped farther and farther away with his brother-in-law. In front of them marched Rita da Fonte carrying the trunk on her head, and on top of it the patchwork bag—multicolored chessboard strident amid the surrounding green. Along they went in the evening sunlight, turning round from time to time and Manuel's big hand waving goodbye.

Amélia and her daughter went on weeping, and they wept louder and more bitterly each time the emigrant turned and waved farewell. There were tears in the eyes of some of the old village women too, and the hardier ones tried to speak words of comfort.

"Now, now, not even five years, and he'll be back again, rich, and sound as an apple. Then we'll be seeing Senhora Amélia in a big house big enough to hold all Frágua."

At last, at the bend in the path where it goes up to Salgueiros, Manuel da Bouça turned round and waved for the last time. It was so far away that he couldn't see the expressions of the people left behind. They were just a confused patch of men and women feverishly waving their arms. Pale with the pang of separation, he stood and looked back, saying goodbye to everything in a daze. Even his own house, though the whitewash was fresh, seemed sad-looking and permeated with the heaviness coming down from the Felgueira and spreading over the whole valley. Far below, they were still waving farewell to him, and he could still make out Amélia, who had moved away from the group to wave and wave to him.

"Come on," his brother-in-law said to him. He complied, and together they disappeared round the bend, to climb up to the highroad. Rita had already put the bag and the trunk down near the telegraph pole.

"Manuel, do you want a drink to cheer you up?" asked Joaquim.

"No, not now, keep it for later. What time is it?"

"I don't know, but we ought to be hearing the bus any time now."

Manuel da Bouça stood looking over the valley. Frágua to the left, half hidden among the pines; then fields, some green, some yellowish, spreading out peacefully on each side of the Caima; in the far distance, clinging to the base of the Felgueira were the buildings of Mosteiro; and, to the right, in Santo António, the red roof of the school and the tower of the new church. Now it all seemed to have a subtle charm, a beauty never felt before, and a melancholy sadness surged up in his heart, rising like a thick fog and choking him. The very sun, which he had always looked upon as useful only at harvesttimes, now exerted an unexpected magnetism that forced him to look as he had never looked before at the white-and-black lace it was weaving under the branches. . . . And Amélia, how was she taking it? . . . Then the panorama caught him again with its charm, and next it dropped a transparent curtain in front of his eyes through which he saw everything shadowy and moist—the pine trees lengthened to an unnatural height with shaggy spines sticking out; the tower dancing, losing its angles and thinning into a sheet; the whole scene was bewitched, as though seen through a rain-beaten pane of glass.

He raised his hand to his eyes and hastily brushed away the tears, the first he had shed, so that Joaquim and Rita wouldn't notice. Were Amélia and Deolinda still crying too?

"It's a long time coming," he said in a hollow voice.

Joaquim listened for sounds coming from the Cambra direction. "I think I can hear something. . . . No, no, it isn't the bus." And he leaned back against the pole, smoking thoughtfully.

Manuel da Bouça looked at Rita da Fonte, who was sitting on the trunk. "You can go back, if you like, Mother Rita. Joaquim and I'll put it in the bus."

"Well, when a body's come as far as this . . . I'm not in a hurry."

A great softness and silence covered the valley and rose up to the highroad, enveloping everything. On the top of the church tower at Santo António the metal weathercock shone in the dying sunlight. Suddenly from the Salgueiros side a boy ran up trundling an old barrel hoop—dirty face, ragged, and half his backside bare. He stood looking at them a minute, and then began legging it again, running after his hoop.

"It's coming, Manuel," said Joaquim moving away from the pole.

The throbbing of a motor could be heard in the distance. Rita got up, and the three of them stood watching the next bend.

When the bus came in sight, Joaquim stepped forward and signaled it to stop. There were just two seats left: one beside the driver, and the other inside where the passengers were all well dressed—because poor people can spend money on this type of transport only on really grave occasions. When the bag and the trunk had been flung on the top of the bus, Joaquim said, "I'll stay outside, and you get in."

Then Manuel stammered out: "Goodbye, Mother Rita! I'll be back someday. Give my love to Amélia and my girl . . ." And once again his voice died away in his throat.

Taking a tight grip, and awkward from lack of experience, he hoisted himself up with an ape's clumsiness. And inside, it was only with difficulty that he managed to edge in between two well-nourished men unwilling to welcome the intruder who was coming to reduce their space on the seat.

The bus passed through Salgueiros—a white house here and there on either side of the road set amid mimosa, oaks, and vines, and Manuel da Bouça shrank in between the two men, self-conscious and diffident. Out of the corner of his eyes, he compared his own best jacket, with its country cut and finish, with the suits they wore, the rings on their fingers, and their general appearance of people who lived in comfort in town or city.

They were already going through Sobradelo before he realized that his embarrassment at being near such fine people had made him forget to look out for the doors and windows of friends he had in Salgueiros. Never mind . . . It's better like that. I hadn't the heart to say goodbye to anyone else.

And once again in spite of himself he fell back into his own thoughts. Poor Deolinda! Poor Amélia! If he could only take them with him . . . If he could only take them along too, but sure of hearth and home! That would be fine, oh, yes, that would be the thing.

Now they were chugging up the Vermoin rise. Fields of maize spread out on either side, with a line of poplars running through them bordering a brook. When he came back, he'd be coming this way, and he'd be alone in Carrelhas' car, because he wouldn't let them know what day he'd get back. He'd give Amélia and Deolinda a big surprise. But how many years would he have to wait for that?

His eyes ran over the twilight countryside, taking it all in more and more avidly. Two of the passengers were talking, and some of their words broke through and lodged in his mind: Well managed, it would give four hundred horse. . . . That's what they did in Zêzere . . . Zêzere . . . Zêzere . . .

Night was falling when the bus entered the Covo woods, sweeping the pines and banks with the luminous jet of its headlights. Manuel da Bouça was feeling cramped, but he didn't like to move for fear of bothering the other two passengers. He felt that he couldn't breathe, with that anxious feeling, like the first night he had lain down in the Barracks of the Twenty-fourth and the lights had been put out.

When they got to town, the bus sounded its warning notes more and more frequently; houses with lights sped by, the theater, the gateway of Dr. Silveira's house, and the trees in the square. Then they stopped at the Post Office building for the mailbags and passengers who didn't want to go on to the station. Then they backed a bit in order to turn and make the smooth run to the station. Here there were more lights, and more powerful, and on the other side of the track the big metal water tank with its iron ladder.

And now for Manuel da Bouça everything passed in a rapid blur: getting the trunk and the bag down, Joaquim paying the bus fares at the station entrance, the buying of his ticket, shadows, female forms, luggage . . . and then a voice, "Only two minutes . . ."

"Joaquim, give a hug for me to Amélia and the girl. And tell them I went off in good spirits. Tell them, and tell everybody that, will you?"

"All right."

"Goodbye, Joaquim! Till I come back, eh? And good luck!"

he croaked, emotion choking him, and Joaquim pressed tight in his arms.

The red eye of the train came nearer, making the rails glitter and the whole station throb with movement.

"The trunk won't get lost?"

"No, but don't lose the slip they gave you; that's to get it back in Lisbon."

Joaquim went up to the footboard with him, and then Manuel da Bouça climbed in alone, provincial and awkward, dragging his patchwork bag through the mob of people boarding the third-class carriages.

Some moments passed, and then, among others, his face appeared at the window, trying to force the full lips into a confident smile, but it was only a wry grimace, a painful twist of the whole mouth.

"Goodbye, Joaquim!"

And the train moved off with a dog chasing after it, barking wildly.

7

A T Lisbon station, feeling timid and awkward in such a
strange place, he held out the slip of paper to the
railway clerks, but they threw only a surly look at it and said:
"Your luggage? It'll be better later. You'd better come back later."
So he went off uneasy in mind. They might lose the trunk, or even
steal it. . . . Later. But would he be able to find his way back?
Why, yes, of course, Custódio de São Martinho would come back
with him.

Somewhat relieved by this thought, he went down the steps
without any fixed purpose, just following other people, with his
poor patchwork bag looking very conspicuous among all the fine
valises.

In the square at the bottom of the steps he got his first big
surprise. So many people! So many cars! And which way should
he go? But with a tongue in your head you can get anywhere.
Nevertheless, he felt bothered and perplexed. So many people!

Not even at the fairs of Senhora de La Salette or São Bartolomeu de Arouca were there so many!

He took several steps forward, jostling people with his awkward shoulders and his bag incommoding all those town legs. Some folk scowled at him, and one fine gentleman—well dressed and with a pin in his tie—turned round and exclaimed, "Can't you see where you're going, you lout?"

He began to feel afraid of the city. He was bewildered by the movement, the lofty facades, the many-changing scenes that met his country eyes on all sides. He felt more and more humble and clumsy, there with his bag on the pavement, his hand fumbling in his pocket for Custódio's address, and looking round for someone who seemed less standoffish, someone poor and simple, more like himself. He settled on a fishwife, but when she heard the almost beggar's voice asking the way to the street written on the paper he held out, she answered in a mocking tone.

"Eh, Dad, you've just got here, haven't you? I don't know how to read, either."

And she went off with her basket on her head, light on her feet, hips swaying rhythmically, harmony in the whole silhouette—a figure stepped down from the bas-relief of some wonderful frieze.

Holding out his paper with the same beggar's gesture, Manuel da Bouça next approached an old man, who stopped a moment, looked at it, and then pointed out the way.

"Let me see . . . Gomes Freire . . . Turn up that way, and halfway up the avenue, ask the policeman."

So he set off, his eyes glancing this way and that, trying to take everything in, then falling to the ground chapfallen, imagining sarcasm on every face, hesitating at every street corner, until—his heart giving a jump of relief—he found himself standing in the doorway of the dairy where Custódio da São Martinho was recommending the excellence of a melon to a customer.

Noticing him there, and recognizing him, his fellow country-man exclaimed: "Why, if it isn't Senhor Manuel! How are things going? I hope it's a good wind that's blown you here. And how's Senhora Amélia? And young Deolinda? Everything well at home?"

"Yes, we're managing, we're managing, God willing!" he answered, gripping the white soft plump hand Custódio held out to him.

"What a surprise! I never thought I'd be seeing you. . . ."

"And you, what a strapping chap! It's good to see you! And your mother sends her love."

"Thank you. She's well, isn't she? I really must write to her one of these days." Then, nodding toward his customer, "If you don't mind, Senhor Manuel, we'll have a talk presently."

"Well, of course, take your time; you must get on with your work," Manuel da Bouça answered and, feeling in his own element again, sat down on one of the benches to wait while Custódio weighed the melon and struggled hard not to give the reduction the woman tried to beat him down to.

When they were alone once more in the small white shop with its benches, counter, and iron tables, with its shelves and walls covered with colored posters shouting the praises of drinks and chocolates, Custódio took up his string of questions again.

"Then what made you decide to come to Lisbon? Have you come to work?"

"I'm going farther than this. . . . I'm going to Brazil."

"To Brazil?"

"To make a living, because the home place is only good for a man who's got something of his own." And as Custódio didn't reply within the natural time limit, Manuel da Bouça went on: "I'd be glad if you'd help me with one or two things here, like going to the Brazilian Consulate, and then to the

boat, because a man's helpless in Lisbon for the first time. . . .
Oh, and I've got to get my trunk too."

"That'll be all right, Senhor Manuel."

"The boat leaves the day after tomorrow, and till then it'd be
a help if you could fix me up with a blanket and bench
here. . . ."

"Well, of course. We must do what we can."

"I can pay what's necessary."

"Now, man, don't talk like that. You won't be as comfortable
as you'd be at home, naturally, but it won't be for lack of good
will. . . ."

"Thank you, thank you, Custódio! You're a good chap!" and
he looked him over from head to foot: the white face with
its plump cheeks, the white shop jacket, the trousers and shoes
such as other city men wore; twenty-eight to thirty the lad
must be, and how he envied him! "And how's life treating you?
You seem to be getting on nicely here. . . ."

"Oh, there are more buts than nuts. . . . I only set up here
two years ago, and the place hasn't got a very good clientèle.
This street's almost a blind alley. The devil take that blank
wall there right opposite! If they'd only knock it down and
build houses . . . That's why, if I could get someone to take
over this place, I'd take another one on Conde Redondo."

"Well, we all have our troubles. But a lot of people from our
part of the world would give a lot to be like you! It's true. And
I've heard you've married a Lisbon girl, too."

"Yes, I'm married, and I've already got a little son. . . ."

"Ah!"

Custódio went to the doorway at the back that opened between
shelves loaded with bottles, and called out, "Margarida! Margarida!" and then went on talking to Manuel da Bouça. "So
up at home there's nothing new? Now, haven't I heard somewhere that Rosa do Marques has got married?"

"Yes, that's right. She married a chap from Coelhosa."

Then a young woman appeared in the doorway. She was pale and thin, but her breasts swelled full under her pink overall.

"Margarida, this is a friend from my village, and he's going to Brazil. But he's only going on board the day after tomorrow. We must put a mattress down somewhere for him to sleep. And then you must look after the counter for a bit, because I've got to go with him to the Brazilian Consulate." Then, turning to Manuel da Bouça, he said, "This is my wife. . . ."

"God bless you!"

With a faint smile she bent her head to acknowledge the greeting. Then a child's cry came from behind the shop.

"Excuse me," said Margarida, and was on the point of moving away when her husband called out, "Remember, our friend's going to eat with us here!"

"There's a queue, Senhor Manuel! We'll have to stay here till dusk," declared Custódio when he saw the column of people waiting on the stairs, right from the street up to the floor where the consulate was. Men and women were huddled together in a dark mass, and spreading out over the steps, and waiting, waiting for the key to give one more turn in the door through which they were going to leave the country. Then the eyes grew accustomed to the dark staircase and could distinguish individual characteristics: the men had big moustaches such as were no longer the fashion in the city, complexions burned by the sun in Virgilian landscapes, great calloused hands, and their whole appearance countrified; the women were clutching their children to them, some with breasts planted in pink little mouths, others awkward and ill at ease, eyes restless under the flowered kerchief covering their heads.

Whole families of them, ranging from newborn mites to weedy adolescents, and from these to red-cheeked young men now free from military service, and ending up with the progenitors of all this offspring—men getting on in years, flesh drained by work and worry, taking the path of exile in search of sweeter bread. They had been waiting for many hours, and so they had already exhausted all small talk, exclamations, laughter. They had grown drowsy, and doubtful whether they would get into the consulate that afternoon, and they were huddling closer to the wall so that persons going up to the Polyclinic and upper floors need not jostle by or tread on their toes. But there was such a crowd of them that all precaution was useless, and those who wanted to pass had to shove their way through the dark human herd.

Custódio managed to find out that it was hopeless for Manuel to join the gloomy troop, because all these people had been there since the preceding night, and many would have to wait till next day because, whosesoever turn it might happen to be, the consulate inexorably closed its doors at four o'clock.

The two of them went away; and that same night, after the meal, which Manuel da Bouça hardly touched because his mind was in a turmoil after the tension of the day, they returned to the building in the Praça Camoes.

It was ten o'clock, and there was already quite a crowd. The tail of the day's queue now occupied the front places and filled up the second flight of the dark stairs. At first only the flicker of two cigarettes could be seen. Then one sensed the resigned animal cleaving to its own kind in defense of its lair. And only the voices showed the different sexes: the women's thin and on edge in the bitterness of complaint, the men's fuller and stronger in face of chance and change. From time to time a sigh came from the gloom.

"Don't leave your place without asking your neighbors to keep it," Custódio advised, and he clipped his meaning with the saying, "If away you race, you lose your place . . . And when it's all finished, come back to my house. You know the way now. But if you can't find it, ask. It's Gomes Freire. Don't forget, Gomes Freire. And now I must go. I'm wanted at the shop."

"Yes, you go, I'll be all right, Custódio."

So Custódio went off, and Manuel da Bouça took up his place at the end of the queue, and leaned against the wall. One more cigarette began to burn the soft black of night. Then a voice came from the step.

"Sit down, senhor, because you'll never last till morning if you stand up."

"I was just thinking the same myself," he murmured in reply, lowering himself down and stretching his legs out on the landing.

Then other people began to arrive, the number increasing till the whole of the lower flight was occupied too. Up on the fourth floor a light was switched on for a moment and the gleam vaguely lit up the dark crowd below. And they all looked at one another; eyes that had grown sleepy opened too; but not one of them spoke, as though they were appalled at their own appearance. Before the disturbing light was switched off again, a baby woke up and began to whimper, and its mother, putting her flaccid breast to its mouth, crooned to it, "There there . . . there, there . . ."

Plunged in darkness once more, men drew in their heads and tried to find a position to sleep.

"What a thirst I've got!" exclaimed a husky voice from the very top steps. Nobody answered. They were in a strange land, without any inkling of helpful ways and means.

Another light shone out, this time from the spacious entrance below. Then heavy steps sounded, and the porter came up.

"It's forbidden to make a noise!" he warned them in an ill-tempered voice. "If you do, you'll all go outside."

The words reverberated in the silence. The porter turned and went down again, put the light out, and closed the door of his small room.

Gradually the hum of noise from outside grew less and less. Individual sounds were more distinct, and the hooting of motors was fairly clear. Then, after a time, Manuel da Bouça could count the striking of a clock somewhere. One . . . two . . . three . . . twelve.

Now there was no glow of cigarettes in the darkness, and snores began to come from the heap of flesh and rags. One was flutelike and very annoying. But Manuel da Bouça couldn't sleep. The thought of his wife, his daughter, his village came back to him. He had forgotten them during the day in the hurry of new sensations. Would they be fast asleep now? No, no; Amélia wouldn't be asleep. He knew her too well. She had to turn and turn in bed before she could close her eyes. . . . Quite distinctly he could hear the little groans she gave sometimes, on nights when she was worried and anxious.

Again the clock struck. One . . . two . . . Two o'clock.

He stretched his arm out on the edge of the step above, and settled his head on it. There was someone else near him who couldn't sleep. There was fidgeting in the darkness, limbs being stretched and drawn in again, and from time to time a sigh of fatigue.

The phantasms of Amélia and his daughter were followed by that of a ship, the one that was going to take him to Brazil. Next, it was the wife of Custódio who came into his dream, with a nose bigger than in real life and surrounded by a swarm of children, all alike, all exactly like the one he'd seen in her arms the day before. It was in the street; a motor car came rushing madly along and all the children opened wings and flew away like pigeons from a country road. . . .

When Manuel da Bouça woke up, dim daylight was showing in the staircase. But how unprepossessing the faces of those already awake; the eyes of some were still heavy with sleep; others sunk and thoughtful with fixed witchlike stare; the cheeks, dirty with a fuzz of beard, seemed longer than the evening before. Above him was an old man with thick side-whiskers, in a brown jacket and wide hat. He had a cigarette end stuck on his lower lip, and it was so dead and black that it looked as though it had been stuck there all night. The only thing of sweetness was the look in a baby's big wide-open eyes as it lay in the lap of its sleeping mother and stared at the smooth whiteness of the wall.

Not far away a man of foresight opened a bag and began to eat. All the people who were awake furtively watched the movement of his jaws, and they all had a hungry look in their eyes. Manuel da Bouça too was lamenting in his own mind that he hadn't had the same foresight. He felt hungry for the meal that Custódio's wife had offered him the evening before and that he hadn't touched for lack of appetite; hungry for the soup and maize bread he used to have in his own house—a deep hunger he couldn't fob off with cigarettes.

All the time the light had been losing its duskiness and growing brighter. In one of the corners of the wall you could see a spider spinning its web. Hungry people were beginning to make arrangements about food.

"If you'll keep my place, I'll go and . . ."

"Of course we'll keep it!"

A beardless young man got up jingling money in his hand. "Would you like something too? And you?"

"What could we get?"

"I don't know, what I can find!"

He gathered up new coins and dirty crumpled notes and finally went off, while the others waited hungrily, each minute seeming long, and each step short, as they followed their savior in imagination. Then he came back with a number of bread rolls and a great hunk of cheese thrust in his pocket.

"And there's still money left over."

Hungry teeth closed on the bread. But before they got down to the crumbs, a fortunate discovery made by the young man while he was outside, and whispered from mouth to mouth, was opening pathways in the crowd. The places of those going out being secured by those who stayed behind, turn and turn about, the reasoning animal quickly went down the steps to relieve itself, and quickly came back.

When the group was in full force again, there was already quite a bit of movement in the building. Doors were being opened, city people were going up and down the stairs, their expressions and gestures different from the expressions and gestures of those who had spent the night herded on the steps. From outside came the same deep hum of traffic they had heard the day before.

All eyes were watching the people who went up the stairs: did this one belong to the Consulate, did that one? Then an attendant came in, then a well-dressed gentleman, a second, a third—and finally the door opened. The head of the queue moved forward, timid and unassuming, with papers sticking out of pockets, hats held submissively in hands.

Then a long time passed before the first emigrant came out again with a smile of relief wrinkling up his cheeks.

"If the boat weren't leaving tomorrow I'm sure I wouldn't have waited here a night and a day," the woman who had got her baby cradled in her lap said querulously.

"Are you going to Brazil too?" asked Manuel da Bouça.

"Oh, yes, my man and I are going." At these words the man turned round, the one with the longest moustaches in the whole group.

"Are you going to Santos?"

"Yes, that's where we're making for."

Manuel da Bouça felt the better for this news; a sudden satisfaction made the long wait seem less uncomfortable.

"Are you going there too?"

"Yes."

The questions exchanged led to a desultory conversation, a

means of killing time and drawing those together who were going to take up life in the same place.

By the consulate clock it was three in the afternoon when a clerk took over Manuel da Bouça's papers.

"Seventy escudos."

"What did you say, sir?"

"Seventy escudos."

"Oh."

He paid the money, and in return got another paper in his hand, accompanied by the words, "And now it's the inspection." As he didn't seem to understand, the clerk explained, "Up the stairs, on the second floor . . ." He wanted to ask more questions, but the clerk was already attending to the next emigrant with the same unchanging formulas.

So he followed hard on the heels of the man who had gone through the ritual in front of him and, having climbed the two flights of stairs, found himself in the presence of a white-coated doctor who asked point-blank in a very official style, "Have you been vaccinated?"

"What?"

"Take your jacket off. Now turn your shirt sleeve up. No, not that one, the left." And then laying hold of his shaggy arm, "How many years is it since you were vaccinated?"

"I can't remember."

"Keep your arm like that." And the doctor picked up the lancet, made the incision, and placed the vaccine. "Now you can go."

At least everything went quickly there. And while he was putting his jacket on again, Manuel da Bouça added the operation he had just gone through to the sum of the many perils a man has to face if he wants to go to Brazil.

Custódio went with his friend down to the quays. Other emigrants were already there, very familiar to Manuel da Bouça because of the wait on the stairs of the consulate. As soon as they were all there, another formality had to be gone through. They had to pass another medical inspection before they left their native land either temporarily or for the last time. And they went off like docile animals to expose their battered flesh to the clinical eye and receive the last official stamp.

When they got back to the open air and the quay, they were still ready for any sacrifice. Once they had left their own hearths, everything seemed inevitable, and they accepted everything without surprise. What, is anything else necessary? No, this time there were no other requirements. They could go on board.

In one group after another, struggling with their bags, trunks and wicker baskets, eyes giving uneasy looks all round, they moved down to the tug in a hesitating flock.

Near the stone steps, Custódio stretched out his arms and said, "Goodbye, Senhor Manuel! I hope you'll have good luck and make a lot of money! And when it's time to come back, write and let me know, so that I can meet you in . . ."

"Who knows when I'll be coming back!"

"Oh, it won't be long! You'll see!"

Affected by the leave-taking, they kept their eyes down to hide the tears that were beginning to well up.

"Goodbye, Custódio! And thank you for everything. I don't know how I could have managed without you. . . ."

"Oh, it was less than nothing! Goodbye!"

Manuel da Bouça went down the steps and crossed the plank to the tug, and, standing on board with a feeling of awkwardness and diffidence at this first contact with a boat, he turned and sent a wavering smile to Custódio who was watching from the quay, with his hands in his pockets.

And Custódio was the only one there to say goodbye to Manuel da Bouça when the tug drew away from land.

Now everything was strange to him: moving over the river Tagus, the vibration of the boat, the iron railings, the grating on the coal bunker, the master's head up at the helm—and, on either hand, big ships at anchor standing out against the hills of the far shore or against the waterside buildings of the city.

He felt the instinctive need to be with someone else, to help him to bear the wonder, almost fear, that the new surroundings awakened in him. In the stern he could see the couple he had talked with at the consulate, and he kept looking in their direction, but they didn't see him. They were taken up with the view, eager not to miss anything coming into sight. There were other people sitting near whom he had seen on the stairs, too, but he couldn't think of any pretext for joining them. Then, tired of waiting to catch the eyes of the married couple, he got up and tried to make his way to them, but he soon gave up the attempt: he couldn't get his balance, and the deck danced under his feet.

"That's the one!" someone exclaimed.

"That one there?"

"Yes, that's it!" And they pointed to a ship with a black hull and white ranges of cabins above, and people looking down in curiosity. There was a swarm of boats round it, and in one of them men bare to the waist and covered with coal dust, sweat making furrows in the crust of dirt, were shoveling coal into a great metal box suspended from a crane.

The slow heavy tug drew nearer, and the other boats pulled off to make way for it. When it came alongside, the emigrants went climbing from its deck in a dark frieze up the steps of the liner. They climbed up, taking every precaution not to slip, feeling more and more diffident and awkward in the strange environment. At each step of the ladder their feet seemed to be treading on emptiness, and their hands clutched the slack rope like talons. At the top, one or two austere, serious officials in uniforms stood like watchdogs, and then with the usual masses of papers the newcomers were checked over.

At last the human herd moved off, bewildered in face of

the general lack of helpfulness and questions that never got a reply, looking for their berths, wandering about—well, if it isn't here, it must be there—and all looking stupidly at one another. They went down black stairways, touched dank handrails, stumbled along dark corridors till they were all stowed in their boxes—yours is there and yours is here, they were told in bad Spanish—one above the other like corpses in a tomb.

When Manuel da Bouça went on deck again, the ship was weighing anchor and beginning the ritual of departure. Along the side facing the city there was not an inch of free space left where a curious passenger could lean. Lisbon lay resplendent: the Estrêla Basilica as though inlaid with plates of gold, the towers of the Cathedral and St. Vincent's outlined against the transparent blue of the afternoon sky, and many-windowed buildings covering the hillsides, beyond the line of factory chimneys on the shore. And the same sun that played over the town, whitening facades, giving a red glow to the roofs and filling angles with shadow, was also laying a great white sheet over the yellowish deck of the ship.

Shrilling, the last tug moved away while the screws of the *Darro* began to churn the emerald water of the Tagus. And all the emigrants were ranged along the ship's side, watching, watching they knew not what, since there was no friendly form to wave goodbye to, no possibility of waving any goodbye that would not be lost like the flutter of a sea gull in the vastness of the estuary. Yet they were nearly all strangely moved by this gentle gliding away along the river under the indifferent gaze of the metropolis.

Near the winches, an old peasant woman was wiping away her tears with a corner of the kerchief covering her head, tears that slipped down loosely one after the other, quietly, with no sobs or moans.

All the emigrants were watching. Only now, when they had cast their lot in the unknown, did they instinctively feel the bond, never realized before, that bound their native villages to this city haloed in sun and sky, shading off in the distance to the vessel's stern. Watching it, they felt moved, and their hearts melted at the sight, as though their native places with their well-known figures and tender memories were all focused in that one spot.

8

THE deck never got dry; it was always black, wet, and slippery, as though it were the liner's backyard. The whole third class was black, a sticky suffocating black. It was like a mine at work with the noise of lifts and pulleys, and its long galleries with shadowy forms moving along them in which great eyes of dull glass let into the wall had taken the place of the mine's red lamps. It all smelled of paint, and the kitchens gave off a nauseous reek of food. Beyond every door were people swaddled in thick blankets or brownish dark-colored rugs that added to the staleness of the atmosphere. To make matters worse, for the first few days the emigrants couldn't open the portholes—if they did, there was a swishing howl outside and water washed over their bunks.

In strained attitudes, Manuel da Bouça and many of his companions would twist in the throes of seasickness and then lie pale and weak with dark circles under their eyes, panting like a dog that has been chasing swallows. Ever afterward the stomach rose with nausea at the thought of the margarine spread on biscuit served with the first mug of coffee taken on board.

And so for the first days of the voyage with the sea growing rougher and the waves swelling more and more into blue rolling hills, the third class of the *Darro* was a floating cattle pen with the herd huddled in it.

Some of the emigrants, with their wives and children, had come down the banks of the Volga and the Neva, and now, in promiscuous gypsydom, with thick beards, and wearing the fur caps typical of cold countries, they were making their way to the tropics, with the veiled look of misfortune in their green eyes. Others had come from Italy and were making for São Paulo or Argentina. Whole households on the march, hungry for peace, comfort, and . . . bread.

At Vigo in Spain, a round hundred Galicians had come on board—strong pink-cheeked men off to try their luck, men naturally sanguine, though why they didn't know themselves, and all of them ready to mint the gold they hankered for out of their own skins.

And a wanton group of Polish women moved about among them all, white-skinned voluptuous women on their way to Brazil to sell their bodies cheap, and quite ready to earn the first coins for their money boxes on board, but the purser was alive to their tricks and had taken strict measures to prevent them.

Portugal had supplied all the rest: the whole queue that Manuel da Bouça had seen at the consulate, and many more besides, so many that they seemed to spring out of the ground.

And they all had the same golden dream. They all had the same maggot gnawing at their vitals, worming its way into their deepest feelings.

Europe, fascinated by the golden image America held up above the blue line of the Atlantic, went marching out in continuous exodus to conquer the idol. From time to time the old continent opened its bosom to the new and handed over, wrapped in rags, what it still had of soundness and promise. There was a continual draining away of its best blood, which went out to blend with other forces in the distant land and there, under the magic wand of ambition and adventure, build a new world.

Almost all of them went out blindly, fascinated by the overseas glow of the loadstone. The prestige of the distant, the mysterious, called them to escape from the clutches of the toilsome poverty they knew so well.

America, holding aloft the horn of plenty from which gold streamed, appeared as the ideal fatherland to those who lacked bread . . . and to those who wanted more bread than they really needed.

Every day a fleet crossed the Atlantic, bearing to the enchanting continent cargoes of human flesh, carrying slaves, not of a pitiless master as in olden days, but of their own ambition, which is more cruel still.

Oh, to be rich, rich, rich! They wrapped themselves in their dream, soaked themselves in dream, building up lives of fantasy and opening the doors of their imagination to a wealth of happy possibilities.

But on board the *Darro,* with the sea swelling in lofty waves, they were only dark shivering forms, shadows that staggered along corridors with twisted mouths slobbering nausea.

When the sea became calm and they had found their sea legs, the Galicians were the first to stretch themselves and explore up and down, and even eat more, because what doesn't kill you fattens you up. The Italians and Portuguese too were not long before they came out and took up life on the upper deck; from time to time they would lean over the bows, above the anchor, watching the progress of the vessel. Only the Russians stayed down below in a silent somber group—the men with their beards thicker every day, and the women with their eyes more green.

When they got over the seasickness and giddiness, some of the emigrants brought out packs of cards and accordions; they played cards during the day, and at night they sang nostalgic songs. Portuguese, Galicians, and Italians came together in the same slow melancholy airs; the voice of folk sorrow rose from the gloomy corridors of the third class and floated over the sea, which swiftly stifled it.

Only once did one of the Polish women come forward to dance and sing to the instrument; the others didn't understand the words, but from her wanton wiles and the rolling of her eyes, they knew she must be lewd, that singing woman. She was low of stature, and fat; her head was small, her face round with a little nose almost buried in the white fullness of the cheeks. Her legs as she pranced about were so fat that they were grotesque. The unmarried men watched her with the bright, avid eyes of a hungry serpent, and the accordionist let the cigarette go out between his sucked-in lips and went on pressing the keys mechanically, his staring eyes binding a rope of desire round the ample haunches of the dancing woman.

The other women instinctively hated the Poles; in fact, more than one of them spat when mentioning the Poles—ugh, what filth! Mothers who in the morning light lifted out their great full breast into the sun and placed it in the little impatient mouth objected more to being seen like that by those women who trafficked their sterile flesh than by the men themselves.

The afternoons were long and boring; those who didn't play cards slept through them, stretched on their backs on deck among coils of rope, under the untroubled blue of the sky. Others wandered round from the side of the vessel to their berths, and from their berths back to the side—and each time they passed they looked at the first-class passengers who had a

dry deck at their disposal, and could walk about at will all over
it.

Two sole preoccupations dominated them: mealtimes and the
thought of arrival. From thinking so much about just these
two things, the days seemed even longer and the stomach always
empty. At the clang of the bell, carrying their tin plates they
hurried up to the big caldron steaming on the sticky deck,
and the English server, wearing a white cap and overall like a
hospital attendant, ladled out a portion to each of them.

Only the Russians held back, waiting till the last; then they
all came up slowly in a group, trailing tragedy behind them,
and in a group they retired again without either gesture or word.
This was the only time they were seen standing; otherwise they
looked as though they had made a vow to cross the Atlantic
seated, held down by some invisible umbilical cord.

Very different from them were the cardplaying champions.
On the forecastle deck, near the great airshafts that ventilated
the corridors where their bunks were, they were always to be
seen, hands and cards tracing small curves in space. They
played from morning till night, using dried beans to mark
their winnings, discussing their luck at length after each game.
And Manuel da Bouça was one of the first to sit down, and
then never got up except to go and eat, and when the light began
to fail.

Then, each evening the clear blue of the sky began to grow
darker—indigo blue, dark blue, it seemed to become damper and
closer to the masts. And the green of the sea was no longer
vivid; it faded and darkened until it too was blue, merging
in a single piece with the great glass dome poised on it. The
foam lost its whiteness: it trailed along in sheets of creaminess,
almost mulatto; it slipped into the hollow scooped between two
waves, then rose again on the crest of billows, surging from
the muffled shock of waters only to die again in dissolution;
then, ever reborn, it increased and spread out in flakes and

strips and bars over the expanse of rimpled blue; it was bloom of almond trees, dust sullied, blown in thick scatter across plowed fields.

In the evening light, with the sun shining horizontally across the masts and the captain's bridge, the lines of the great oval of the vessel became clearer, standing out as though the ocean were no more than this, as though it didn't stretch farther to where the last tatter of blue sky merged with the last tatter of blue water. The *Darro* seemed to be intent on racing at full speed toward some imaginary frontier, moving of its own volition, haughty and imposing, sure of winning some fabulous challenge. There was something vindictive, omnipotent, implacably dominating in the line of its bows cutting through the undulating water, cleaving the ocean and making it moan in giant copulation. The sound of this continual act of possession rose clearly and distinctly up to the third class, pervading the whole of it.

The sun had become half of a golden monstrance showing on the line of the horizon. The blue of the zenith became more opaque, while the blue nearer the horizon was illuminated by the last rays of the sun. A straight luminous path, gold-glittering, opened up from the ship to the decapitated sun. The foam was touched with gold, and it seemed as though some waves were forming and surging up merely to receive the last kiss of light.

Along the first-class deck, feminine forms—book in hand and flutter of scarf—were lazily stretched out in deck chairs and basket chairs. A stocky man, round glasses under a white cap, dark jacket and light flannel trousers, was placidly promenading to and fro. And from the tearoom, swelling a moment in space, and then fading away, a few bars from *The Bohemian Girl* came wafting.

In the third-class section were groups of men and women: heads bent in homesickness, shawls, faces of babies, breasts revealed—gray mass growing dark and gloomy to the point of fear. If only they were already there! And the future? How was it all going to turn out?

The sun had disappeared, but someone had thrown a match after it into its grave and caused a monumental conflagration. A huge ruddy reflection rose dazzling from the line of the horizon into the sky, flames twining in clouds, shreds of fire floating in ecstasy. Gradually it seemed to grow red-hot, blood-red, glow of a mighty pyre burning on the edge of the sea. It rose from a point of absolute stillness, from behind something insubstantial yet prismatic—a screen of pollen warding off the fire. The splendor of it rose up to the center of the lofty dome, and there it was a scarlet diaphanous veil through which the bluish depth of the sky was visible as in a swoon.

Slowly the sea put out the conflagration, the blood was washed away by water, and under the darkened firmament the hills and curves of the waves could no longer be seen.

On the *Darro*, electric lights were switched on and the players gathered up the pack of cards. Manuel da Bouça got up and stretched, while the others went on gossiping. For him, this was always the difficult moment of the day. The whole afternoon spent at cardplaying gave him a headache at night. And, not knowing how to play the accordion or sing, he spent endless time without any fun, without sleep, without fatigue—hours on end watching the faces of the others, yellow in the light down below, or shadowy in the gloom of the deck. Sometimes his companions talked; the women made strings of complaints, but he didn't hear them, his mind far away wondering what Cipriano would do when he went up to him—Here I am, I'm looking for work!—and about the kind of life waiting over there for him, shy at showing itself, and glimpsed only indistinctly, like a patch of cultivated ground under thick fog. Then came the racking memory of Amélia, Deolinda, his home—somewhere out there, he didn't know whether to right or left, east or west. If the ship were his, which way would he have to turn?

When his mind came back to the present situation, the example of others gave him courage. Lopes, like himself, was going out to meet someone he knew—and he was taking his wife and children too. And Nóbrega? And the Galicians? They were all alike, all in the same boat.

So optimism came back, made him conjure up scenes of happy return—and kept sleep from him.

One afternoon a plain pinewood table was set up on deck, and the purser of the *Darro*, clean-shaven and serious, took up his post behind it. It was Thursday, and the purser was wearing a white uniform—two green stripes at his throat and on his cap.

The herd was assembled, and all the emigrants, called individually by name, went passing by the table piled with a mass of papers.

All the exits from the deck were closed, and down below members of the crew were poking their noses into corners and hiding-places.

The purser was comparing passports with their bearers, who then passed over to the left, silent and docile. In the middle of this formality a steward and a waiter came up pushing two men in front of them, men with the scared faces and guilty attitude of poor-spirited thieves caught in the act. One of them was still only a youth, a lad with his shirt open at the neck showing a white plump throat, and his head uncovered except for thick long hair. The other one, wearing a dark beret, was about thirty, with dry features, short moustache, and thin lips. He looked as though he had spent his days in lightless factories in a continual struggle for daily bread.

The steward came forward and said that both men had locked themselves in the bathroom, trying to escape the roundup. With an abrupt gesture, the purser ordered them to wait, and went on imperturbably checking the passports.

The herd couldn't take its eyes off the two prisoners standing by themselves near the stairs, for all the world like captives about to be shot. But papers went on passing from one end of the table to the other, and when at last they made one big pile, the purser ordered the deck to be cleared, and remained alone with the two clandestine passengers, the steward, and the waiter. Now his expression became more disagreeable; his eyes lost their look of detachment and took on a harsh glint.

The steward reported again how the two men had been found, how he had banged on the bathroom door but nobody had opened or answered, and then the panic of the two men inside. Harshly looking them up and down to guess their nationality, the purser asked them, in a mixture of English and Spanish, where they had come on board.

"At Vigo."

"And your passports?"

"We haven't got any."

Shakily, and speaking in a humble tone of voice in answer to the brief questions of the Englishman, they told the story of their coming on board.

The younger one was Portuguese from the Minho district, Manuel António de Sousa by name; he had crossed into Spain to try to better himself, and days after was still tramping hungry about the streets of Vigo. The other man came from Bilbao, workman in a sawmill, and had been dismissed after a brawl. He had gone to Galicia in search of work, but he hadn't found any; he had only heard talk about Argentina. He wouldn't have had the nerve to get into the hold of a ship by himself, and without either papers or money. But he had come across Manuel António; they had been drawn together by their ill luck, and so he had been willing to try. With his last pesetas handed over to a man he knew, he had managed to get hold of two visitors' tickets for the *Darro,* proper tickets issued by the proper people, and he had gone on board with his companion. When the bell rang warning visitors that it was time to leave the ship, they stood among the emigrants who had just come on board. They didn't know how they were going to get ashore on the other side, if they weren't discovered during the crossing; but they had been told that the ship anchored near land, and they both knew how to swim. They begged him to do them no harm; they were poor Christian bodies without work, and all they wanted was to earn their living, because in Portugal and Spain a poor man couldn't get on in life.

When he had finished questioning them, the purser picked up all the papers and, in a harsh voice, ordered them to leave the deck in front of him, and they went off as though being led to the scaffold. And soon the emigrants, watching from a distance, saw them disappear along the corridor connecting the third with the second class.

Until nighttime they heard no more of them, except tales about lashes and fetters in one of the dark holds. But at eleven o'clock one of the Galicians came along with the news that he had seen them down in the coal bunker, and he had to turn back at the head of the procession that formed and lead the way along the devious route by which the engine room could be reached without breaking rules.

And there they were. Bare-chested and black with coal dust, the man from Bilbao lean and the Portuguese youth plump-chested, they were heaving shovelsful of coal into the red gullets of the furnaces. They felt the eyes of the others staring down at them through the grating, and they looked up, but at a gesture from the stoker in charge they turned back to their task.

Great drops of sweat channeling the filth ran down their bodies and arms. And the furnace was insatiable, a monster ever demanding more and more shovelsful of coal, which it rapidly devoured. A hellish glow came from it, glittering on the black smooth lumps of coal lying in heaps, and the two men were always bent double, feeding the fiery maws. The time came when the weak chest of the man from Bilbao gave out; he straightened up, panting, and with black spittle running from his mouth. The shovel fell from his hands, and his exhausted body slipped down onto a heap of coal. The red glow played on him from head to foot. Mouth and nostrils were wide open, gasping for breath, and his lids closed over eyes that were so quiet that they seemed dead. The stoker looked down at him for a moment, uncertain what to do; then he bent down, tapped the man lightly on the shoulder, and told him to get on with his work.

Then the onlookers began to leave the grating, attracted by the sight of the machines in operation nearby. They were in a vast well of space, railed in by white-painted iron bars; hundreds of parts could be seen, and hundreds more guessed at. Some were small and delicate like fine clockwork; others huge and powerful like the tireless arms of titans. Some were still, as though in a numb, useless immobility; others were in perpetual labor: rotating of dynamos, to-and-fro of levers, turning of shafts, risings and fallings—a continual movement subdivided into many parts; unending intricacy of outline; a thousand curves, a thousand straight lines, a thousand different facets in a single instant, and a marvelous unchanging rhythm governing everything, bearing witness to the power of the human brain. The iron steps that connected the two decks gave a good general view over the mechanics of the *Darro*. On one side, in gleaming copper, great bulge and great turbine set up like an intestine. On the other, the mighty gear, the great cogwheel into which others gripped with iron teeth, turning in a mutual production of power. In the center, a man in overalls was moving about, thrown into relief by the reddish light falling on him from above, casting shadows here and there, and glitter wherever the machines had a polished surface. On the second floor, this light merged with the light shining from below and flowed round the parts in motion, revealing some with clean distinctness of outline, enlarging the contours of others in dark, impenetrable places.

Near the telegraph dial ribbed with yellow metal was the clock, visible from all parts and also cased in metal. And there were other things, too, of the same color: couplings, plates, handrails, a flash here and a flash there among the polished steel and the shafts, dripping oil, of the tireless monster. Some detail attracted the attention; then it was soon forgotten in the profusion of other details. The emigrants had the impression that there in front of their eyes the impossible had been realized, to be accepted without any question, but which they could never have believed if they had not seen it for themselves. Glued to the bars, their faces too were lighted up by the reddish glow, lost in admiration.

9

ℑT had been said that land would be in sight at peep of dawn, so a good number of the emigrants got up early. Pale stars were still in the sky when Manuel da Bouça came on deck turning up the collar of his jacket against the cold. The Russians were already there in a compact silent group, looking at a sea so calm that it seemed to be asleep. Other emigrants were there too: shadows leaning against the sides, eyes fixed straight ahead on the lookout for the new continent.

Manuel da Bouça recognized a companion from the card table, Afonso, a tall chap who was going ashore at Rio de Janeiro, so he went and joined him.

"Can you see land yet?"

"Yes."

"Where?"

"Over there."

"I can't see anything," said Manuel da Bouça, staring hard in the direction indicated.

"Over there, look. Can't you see a light flashing on and off?"

"A light? Oh, yes, now I can see it!" And he stood looking far ahead where stars were sinking down to kiss the ocean, and where he could see a luminous point of light that differed from the stars only by its flickering in and out.

"That's a lighthouse. I can tell them miles off, because I've been tunny fishing in the Algarve."

Other figures came up on deck, dark forms scrutinizing the Atlantic over the bows of the *Darro*. Then the whimper of a baby was heard from the stairs; next, mother and child came out, the mother disheveled and anxious, asking to right and left, "Can you see land? Can you see land?"

The stars were fading, the sky had become lead-colored, and the gentle undulation of the water could be seen far ahead. The two lights on the captain's bridge, the one green and the other red, lost their brightness and the metal rims round them became visible. And then, by light that was no longer artificial, the whole outline of the *Darro* came into view from the fore anchor to the top of the masts, and from the top of the masts to the first-class deck—still empty.

The lead color in the sky turned to purple, and the stars were everlasting-flowers closed and faded. Like a magic castle the first white cloud appeared and, at the same time, an irregular shadow along the line of the horizon.

"Look, look," exclaimed Afonso, "land ahead!"

The sea was becoming more and more tinged with green, and Manuel da Bouça watched the huge camel's hump rising vaguely and shadowily from it. Other emigrants near him focused it too and stretched out their arms, pointing excitedly toward the Brazilian coast.

"Shall we be long getting there?"

And Alfonso replied authoritatively from his fisherman's experience, "A boat that sights land and doesn't reach it within three hours has either sprung a leak or got its keel in the air."

The lights of the *Darro* went out, and near one of the white lifeboats an officer was forcing his field glasses on the horizon.

More rose-colored patches had appeared in the sky and great plains of blue—a faraway fresh blue giving an impression of immense height between it and the green-washed sea.

Now the whole herd had assembled on deck: medley of trousers and skirts, adults and children, some people solemn, others yawning in the early morning—but all waiting as though something extraordinary were going to happen. You couldn't seize on any special detail, but the thing as a whole made the impression: large-scale engraving of a dark, wretched group of people, with pathetic faces turned to the land toward which the vessel was heading. Then, armed with brushes, canvas buckets, and hosepipes, a swarm of sailors came along to swab the decks. Water began to run in all directions. Balked, many of the emigrants went below, while others tried to find a perch among the coils of rope or along the sides up on the foredeck. But as soon as the sluicing was finished, they all came back again, growing more and more curious, more and more intent on the black brushstroke that was growing bigger on the horizon, though at times their attention was distracted by a school of big fish that passed in rapid curves of gleaming backs, now diving now reappearing on the surface of the water. And then two sea gulls came up from the distance, and hovered over the vessel, very self-assured, as though they were carrying out some usual assignment.

The rose-colored wisps had disappeared, and the sky was now all blue with snow-white clouds—great downy flakes wafted in whimsical patterns by a gentle breeze. And then the tropical sun, level with the waves, rose from the sea in a burst of rays that made all colors lighter. The foam became white, and on the captain's bridge the glass of the lights glittered. Now a woman's form, intently watching land, could be seen on the first-class deck. More sea gulls came up, and on ahead another boat was coming toward the *Darro* with a shimmering crown of smoke lying over it in the clear air. Next, the sail of a canoe became visible near the coast. The dark wedge of land grew more distinct, and sharp eyes could make out the outline of the rocks.

Those who were landing at Rio began to leave the deck; then they came back wearing other hats, and they placed their bags and trunks in piles. More people came out on the first-class deck, and both fore and aft there was the same intense curiosity—a long row of heads turned toward land. Along the shoreline isolated white villas came into view, and the steep coast changed color, passing from black to dark forest green.

The *Darro* had now put to starboard, and for more than half an hour novices had the impression that it was going to strike right into land, so unbroken did the coastline seem to the naked eye. Little by little, however, a wide canal opened in the greenish mass, and the vessel slowly moved in deep water overshadowed by hills. Someone shouted, "There's the Sugar Loaf!" And the emigrants passed the word from mouth to mouth. The Sugar Loaf! The Sugar Loaf! It was a great dark rock bare of vegetation, a giant egg rising from the water, and terminating in iron scaf- folding like a weird gallery for dream musicians. Someone made the remark that, however close the vessel passed, you couldn't hit the base of the hill with a stone thrown from deck. And to test the illusion of nearness, more than one missile cut through the air in an impotent curve, only to fall short in the dark water.

There was a spate of binoculars on the first-class deck and much ado among those who were going to land. Guanabara came into sight, a jewel hidden in a multicolored casket. After feasting on the amazing scene as a whole, the eyes were next enchanted by its many different facets. Light, color, and line took the fascinated spectator by surprise and evoked the inevitable Ah!

Urca followed the Sugar Loaf, connected with it by an aerial railway, and in the distance the cabin looked like a child's toy moving under the wire. Then came Praia Vermelha, Botafogo, Flamengo—bay glittering in a clean graceful curve and dotted with houses and trees. Rising on different planes were more villas and trees—an amazing polychrome ending in the clean-cut outline, the huge tooth of Corcovado rearing into the sky. And caught on the tooth, like a great banner, an opal cloud.

An unexpected inlet opened on the right, rather more hazy in the distance, an intimate corner reserved for Guanabara in the midst of the panoramic vastness: Saco de São Francisco and Icarahy beach. Farther along the same shore, the white house cluster of Niterói with its ferryboats, old-fashioned paddle wheels turning. Directly ahead the forests of masts grew thicker, the majestic outlines of ships standing out against small islands became more numerous; the sight couldn't pass beyond them, and so came back to feast again on the left-hand side of the bay.

The wide avenues of Botafogo, with automobiles rolling along as in a vast park, serving as a setting for the magnificent lake, were lined with monumental edifices, some only glimpsed by a corner, others on the Avenida Rio Branco guessed at from the cupolas and towers rising above the buildings on the shore. Both city and bay lay glittering under the splendor of the sun, a sun pulsing in apotheosis and scattering rich gold dust everywhere.

The engines of the *Darro* stopped; the steps were fixed in place, and two launches that had come out to meet the ship came alongside. Men in light suits, glasses, Panama hats, and with briefcases under their arms came on board; then others in uniform, from the health authorities and police, to make the customary visit.

A little later two stewards went through the third class calling those who were landing at Rio to go up for inspection. Afonso came up and put his strong arms round Manuel da Bouça's shoulders.

"Goodbye, old chap, and may you be lucky!"

"And you too. Goodbye!"

Other farewells were in progress, and bags, blankets, and trunks were still piling up on the third-class deck. The Russians, as usual in a single silent group, the men in black and the women now in their best dresses, disappeared along the corridor leading to the middle deck where the inspection was to take place.

More than an hour went by. Manuel da Bouça had spent the time admiring the various aspects of Ilha Fiscal—twenty meters of land out in the bay with the Customs in the center and fans of palm trees shading it; Pharoux Quay with steps and square higher up; the ships anchored near the *Darro* and the small boats picking their way among them; he was admiring everything the eye could see, when Afonso suddenly came back and stood at his side.

"This isn't the place yet," he said. And as Manuel da Bouça didn't gather what he meant, he explained. "We don't land here. The ship's going to touch farther up, at the Mauá Quay, wherever that is!"

"And will it be long before we get there?"

Afonso shrugged his shoulders to indicate that he didn't know, and then he said, "You know, the two stowaways, they've already been handed over to the police."

"But I thought it was said they wouldn't be detained, considering they'd worked. . . . And heaven knows the work was enough to make anyone run!"

"I don't know about that. Anyway, it was the captain who handed them over. I saw the young one crying. . . . Look! Look! There they go!" And Afonso pointed to the police launch moving off with the two stowaways surrounded by men in uniform.

"Poor fellows! I'm sorry for them," murmured Manuel da Bouça.

"So am I. They may still get it on the knuckles for coming on board without a ticket."

The other launch stood off from the ladder, and the *Darro* began to vibrate again and move along the bay. Here the shore was less attractive. Old narrow streets could be glimpsed in the distance, buildings darkened by time, reminders of the early colonial city. Then, their modern outline loudly proclaiming the age of reinforced concrete, came the row of warehouses, the customs depot, and the dock for the big transatlantic liners with its clusters of cranes, trucks, blacks, half-breeds, and whites.

The *Darro* went through a slow careful maneuver till the gangway was well in place on the long quay. And then, while a crowd of people came pressing round the exit to meet friends returning from Europe, almost all of them from the first class, there was also a bustle from the third class, a tugging at bags and trunks; they didn't want to leave anything behind, and there was nothing to wait for, either. The Barcelos couple came up with their children to say goodbye to Manuel da Bouça; then Ernest and Costa shook hands with him; and last Afonso came along grumbling.

"Now that's a fine thing! So we're the only ones who have to go to the Ilha das Flores!"

"What do you mean?"

"We've got to go to the hostel or whatever it is. But only us, the poor people. The first-class folk can go straight into town. As though we weren't all alike! They say we get board and lodging. But what I want is to get on land. I came to work, not to waste time. Anyway, goodbye once again, Senhor Manuel! Keep well, and good luck!"

And he went off with those who were making their way in a huddled group along the corridor to the middle deck.

Some minutes passed. People were still going ashore from the first class, and down on the quay more friends were joining the waiting group, colorful with the parasols of women and effervescent with noisy greetings and enthusiastic hugs of welcome.

Then, changing his place, Manuel da Bouça saw his own shipmates leaving the vessel. On the bay side, a tug was waiting to take the emigrants into quarantine on the Ilha das Flores. The Russians were the first to go down the steps carrying suitcases and rolls of blankets, their eyes anxiously glancing all round to get their bearings. After them went the Portuguese families: men in big rough shoes, brown trousers, and jackets of country cut; women in dark full skirts and kerchiefs on their heads, some in colorful smocks and others wrapped in shawls; children in a medley of nondescript clothing, hardly distinguishable from the luggage. Then, filling the shaking steps with flashes of white went the voluble Polish women, stepping out lightly from one boat to the other. And the Galicians went last of all, straight-backed, breathing health and firm resolve.

When the herd was assembled again in charge of the four officials, the tug moved off to the sound of a shrill whistle. Off they went farther and farther over the bay, some waving last goodbyes to those left behind on the *Darro*, others with their eyes staring ahead as though on the lookout for some seasonable help that was taking its time, that had not come, that would not come. . . . What's happened to Santiago! And Mariano! I thought he'd come and meet the ship, but after all . . . The best thing is that with a tongue in your head you can find your way about anywhere.

They hadn't been prepared for this, and they were surprised at the absence of fellow villagers who had emigrated earlier, to whom they'd written one or two letters, or who had persuaded them to come out; and now they weren't there on the quays to give the warm welcome the newcomers had been imagining. . . . Welcome, welcome to Brazil! . . . Well, here we are, my lad, all ready to get going!

But what troubled them most of all was the unexpected stay on the Ilha das Flores that would divide them several days longer from the land, which seemed even more tempting now it was so near, there in sight, with the glamour of wealth round it attributed by tradition.

When the tug was a long way off, Manuel da Bouça crossed the deck again and went back to lean over the quay side of the ship. The last passengers from the first class were disappearing, the last parasols were turning the corner by the warehouse with its sliding doors wide open showing pyramids of boxes inside. Soon, on the long esplanade, there were only dockworkers left, a black dog, trucks, and the powerful crane that was swinging slings of luggage from the hold of the *Darro*.

Someone came and leaned over the side at Manuel da Bouça's elbow.

"Well, shall we have a look round on shore?"

It was Janardo; he was going to Santos too, and the two men, drawn together because they were going to the same place, had got to know each other during the crossing.

"No, we should only go and get lost."

"Of course we shan't; all towns are alike. In Oporto I used to move round just like walking about in my own house. So let's just go and have a look round, only to see what it's like, and we'll be back in an hour's time."

"And what about the ship?"

Then a bell rang close by.

"There, that's lunch. Let's go and have lunch, and we'll go ashore afterward. The ship's here till night, so what about it?"

Manuel da Bouça agreed. His companion had shown general resourcefulness during the voyage, and he relied on his judgment.

After the meal the two of them went off, Janardo taking mental note of things on the way to serve as landmarks for the return. They crossed Mauá Square, and then their attention was caught and held by the pulsing, dynamic, multiform life of the Avenida Central. Lofty buildings of different styles with a display of commercial signboards on every story gave the great artery a pronounced air of wealth and magnificence. Everywhere, from window to window, on the balconies and doors, even on the roofs, was a profusion of company names and publicity, trademarks and trade names and articles on view. Here a splash of green; farther on the gilt of a facade, and then splashes of all kinds of colors mingling with the glitter of glass, showing up the curves and angles of the buildings, towers, domes, and fluttering flags, to the point of hallucination.

And under all this, along the wide and tree-lined walks, a restless, eager crowd of people was moving this way and that way. In the middle of the gleaming roadway, a mass of vehicles, four uninterrupted lines of cars and buses—one side moving up, the other side moving down. More dazzle of glass and metal, more cluster of advertisements and signboards near the lamp-posts and among the trees—everywhere. And from the many-sided uninterrupted movement of this astounding scene rose a deafening hum—the rhythm of group life issuing from all the crevices of the city, orchestrated into a tone poem of strength and achievement.

Overwhelmed, Manuel da Bouça pressed Janardo's arm. "This, this is something like a country!" he murmured.

But Janardo, in his black shiny suit and black hat with brim pulled down over his eyes, this barber who looked just like a provincial clerk, damped his enthusiasm.

"Oh, this doesn't impress me. I'm used to cities. Do you know Oporto?" he remarked in a superior tone of voice.

"No."

"If you could only see it, that's something like a town!"

"I've only seen Lisbon. . . ."

"I don't know Lisbon very well. But Oporto! You should see its Praça da Liberdade and the Rua Trinta e Um de Janeiro. . . . And it just teems with people."

But Manuel da Bouça was all eyes for the Avenida and wasn't listening, so Janardo began to look round too, forced to admire in spite of himself, but stealthily so that his attitude shouldn't give the lie to his words.

Attractive women passed by, dainty as little statues, dressed in clinging suggestive silks that revealed rather than covered; and there was a provocative look about their red mouths and sensuous eyes. On the front walk a group of young rogues was having a fine time watching the women's legs in silhouette when the sun shone through their thin dresses.

Almost stupid with astonishment Manuel da Bouça watched them pass by and then, against the panorama of the magnificent avenue, he caught a sudden motion-picture flash of his own village. Where could it be? In what direction did it lie? On what side would he have to stretch his arm if he wanted to show

Janardo which way it was? And his memories seemed to be fading in his mind, as though he were dreaming.

"No loitering there!"

Manuel da Bouça looked up. The voice was speaking to them. At his side a policeman said again gravely: "You can't stand here. Either go to the edge or the inside of the walk." Manuel was frightened, and quickly looked round for Janardo's protection, and saw him moving off to lean against the wall, putting on an air of unconcern as one quite used to these town whimsies, and making signs for his companion to follow him. So Manuel da Bouça went up to him and got his breath back after his shock.

But they didn't go any farther. Janardo was beginning to sense the depths of the city. All the street corners and side streets looked like a huge, complicated chessboard, and he felt responsible for his companion if they should lose their way. So they both leaned against the wall, and Manuel da Bouça, in his slow, obstinate way, took up the thread of their conversation.

"But are there as many people in Oporto as there are here?"

"As many . . . well, I wouldn't say as many." Then, giving a twist to the truth, "But not much less. I went there when I was a kid and never wanted to come away again. Lisbon folk say that Lisbon's better, but I don't believe it."

"I've seen Lisbon."

Then he stopped short because he couldn't fix on any point of contrast. He suddenly realized with surprise that everything that differed from the kind of scene his eyes were accustomed to looked the same to him and provoked the same strong sensation of respect and mental stimulation.

They didn't stay there much longer. Janardo didn't want to risk any further excursion, so he put a brake on curiosity and muttered, "Let's go back." And to justify his lack of enterprise he quibbled again. "You know, from here onward it'd just be the same sort of thing all over again."

So they turned back: Janardo looking for the landmarks he'd

noted on the way out; Manuel da Bouça relying on him, and full of admiration for everything he saw.

When they got back Mauá Square it was less busy. Buses came up and stopped, took other passengers on board, then turned and went back the way they had come. Buses leaving the Avenida accelerated; those arriving slowed down, and there were not nearly so many people. But Janardo didn't feel really at ease till he saw the warehouses on the docks and, behind the first of them, the funnel and masts of the *Darro*. Then he let himself go about all they had seen: the beauty of the women, the line of the Avenida, all the things that had struck him most—though they had only just scratched the surface of the great work that that branch of the human race was creating and developing with febrile energy and feeling for civilization on the other shore of the Atlantic. Manuel da Bouça heard him out in silence, because he too had found everything first-rate and worthy of admiration.

"But in Oporto, if there was a mob of people like there is here, there wouldn't be only two bridges, there'd be . . . I don't know what!" Janardo ended up when he set foot on the ship's gangway.

On board, the atmosphere was quite different from what it had been hitherto. In the first class, not a living soul; the deck deserted from end to end, and the captain's bridge deserted too. If they caught sight of anyone, it was an officer or a seaman, and always in a hurry, coming out of one door to disappear through another. In the stern, the only movement was from the hatchway which kept on throwing up trunks and boxes, boxes and trunks. And in the third class everything had a temporary look: the herd had been broken up and those who remained—the Italians, some Galicians, five Portuguese, and about half a score of women— looked as though they were waiting for a funeral to set out, after which they could give a new direction to life and establish a new routine. On deck there was more sunlit space; something seemed to be missing; the spoken word had a different sound; there was more silence and a great emptiness. There were still quite a few people left in the third class, yet it seemed deserted.

A steward went by, and Janardo boldly stopped him to check whether what he had been told about the departure of the *Darro* and the time of arrival at Santos was exact. The steward answered in a mixture of Spanish, Portuguese, and English, and when Janardo didn't immediately grasp what he meant he repeated it all again with a bad grace.

"Yes, it's what I thought," said Janardo, returning to Manuel da Bouça. "We leave here at six this evening and get to Santos tomorrow at three in the afternoon."

"Is anyone coming to meet you?"

"No. I've got a cousin there, but I don't know where he lives; I'm just going to look round for him. And what about you?"

"I haven't got anyone to meet me, either. I wrote to a friend, but I didn't tell him when I was coming. . . . Perhaps you could help me to look him up; I've got his address. And then I'll help you look for your cousin."

"Yes, that seems all right. We'll both go along together."

All through the voyage Manuel da Bouça had been worrying about the business of going ashore, and now he felt real relief. Janardo, with his cocksure air of a man used to cities would be quite equal, he thought, to this tricky proceeding, and his being there was a real godsend.

$\mathcal{A}$FTER the wonder of Guanabara the entrance into the port of Santos looked less pleasing to the eyes of emigrants who had been imagining all sorts of marvels during the whole crossing.

Near the Ilha das Palmas the *Darro* stopped to take a pilot on board, and then it doubled the tongue of land and slowly entered the canal.

Soon, to the left, they could see the beach of José Menino, a ribbon of pleasant-looking houses, and wide avenues connecting it with the city. Motorcars were driving along the sand and, higher up, tramcars could be seen quite distinctly running towards São Vicente, which stood hazily in the background in a recess of the bay.

The canal gradually narrowed, and the *Darro* moved more and more slowly till at last it came to a full stop some way from the docks. Three launches set out across the dividing space and came alongside. And then, in the third-class section, the Rio scene was repeated all over again, and the emigrants were called to the second-class deck for the ritual of inspection. A number of Italians dressed in dark blue suits came first; they were going to São Paulo. Behind them came the Spaniards, and then the five Portuguese. Manuel da Bouça was swinging his flower-patterned bag in his hand, so Janardo said to him, "Why, man, what are you carrying that for? We're nowhere near landing yet; the ship isn't even in dock." And when Manuel da Bouça looked a bit doubtful because the other emigrants were carrying their small luggage, Janardo went on: "Just a lot of idiots! There's still a long time to wait."

"But just now . . ."

"Oh, do what you like, then," said Janardo, shrugging his shoulders.

At the end of the dark passage were two tables and men sitting at them, some stern, others supercilious, and almost all in uniform.

In a dingy batch the emigrants filled all the space between the hatchway and the ship's side. Here and there among the cluster of heads was the humble face of a woman and the soft rosy cheeks of a baby held tight in the maternal arms.

One of the men in uniform was going through a mass of papers, shuffling, separating, and placing them on the table. When they were ready he passed them to the second man and said, "You can call now."

And the other man, tall, white suit, Panama hat, and gold tooth glittering in his thin face, began the roll call:

"Giuseppe Cappelli, Giulia Ubaldi Cappelli e figlia."

The three of them came forward, the man with dark dry features, the woman very fair, holding her daughter close to her breast.

"Pietro Verga; Giovanni Frascesco . . ."

And still more and more of them.

When all the Italians had been checked over, the man who

had given the order for the inspection to begin stretched his neck from the collar of his uniform and harangued them in their own tongue.

"The State of São Paulo prides itself on possessing the most complete, the most liberal, the most humane legislation with regard to emigration of any which exist in other countries. Immensely wealthy, with land of amazing fertility where nature takes upon itself to facilitate the labor of man, São Paulo gives full protection to emigrants from the time they reach Santos until they are in a position to earn their own living. The State gives them transport, shelter, food, and finally finds them work—the sole condition being that they must take up work on the land."

He paused, glanced over the group, and then brought his speech to a conclusion.

"Those who want to avail themselves of these advantages must say so immediately. Those who do so cease to have any kind of anxiety from that moment."

At first the Italians said nothing. Then a dull murmur arose, remarks timidly exchanged among themselves in low voices. Janardo had gone off to find out what he could; then he came back and passed the information on to Manuel da Bouça.

"That's the Inspector of Emigration."

"Who is?"

"The man who's been speaking."

By this time the Italians had made up their minds.

"Si! Si! Si!"

"Tutti?"

"Si! Si! Si!"

Only one man came forward to refuse.

"Io, no." And he explained that he had come out at a relative's request.

The man who had called out the list began to scribble on papers, while the doctor led all the Italians away to the other table.

Then the Spaniards were checked over, and the inspector, with the careless ease of one who knows his speech by heart, said in Spanish what he had just said to the others in Italian.

"Now that's something like!" whispered Janardo. "I had a customer once who talked like that."

"What did he say?" asked Manuel da Bouça, who had understood nothing of the speech.

"That they'll give us everything, if we agree to go and work on the land."

"And what does everything mean?"

"Transport and work."

"Are you going to accept?"

"Me? Do you think I've come out to Brazil to be clamped to the end of a mattock?"

When the bored official repeated the offer a third time to the five Portuguese emigrants, only the couple came forward (the woman carrying the child in her arms) to declare that they accepted official protection.

"I've come with somewhere to go!" said Janardo firmly.

But Manuel da Bouça, standing alone with his bag in front of the inspector, felt very unsure of himself.

"I . . . Could you tell me, sir, what people do there?" he stammered out.

"What people do there? Where?"

"On the land."

"Oh, they grow maize and wheat, and there are coffee plantations, and so on."

"And how much do they earn?"

The inspector looked him up and down, and answered shortly. "Depends. Hundred and fifty to two hundred milréis a month."

Manuel da Bouça stood a moment in thought.

"Well?"

"No, no, thanks."

"Have you got a recommendation?"

"I've come to see a fellow from my village."

The inspector turned back to the table to gather his papers together, and Manuel da Bouça stood ruminating over the questions and replies. They must be making a fool of him. . . . To come to Brazil to earn one hundred and fifty milréis a month! At that rate, when would he get back to Portugal?

"Manuel Joaquim dos Santos!" another man in uniform called out who was with the doctor. But he had to call again before Manuel da Bouça came down to earth and recognized his own name.

"Here I am!"

The doctor examined him, looked at his papers, asked the usual questions, and then, at a sign that he had finished, his assistant took over.

"Where are you going to stay?"

"Where? I don't know yet, sir." And he smiled, taking the words of the port health official to be of no consequence.

"Without a fixed address, nobody can land!" the official warned him, putting on a severe look. Then, at the sudden despair and scare that showed on Manuel da Bouça's face, he took pity on his ignorance and added, "Haven't you come out to some relative or friend?"

"Oh, yes, I've come out to a chap from my village."

"And where does he live?"

As though his very life depended on it, Manuel da Bouça began fumbling through his pockets for Cipriano's address, but everything his fingers got hold of was beside the point; his heart sank more and more at not finding what he wanted and having to make the stern gentleman wait. At last he brought out a folded piece of paper and handed it to the health official.

"Here it is! It's this fellow's house. Please look."

"Rua do Rosário 159," he read out. "Is that it?"

"Yes, that's it. Rua do Rosário 159. And to think that I'd learned it by heart!"

The official scribbled out the address, filled in the counterfoil, tore it off, and handed it over.

"You have to go for medical inspection as often as marked on this paper."

Manuel da Bouça stood perplexed with a series of questions jostling in his brain that he would like to ask. What kind of inspection? Where? When? On board? On shore? But they were already calling out the next name.

"Gervasio da Costa Janardo!"

"Here I am," replied the barber in a firm voice, going forward to the table. At the end of the ritual, when he was asked where he was going to stay, he answered without any hesitation. "At Rua do Rosário 159." Manuel da Bouça was dumbfounded at this reply, but he didn't like to contradict his companion.

After they had all been authorized to land, Janardo came back to the third class and apologized.

"I gave your friend's address, but you know it won't cause any trouble at all. I don't know where I'm going to find a perch yet, and it's only a formality. . . ."

"But this thing about inspection, this paper?"

"Oh, that's to see whether we're in good health. We have to go to the department every three days," Janardo answered, unfolding his piece of paper. "It's the Public Health Department. But that's on shore. Good, wait for me here, while I go and get my case."

Manuel da Bouça put his bag down and leaned over the side of the ship. The three launches pulled off from the *Darro,* which then began the operation of coming alongside. A long row of warehouses and a great quay came into view—the famous modern docks, the legitimate pride of the city. And with them came the first huge surprise the port of Santos provoked in the country mind of Manuel da Bouça: innumerable plump sacks, crammed to the brim, were being carried along on a wide woven band and pitched into a sloping chute that bore them down to the hold of a ship. However hard he looked, he couldn't find the mighty hand which was working the wonder; it looked as though it was all being done by magic—black magic to bemuse Christian eyes.

With shouts fore and aft, a cable thrown toward the quay and falling short into the lapping water, retrieved and thrown again, slowly the *Darro* came alongside to take its place between two steamers—an expert, close-judged maneuver because ten feet to one side or the other might cause a rip in its hull.

Janardo came back with his case, set it down beside Manuel de Bouça's bag, and leaned over the side too. He took in the new position of the liner and drew a breath of satisfaction.

"So at last, here we are!"

The gangway was put across and, moving and treading with care, the first- and second-class passengers stepped out on the stone quay. Conspicuous among them was a short fat man with a round red face, wearing a morning coat and bowler hat. Small cases and hatboxes tapped against women's hips and then were handed over to porters. More and more feet went stepping gingerly along the gangway, more and more people—and there on the quay, what embracings and glad cries of welcome.

"Now for the new life, Senhor Manuel!" exclaimed Janardo when he saw that it was time for the third-class herd to go ashore.

And away they went stepping along the corridor. At the top of the gangway they were again asked for name and address, and then at last, after one more glance at the books, the man in uniform let them pass.

Now, on quitting the moving deck of the liner and leaving the ship, Manuel da Bouça experienced a strange feeling, like the cessation of all his senses. For the first time the land of exile rose before him like a great question mark that he hadn't perceived or realized properly till then, though it had been working subconsciously in his mind. He felt a sudden inexplicable swoon in his chest; there was a sudden emptiness, a fluttering vacuum that was expectancy, satisfaction, and apprehension all at the same time. It seemed as though he were walking on cotton, that he had turned into rubber, and that people and things had lost their usual appearance.

The opening of his bag for the searching eyes of the customs, the measures Janardo took for both their trunks, crossing the quays and going out into the streets of Santos: it all seemed unreal, something performed by another self far away, something that was not part of the life felt in his vitals; something that, as his simple mind couldn't put it into words, he exteriorized in a silly, happy smile.

Janardo passed voluble remarks about various aspects of the city as he noted them; but Manuel da Bouça answered only yes or no mechanically. Janardo pointed this or that out, but Manuel looked without seeing anything. Janardo stopped people in the street, asked questions, and waited while they replied; and Manuel stopped too, but heard nothing.

At last he was roused from his trance by a concrete statement from his companion.

"This is it."

"What?"

"Rua do Rosário."

"Oh, and Cipriano's house?"

"We're on the way now!"

Then Manuel da Bouça became all curiosity, all interest; his eyes kept darting from the doors they were passing to Janardo's face, on the lookout for the "Here it is!" that had to come. But Janardo moved on imperturbably, stopping here and there to see what was inside the shops; then he turned and glanced back over the length of street they had already come.

"There's no comparison between this street and the Trinta e Um de Janeiro and the Rua dos Clérigos seen from Santa Catarina. That's where I had my barber's shop."

In his eagerness to get there, Manuel da Bouça thought that this retrospective vanity that was delaying them was absurd, but Janardo began to move on again and count out the numbers on the doors.

"103, 105 . . . 109, 111 . . . 117, 119 . . . 125 . . . 133 . . . Here we are at last! *Ecce homo!*" His companion looked at him openmouthed, so he explained, "This is where our man must be!"

He pointed to a corner house with three doorways, where there were bags of dried beans and rice, with the sacking carefully folded back at the mouth of each bag; boxes of potatoes with the price per kilo and place of origin—Guaranteed Portuguese—marked on a card; and, hanging from the ceiling, various kinds of hams.

Inside the shop, a rapid glance took in shelves full of bottles, tins, and boxes with colored labels; and beneath them, on a part of the counter, more bags and a shining pair of scales.

Janardo, standing with his hands in his pockets and a cigarette waiting to be lighted stuck on his lower lip, read out the black lettering painted on the wall. " 'Family Grocery of Albino da Silva Fernandes. Moderate Prices.' The shop seems to be well placed, so they must do a good trade. Is Fernandes your friend?"

"No, not Fernandes. My friend's name is Cipriano."

"Oh, yes, so you said. Cipriano. But the name here's Albino. Perhaps Cipriano's a partner, or maybe he's just taken over the business from the other man."

They both crossed the street and went through one of the doors into the shop. Inside, there was a fat oily man with a round red face weighing out sugar for a boy whose head hardly reached the rim of the counter. But Manuel da Bouça's eyes searched the place in vain. Cipriano wasn't there. The grocer handed over the sugar and took the money, and then asked him what he wanted.

"Isn't this where Senhor Cipriano Soares lives?" he asked timidly.

"Senhor Cipriano works here," said the fat man in a surly voice, after looking him over a bit.

"I'd like to speak to him. I've come from his home village."

"He isn't here."

"Will he be long?"

"No. He shouldn't be long."

And keeping the same unpleasant expression on his face, he went and sat down at a desk and, with a pencil grasped in his fat hairy fingers, began to scrawl in a book.

Janardo, who had already looked through the door three times and moved off again, at last came to the end of his patience.

"Well, Senhor Manuel, now we've found your friend's address, I'm going."

"But I wanted to help you find your cousin."

"It doesn't matter. I'll find him somehow, don't you worry! So goodbye! We're sure to come across each other sometime. Santos is certainly no bigger than Oporto, and over there I used to run across friends every day. Good luck to you!"

"Thanks, and good luck to you too! But if you want me to go with you . . ."

"Oh, no, it isn't necessary!"

And, disengaging his hand, he went out unconcerned. Manuel da Bouça, standing among the bags, watched him go off round the next corner with a firm tread, puffing out spirals of smoke.

Cipriano turned up soon afterward. Bareheaded and in his shirt sleeves, he came in from the street carrying an empty case on his back. At sight of Manuel da Bouça he stopped, hesitated, and would have gone on doubting if Manuel had not stretched out his arms.

"Cipriano! Don't you recognize me? You've grown into a fine chap, you certainly have!" he exclaimed.

Cipriano allowed Manuel to clasp him in his arms, and he was evidently surprised, but he didn't respond to the warmth shown by his compatriot.

"When did you get here?"

"I've just arrived."

"And back home, is everything all right?"

"Yes, and I've got lots of things to tell you—"

"We'll have a talk soon. Just wait a minute."

He went to the other side of the counter with the case and

deposited it in a corner. Then he went up to the fat man and meekly exchanged a few words with him.

"Well, yes, but don't be long!" Manuel da Bouça heard the man answer in the same bossy voice in which he'd spoken to him a short time before.

Cipriano disappeared behind the shelves, and when he came back he'd got his jacket and hat on.

"Come along," he said to Manuel da Bouça.

The two of them went off, the one saying "Well, my boy!" and the other "Well, Senhor Manuel!" and they came to a halt in a street not far away. Cipriano pushed a door open, and they went up the steep staircase inside. At the top of the stairs was a passage, and at the end of the passage another door, which Cipriano opened with his key.

"This is my room. Put your bag down here, and make yourself at home."

Within the compass of the four filthy walls was just space enough for an iron bed, a small trunk, and two small packing-cases, on one of which a black bottle with drops of wax down its sides served as a candlestick. The small window looked over the backyard.

"Sit down, Senhor Manuel, sit down!" And he pointed to the trunk, while he himself sat down on the bed.

"You've put on flesh and seem to have grown!" exclaimed Manuel da Bouça, looking at his friend's lean face, big straight nose, and hair cropped close. "Of course, that's not surprising; you must be about thirty now, aren't you?"

"Twenty-nine."

"Yes, that's about it. And have you got on well? If you'd stayed at home, you wouldn't have prospered!"

"No, you don't prosper there," stammered Cipriano as though talking to himself. And hesitating more and more, he went on, "So it's true. . . . So you've come out here. . . . It's true. . . . Didn't you get a letter I sent you?"

"No, you never wrote to me!"

"It was only a short time ago, when I got yours saying you were coming."

"Oh, I took ship only two weeks after I sent that letter."

"And so, when mine got there, you'd already left. So that's it. . . . And is everybody well? Senhora Amélia, and Deolinda, and all?"

"Yes, they're all well. And over at Lordelo, too. They talk about you a lot there. You know, Mariquinhas da Venda's dead."

"Marquinhas da Venda? Poor woman!"

"Oh, and I was forgetting, your mother's sent you some apples. I've got them in my trunk. They're all well at your place, thank God."

"Thanks. So that explains it. . . . In the letter I sent you, I told you not to come."

Manuel da Bouça's expansive mood was cut short by this astounding announcement, and as Cipriano—who looked as though he were confessing a crime—didn't add anything more, he asked him why with some apprehension.

"Because here, like everywhere else, the situation's not good. You can hardly earn a living here."

With bright eyes and trembling lips, Manuel da Bouça, who was shaken to the core, anxiously waited for his friend to give some further explanation, and as this was not forthcoming, he probed further.

"But have you done well?"

"Me? No. I've been here getting on five years now, and the only money I've been able to save is the hundred milréis I sent my mother for Christmas and Easter."

"But back at home, everybody thinks you've set up on your own."

"Oh, yes, I got someone to say that. Everybody here sends news that they're doing well, but that's because we don't want the family to worry, and so as not to look fools to our friends."

"So the shop where you are?"

"Belongs to Senhor Fernandes, the man you saw. And I'm lucky to have a job. There are lots of people here with more time than they want on their hands! They spend months and months without finding work. I've been forced to the conclusion that it's not worth a man's while to leave home."

He stopped talking, with his eyes fixed on the ground and his hands gripped between his legs as though ashamed of his own words. Manuel da Bouça stared at him, anxious not to miss a word, so astounding it all seemed, but as Cipriano didn't go on, he floundered into speech.

"But . . . but . . . I thought . . . I thought you were doing well! So there are a lot of people without work, are there?"

"Oh, yes, a lot. And more come over every day. Some even go hungry."

"Does that happen here, too?"

"If you don't know anyone, there's no work to be had. So what are you to do? Steal? In trade, it's almost impossible to fix up anything. Before a man can find a job, he has to sweat for it, I can tell you."

Again he remained silent. And Manuel da Bouça too. He was preoccupied, seeing everything in a jumble: the land he wanted so badly on the bank of the Caima, his own house, his wife and daughter, the faces of Cipriano and of his employer, the streets of Santos, opaque patches, dark blocks that were tumbling down, slowly, slowly, as in a dream. Then he pulled himself together.

"How much do you earn?"

"Eighty milréis a month."

"Is that all?"

"Food, too."

"Eighty milréis and food?"

"Yes, I pay for my own room and laundry."

Manuel da Bouça had a hard struggle to accept the harsh truth. He couldn't believe it! To be able to believe that, he'd have to be able to believe in the incredible, in what was beyond

imagination, in something worse than phantoms and were-
wolves—because he believed in the devil. To be able to believe
that, he'd have to believe in those incredible things too.

"Do other people earn as little?" he asked, his eyes wide
open, almost panic-stricken.

"They earn more in drapery stores and offices, but they have
to pay for their own food. If you want to earn three hundred
milréis, you have to have a lot of qualifications, and what's the
use if you have to spend it all on clothes and food?"

"But like that, you can't save anything."

"No, nothing. The only thing that keeps me from going
back home is the disgrace of it."

"But, Cipriano, a lot of people come back rich!"

"It's a matter of luck. Some are lucky, others aren't. What
I do know is that when you see one come back with money,
you forget all about the others. Before, employers used to take
their head assistants as partners, it seems, when they had good
experience and conduct, but nowadays . . ."

"What?"

"If a man gets worn out at his job and then is careless one
day, well, it's out into the middle of the street with him. Shops
close at night because that's the law, but you have to go on
working inside till late, tidying up, cleaning the scales, opening
boxes and bags there's been no time to attend to during the
day. And on Sundays it's exactly the same thing. The only bit
of rest you can get is in the afternoon."

"For eighty milréis, no, it's not much," murmured Manuel
da Bouça.

"What are you thinking of doing then?"

"I don't know. I was hoping you'd be able to tell me. . . .
I don't know. What do you think?"

"I don't know either. It's all such a mess!"

"It's a real knockout blow, the very devil of bad luck! On
the boat they offered me a hundred and fifty to two hundred

milréis clear to go and work on the land, but I didn't want to do that. There's no future in it. I wanted to stay here four or five years, but to make something worthwhile!" He stopped, and then after a moment added, as though to give himself courage, "Even though I had to work like a nigger!"

"That isn't enough! I thought of unloading coal, but I saw it was no good. They earned six milréis a shift. And now I'm quite certain that hard work alone never got anybody rich!"

"But is it like that everywhere in Brazil?"

"It's like that all over the world, I tell you. When you're poor . . ."

Once more both of them fell silent. Manuel da Bouça drew a red handkerchief from his pocket and began wiping off the sweat that was trickling down his forehead. His chest was burning. The faint sunrays had disappeared from the yard wall outside; daylight was fading in the room, and in the increasing dusk only the candle and the whitish wood of the cases were clearly visible.

"If I were you, Senhor Manuel, I'd accept what they offered you on the boat. To begin with at least, while you get your bearings. . . . Then later on you can see."

"Do you think so?"

"I don't see any way of getting you a job in the commercial line. Can you read and write?"

"No."

"That makes it worse. There are so many people who've passed exams, and even they can't find jobs. So if I were you, that's what I'd do. Unless of course you've got something else in mind . . ."

"No, I wasn't thinking of anything special. I thought there was plenty of work here, and that a man only had to come with a mind not to be idle. At home, everybody talks about Brazil and America."

"Yes, they all talk."

Manuel da Bouça began to roll a cigarette, very slowly, as though to give himself time to roll up some of the resolutions he'd brought with him, and fold them away like defeated banners.

"Haven't you any friends who could see about finding something for me?" he asked.

"Yes, I have friends. But they'll all tell you the same thing, you see if they don't. They're all like me. Unless you've got a protector . . . but who'd bother about the likes of us?"

"But now I've said no, I don't know whether the men from the boat would take me on now."

"They ought to. Were they the emigration inspectors?"

"I think so."

"They ought to. We'll ask my boss if he knows anything about it. And I'll have to go back now. I said I wouldn't be long. I just came to show you my room and so that we could talk a bit. You can stay here till you find something. The bed's small, but we can always manage. As for food, I haven't got anything here, but you can buy a bite of something outside."

"Thanks, Cipriano. I had a meal before leaving the boat, and I'm not hungry. All this has taken my appetite away."

"All right, we'll see about the eatables tonight, then. Why, Senhor Manuel, you're crying!"

"No, no. Let's go and see your boss." Ashamed of his weakness, with the back of his hand he hastily brushed away the big silent tears that were rolling down his cheeks.

"Why are you crying?"

"Oh, it's nothing . . . nothing."

While Manuel da Bouça got up, Cipriano sat looking at him without speaking. Then, in a friendly voice that showed his own emotion, he said, "It's because you were expecting something different, isn't it?"

And the other replied with an effort, as though he found

it hard to get the words out. "Yes, that's it. But what can we do about it!"

"It was the same with me, Senhor Manuel. I thought I was going to get on in a short time, too; and then, in the end . . . Sometimes, when I think over what I felt when I left home, and the way my mother's still crying over me, I feel like doing something crazy—I don't know what! But what's the use of fretting about it! Everywhere you can make some kind of a living, and then, if you're lucky . . . What I've been telling you, Senhora Manuel, doesn't mean that you won't manage to get good money together and even grow rich. Everything depends on a man's luck. And a lot of people have made money." Then, getting up in his turn, he went on, "Come on, we'll go to the shop now, if you like."

"Yes," murmured Manuel da Bouça very humbly, his face lined with disappointment. "Yes, let's go. Can I leave my bag here?"

"Of course. Didn't you bring anything else?"

"I've got a trunk, but I couldn't bring it away. Something or other has to be done."

"Oh, yes, I know. It's the customs. We'll look after that later, or we'll get a carter to look after it. Let's be off now."

They went downstairs, hurrying along so that the boss wouldn't be angry and give two or three of his bellowing shouts, and Cipriano asked more questions about the people at home while he showed Manuel da Bouça the way back to the grocery.

There were two customers at the counter; Senhor Fernandes was serving one of them, and he gave Cipriano a sharp, almost angry look as soon as he came through the door.

"Just wait a minute, Senhor Manuel," and Cipriano ran off to remove his hat and jacket and then came back to attend to the other woman.

Then other customers came in, and Manuel da Bouça, leaning against the doorpost, had ample time to examine all that part of the street again and again before Cipriano managed to apologize to Senhor Fernandes about being late and tell him about the position his compatriot was in.

"Well, what does he want? Is he another of those chaps who come here and think that, because they're wearing a tie like a lord, they can pick up a fortune in five minutes?"

"Oh, no, he's not like that. But he doesn't know how to set about things."

"Then why doesn't he accept the offer they made on the boat?"

"He doesn't know whether they'll still keep it open. But if you please, sir, I think the best thing would be for you to speak to him yourself." Senhor Fernandes didn't say anything to the contrary, so Cipriano shouted, "Senhor Manuel, Senhor Manuel, will you come over here, please?" When Manuel da Bouça came up he explained, "I've already told my employer all about it, and he wants to know whether you're willing to go and work on the land."

"God bless you, sir," said Manuel da Bouça, pulling off his hat.

"Good afternoon."

"Please, sir, I don't know what's the best thing to do. Cipriano has just been telling me that times are hard. . . . But, on the other hand, to come right from Portugal to earn so little . . ."

"How much did they offer you?"

"They mentioned a hundred and fifty to two hundred milréis."

"And you call that a little?" exclaimed Fernandes. His shirt sleeves were half rolled up, and he leaned his fat hairy arms on the desk. "So you think that's a little! You know, when I first came over here, I began by earning twenty milréis a month. That was thirty years ago. And nobody grumbled. Things aren't very bright here, it's true, but people who come over today have such a big opinion of themselves. In the old days, we used to work day and night, Sundays and holidays, and nobody grumbled about wages. Yet a lot of people made good. Today . . . it's what you see. I even got kicks from my boss."

Manuel da Bouça listened passively to this flow of words, and only when Fernandes, from the height of his domineering girth, seemed to have come to an end, did he dare to speak.

"Then it's your opinion, sir, that I should go and work on the land?"

"No doubt about it. No doubt whatever. Those who work and do their duty always attain their end. . . . I got here with two silver bits in my pocket that my godmother gave me. . . . You look healthy enough."

"That's so, thanks be to God."

"Well then, you're healthy, and you're not old yet. You've still got time to get on well. But if I were the Portuguese government, I wouldn't let anyone come out to Brazil over twenty. This is a place to come to while you're still young, with long years ahead to build up a good living. But the others had better stay at home, because there's quite enough sadness and trouble in the world as it is!" Then he turned to Cipriano. "Just mind those bags. The sun's shining right on those beans."

"But I don't know who the men are who came on the boat. I don't know whether they're still willing to take anyone on."

Cipriano left off moving the bags to come over and explain. "He means the emigration inspectors, sir. If you could only find out whether they'll still accept Senhor Manuel . . ."

"The Emigration Department," said the grocer thoughtfully, "Emigration . . . Now there, look after those bags! Well, it must be Lieutenant Eleuterio, or I'm very much mistaken. I don't know him personally, but Costa knows him. I'll speak to him about it." Then he said firmly to Manuel da Bouça:

"I should think it's likely myself. The devil, if you suited them on board ship, you ought to suit them now on land. I'll see about it tomorrow."

"I'll be very much obliged to you, sir, very obliged indeed. Whatever happens . . ."

"Don't you worry, man! You'll see that it's still possible to get what you want! You'll see! Life belongs to those who know how to work!"

11

*W*HEN Manuel da Bouça appeared at the counter of the Emigration Inspectorate, with Cipriano's head looking over his shoulder, the official (lean, swarthy, and with a monocle at one side of his wide forehead) reprimanded him.

"So you didn't find any use for the hostel yesterday, but it looks better today, eh? Do you take this for an easygoing sort of place where you can come at your own convenience?"

"I didn't know," said Manuel da Bouça in excuse.

"You didn't know! But as soon as you saw that the money-tree didn't exist, then you knew all right! What I ought to do would be to send you to the Labor Exchange, then you'd see whether there'd be any hurry! If you had to hang round for two months, it'd serve you right. It'd be a good punishment for you."

Manuel da Bouça listened, out of countenance and hanging his head to have made such a blunder, while his critic angrily finished scribbling on a paper.

"Take this," he said, handing it over. "It's for the train at half-past three. Show it to the man in charge of the emigrants' squad, at the station."

"Yes, sir. Thank you, sir."

"Good afternoon."

"Is anything else necessary?"

"No."

"Thank you and much obliged, sir."

The official once more leaned over the papers on his desk, and Manuel da Bouça and Cipriano went off.

Out in the street, where the tropical sun burning over the city was flooding both pavements with a yellow wave of fire, Cipriano began to turn the thing over in his mind.

"If it weren't for the boss, Senhor Manuel, I don't think you'd have got into the Emigrants' Reception. It's evident, in this matter, that it's either yes or no upon arrival."

"That's true. Senhor Fernandes doesn't seem such a bad sort after all."

"Oh, that's because it was a case of work," retorted Cipriano. "It's because he thinks you'll have to work hard out there. If it were a case of getting an easy job for you, he wouldn't lift his little finger. The boss has a mania for making other people work. He'd like everybody to work day and night, and he wouldn't be satisfied till they dropped."

Manuel da Bouça looked pensive. He walked along beside his companion with his eyes down, feeling languid because of the "northwest," a climatic condition very common in Santos, the effect of which was to rob you of energy, relax muscles and will, and almost suffocate you, as though a burning wave of sleep were rolling over limp defenseless bodies. Suddenly, in spite of this lassitude, Manuel da Bouça came to himself in a panic.

"Whom did he say I had to give the paper to?"

"The man in charge of the emigrants' squad."

"And who's that?"

"We'll find out at the station."

"Cipriano, are you sure my trunk and bag will be all right?"

"Don't you worry, they won't get lost. When I handed them over, good note was taken. And the boss wouldn't have told me to take them if Costa hadn't told him there was no hitch. By the time you get to the hostel, it's quite likely they'll be there waiting for you."

They crossed the Largo do Rosário and, even though it was the peak hour for business activity, the square was almost deserted because of the "northwest." Only a few thirsty people were indolently sipping iced drinks under the awning of a bar. And whoever was daring enough to cross did it quickly, making for the shade or the semicool protection of the shops.

Cipriano caught sight of a clock in passing.

"We'd better make haste. It's already five to three."

"Is the station far away?"

"No, but we'd better get there early, to give us time to look round for the man in charge."

But a few steps farther on, Manuel da Bouça stood stock still in surprise. Coming toward them were two little men dressed in white, with yellow faces and slanting eyes, and he didn't move again till they'd passed by talking in easy conversation.

"What ugly devils they are!" he then explained.

"They're Japanese," said Cipriano with a smile. "Haven't you ever seen any before? There's lots of them here, Senhor Manuel."

"No, I've never seen anyone like that before. If I ever met a face like that at a lonely crossroad at night, I should take to my heels."

When they reached the station, they found that the emigrants' squad hadn't arrived. Manuel da Bouça admired the easy way Cipriano walked about. Then, about twenty past three, a train whistled and uttered its final steamy hoot and, at the same time, they caught sight of the dingy band of hostel protégés.

There were more than a hundred of these poor pilgrims from over the sea: women and children, and men who walked with slow steps, glancing round to take everything in. Some of the men were already bent-backed, while others held their heads well up, facing the destiny they had chosen. There was an air of long-standing promiscuity about them, and they looked as though, under their clothes, they were covered with dust and sweat, their ears, necks, and hands untouched by soap and water. There were great nailed boots that seemed to have tramped down from the Abruzzi, and hoods that had seen scorching days on torrid heaths. But the greater number wore corduroy and caps, and the whole formed a dark-blue restless mass the rough monotony of which was broken only by the colorful clothes of the women.

At an order from the half-breed who accompanied them, they halted inside the station and huddled together till only those who stood on the outside of the group were clearly visible.

"That must be the man in charge," said Cipriano, pointing out to Manuel da Bouça the tall chap with swarthy cheeks who was walking to and fro between the squad and an inside door, nobody knew why.

"Cipriano, come with me." And Manuel da Bouça stopped the half-breed as he went by. "Are you in charge, please?"

"Yes, what is it?" he answered quickly. And when he saw the paper, he added, "Go over there."

So Manuel da Bouça joined the flock, with Cipriano waiting at his side. Meanwhile the anxious shepherd had gone back to the door and again looked inside.

"Is it time?" he asked someone they couldn't see. There must have been an affirmative answer, because he turned to the group and gave the order, "Off we go!"

The mass began to move, the dark blotch spread out, and Cipriano put his arms round his friend's shoulders.

"Good luck, Senhor Manuel. And if there's anything I can do, you know . . ."

"Thank you, Cipriano. I don't know why, but it's just as though I were setting out for Brazil a second time."

Slowly the emigrants went disappearing through the high doorway till they were all on the platform beside the waiting train. The man in charge pointed out special carriages for the majority of them, and the few who, like Manuel da Bouça, hadn't got a seat in them, were put in another carriage with the private passengers.

And the train set out, passing through the usual type of scenery: level tracts of mangue and banana groves, buildings glimpsed in passing, a road running parallel with the railway for a few minutes, more houses, a few trees just stuck down in the landscape, and a factory chimney in the distance smoking to the sky.

The train stopped at Cubatão, and the attention of the passengers on the left was attracted by something outside. Almost all of them got up and leaned out of the windows and, whatever it was, those on the other side came and looked over their shoulders too.

There, outside, a few yards from the track, was a camp of ragged men, women, and children, a promiscuous rabble. Squalid faces, tangled hair, bare skin showing through their fluttering rags; here and there one or two long beards with ivory-colored noses above them and eyes hollow and dejected with fatigue—they looked like the population of a cemetery just risen from their graves. The children were naked and seemed weighed down by bellies swollen with paludism, bellies that bulged out between skinny chests and lean little legs. Except for their crying destitution, they might have been taken for a tribe of gypsies. The sun shone on a mound nearby, its soft light revealing repellent refuse: detritus, crumpled papers, human rags—all the drama of the cesspool. The women, sitting on the ground, had a lost, forsaken look, eyes vaguely watching the distance in a dark, hopeless dream. Some of the men, slumped down on their arms, were sleeping like brutes, while others looked sunk in preoccupation, as though, after chewing their last crust of bread, they were now ruminating their own entrails.

This striking scene stirred all hearts on the train, and the more people gazed at it, the deeper was the impression etched on their mind of black misery embedded in the filth of a pigsty rigged up along the arduous road.

"They are foreigners," someone said near Manuel da Bouça.

"They are Rumanians," said another passenger as he came away from the window. "I've just read all about the sad case of those poor folk in the paper. It seems incredible that it could be allowed to happen. Do you want to read it?" And he passed his newspaper on to the other man.

These Rumanians, fascinated by the mirage of gold, had left their native land one day and set out for distant Brazil, expenses paid by the Government of São Paulo. Seven families had torn up their roots in search of better soil, seven families in which there was a tragic preponderance of women and children.

There was a shortage of labor in São Paulo, and for the good of the state the government had offered facilities, promising everything necessary not only to these but to hundreds and thousands of families willing to go and till the virgin soil. But the agents had carried out their orders with an excess of zeal and, instead of an honest promise that could be executed, they had painted palaces of gold to make the prospect more attractive; they had suggested to these simple people that wealth was easy to obtain once they got to São Paulo. The government would give them big grants of land that would be theirs for ever and that would make their fortunes in a very short time.

Hypnotized by the golden serpent, the seven families had extinguished their home lamps, and one afternoon the liner *Sofia* had set them down on the quay at Santos. The Emigration Inspectors had docketed the herd and dispatched it to the Emigrants Hostel in São Paulo. There they had one day in which to enjoy the bloom of their colonial dream, the promised land with its glimpse of gold; then they were sent off to a distant fazenda.

The facilities, promised far away in their own land, on the spot turned out to be hard work with no time limit and no protection, because the colonel who owned the property wanted to get rich quick and knew that the more others toiled for him, the more wealth he would get. And so the gold the Rumanians had dreamed about dwindled in their hands and turned into a much less precious metal—a silver coin of one milréis as wages for their toil. Wide fine lands with rich soil that sang the dazzling wealth of the new world did certainly exist; but, just the same as everywhere else, they didn't produce for those who did the work and watered them with their sweat. Others enjoyed the wealth.

And the laws covering emigrant work and welfare, which humane Brazilian legislators had drawn up in a feeling of human solidarity and pride in their native land, were ignored in the interior of the state, in the very place where their protection was most needed.

One day the seven families, drained to the marrow, laid down their farm implements and left the fazenda; and, still drawn by the wealth they had dreamed of, set out for Orlandia in search of better pay. They had gone wandering through the state, and then, at sight of their misery, a general collection had given them the means to get to São Paulo in quest of work and generosity.

A powerful English company had given them work in the capital for a short time; then, when their help became unnecessary, dispensed with it; and once more, with all their resources vanished, the Rumanians set out again, stumbling over hill and dale till they got to Santos, where the sea was an outlet and possible way of return.

And there they were: broken-backed, hungry, ill, amid the continual crying of the newborn and the wails of scrofulous, famished children. There they were with their inflamed eyes fixed on the vague hope that the Consul of Rumania would take pity on them and give their sick flesh transport—some, still fascinated by the idea of gold, to North America, while others wanted only to get back to the land where they were born.

After reading the paper aloud, the passenger handed it back to its owner.

"Really, it's a terrible thing," he said.

"Yes, but it's also a fact," replied the other, "that when these people get here, and see that money isn't to be picked up in the street, they lose interest in work."

Manuel da Bouça was not used to the Brazilian way of speaking, so he didn't catch all the words. But he understood the main drift and began to turn the puzzle over in his mind. If there wasn't plenty of money in this country for the poor too, then where did it exist? How was it that some people in all parts of the world got rich? It wasn't with the daily wage a man earned in Portugal, or with the wage he was going to earn here, that you could get on and lift up your head.

This uneasiness was followed by an agreeable presentiment, like a certitude inside him, that he would be lucky. He couldn't foresee how, but it seemed to him that he would make money and not wander about taking tumbles like the Rumanians. He was healthy, strong, willing to work. And even though Cipriano had said that a man couldn't make money by work alone, he himself had heard of a number of people who'd grown rich just by hard work—and, of course, by being thrifty.

The train set off again and, a little farther on, at Piassaguera, began to climb the mountain range that took its rise there. As the carriages mounted two by two, the landscape became majestic, imposing. Wide horizons opened up on the other side, the vista becoming more and more extensive till the sight, strained by the vast expanse, took in the whole, knitting up the blue draperies of the sky with the visible fringe of land.

Down below, the old railway track still stretched out, rusty from disuse, and with thick tufts of wild plants growing between the crumbling sleepers. Then the base of the mountain range linked up with a neighboring hill, and the eyes were able to embrace it all: here stretches of rough ground, there the green tresses of tree clusters, oases in the blackened bareness. Here and there, also, were gray cottages roofed with zinc, like watchtowers in the hilly desert, but drowsing in the sun's deep hot throe.

It was an impressive landscape of stately beauty that the train unfolded to the eyes of the passengers; but Manuel da Bouça was more interested in the mechanical secret of the climb—that stimulated his peasant's curiosity more than the wonderful panorama spread out before him.

The steel cables, the wires, and various levers, and the great iron teeth that could be glimpsed from time to time between the tracks were an endless source of surprise, and the subject of lengthy study that came to an end only when the train stopped in the station smiling to the sky at the top of the mountain range. From there onward the route was level and, except for the exotic trees, was like a summer landscape in Europe.

Manuel da Bouça began to feel sleepy. . . . When he opened his eyes again, weary eyes like those of a ruminating ox, they saw beyond the banks of the railway line a superposition of redtiled roofs and a forest of factory chimneys that cut off the horizon. A humming beehive could be sensed behind the barrier, something hidden from sight but pulsing with activity, something that throbbed with a monstrous, dynamic vitality.

Then on the outskirts of Braz everything became congested: following in swift succession came walls and corners, bright colors, brick walls, trucks and company names; farther away, outlines of modern buildings, placards and patches of sunlight; slipping along outside the train windows, more factory chimneys, more ridges of roofs; and a strange rhythm, muted yet dense, dominated that of the locomotive and came purring from the city's flanks—music of the titanic epic of industry.

When the train stopped and the herd reformed its ranks, Manuel da Bouça let himself be led along in a daze, too far gone to be surprised, too tired to wonder at anything else. Now and again some of the other emigrants stopped to marvel at what they saw, holding up the procession, and then the man in charge said: "Let's keep moving. You'll have time to see everything later." And they moved on again obediently, though still eager to gaze at all the new sights.

Manuel da Bouça felt isolated among his companions because they spoke a different language that made him feel more of an exile than before, and this feeling of loneliness was relieved only when they passed through a wide gateway where the hubbub of the streets died away, and great peace, great silence, cool and welcoming, suddenly surrounded them.

They marched through a park with wooden benches and rounded shrubs rising from carpets of green lawn. To their left lay the ample quarters of the Emigrants' Hostel: row of windows above and wide veranda below. It was a lodging place for poor, unprotected people come to seek a slice of bread in a strange land, and so there was no dazzling ostentation, no pretentious architecture. But everything was clean and neat, and the simple plants and creepers, the soft color of the walls and the shady veranda came like a sweet, comforting smile.

The herd, which had straggled out while crossing the park, went into the building and closed its ranks again in order to get into the reception room. No one was accepted without being vaccinated, and so one by one, holding out their arms, they passed before the doctor's lancet. Then they were given a residence card with their name and other details scribbled on it, which authorized them to spend six days there at government expense.

And finally the dormitory was pointed out to them, a roomy place white and hygienic as an infirmary ward, and they didn't know what to do with themselves. It was too early to go to bed and forget their weariness and new experiences. And nobody seemed to know how to set about killing time. So there they were among the white-painted iron beds between the white-painted walls, growing more and more dejected; and there they would have stayed for hours on end if a charitable official passing by had not said: "You can go outside, you know. A bell rings for dinner." Only two or three of them understood the saving words, but the getting up and going out of these knowing ones showed the way to the others.

Outside in the park Manuel da Bouça recognized the Italians who had traveled with him on the *Darro,* and the friendly glance he exchanged with them made him feel less alone among so many strangers. What a pity they speak the devil's own tongue and it's impossible to understand them!

At the hostel, it was language that drew people together, and made them form into groups, creating a fellow feeling they wouldn't have felt in their own country. The Italians were the most numerous. More than fifty of them had grouped themselves round two benches, in the grave evening quiet. Some of them had come from the remotest provinces of Italy, each perhaps with its different customs and traditions; but here, lonely and far away from home, they could always find some detail or memory of common interest. Those who had been there some time went over to join the new arrivals, shy at first, then with less restraint, and soon affinity leveled them into the common stock.

After the Italians came a compact group of Serbs, Croats, and Slovenes, melancholy, reserved people who settled in a corner and broke the silence from time to time only with some casual remark brought up from their private rumination. Only the Galician and Castilian fellows were noisy, gesticulating as they walked from end to end of the park in loud conversation, as though quite at home. And other, smaller groups were dotted about: two or three people talking in low voices, a thoughtful married couple, and more than one isolated figure at the end of the park absentmindedly poking the ground with the toe of its boot.

Manuel da Bouça wanted to forget the weight that was lying on his heart, and he strained his ears trying to catch some talk he could understand and in which he could join. But there was nothing, nothing! The devil if these people didn't talk more strangely than the Englishmen from the mines at Nogueira do Cravo! Not even from gypsies, dancing-bear or monkey showmen had he ever heard such jargon as this. It didn't seem human. Feeling like a prisoner there, he smoked cigarette after cigarette, and grew full of homesickness, with patches of his native countryside and the familiar faces of his wife and daughter continually misting in front of his eyes like colored cataracts.

The very evening was turning despondent! Beyond the wires that crossed the park, pink was showing in the sky, a dull faded pink of mysterious sweetness. A flight of pigeons came and settled quietly along the edge of the hostel roof. City life was throbbing nearby, but its vibration seemed to be a long way off.

Night was falling and bringing deeper melancholy when the bell rang for dinner. Those who had already spent some days there showed the way along the veranda and corridors to the spacious dining room. And only then did Manuel da Bouça hear another emigrant, on the other side of the table, speak the language he understood.

"I sat over there yesterday," said the exile to the waiter.

"That doesn't matter. Sit here today."

Manuel da Bouça watched how the others behaved so as not to seem a vulgar fellow without any manners, but he kept his eyes on the compatriot whom fate had placed in his path after an evening of utter loneliness. It was the man he had seen in the distance, alone at the end of the park, scratching the ground with the toe of his boot. About his own age too, but he showed it more, with a lot of wrinkles at the corners of his mouth and eyes. When the meal was over, Manuel da Bouça went out behind him and followed till he found a chance to speak to him without the presence of strangers, so that he wouldn't be shy.

"Have you come from Portugal too?"

"Yes." The man took a better look at Manuel da Bouça. "But I didn't know there was any other Portuguese here besides myself."

"I only got here today."

"I got here last Friday. It must have been an unlucky day, because there was nobody to talk to in my own language. There were some Spaniards, and I can understand a bit of their lingo because I've worked in Buenos Aires, but they went away yesterday. And you? Did you land today?"

"No, the day before yesterday, but I've been in Santos. It's been very dull this evening, not having anyone to talk to."

"Yes, it's like that. There doesn't seem to be a Portuguese soul here. But that's not surprising. They all go into business, but now that trade's bad they'll have to come. Round here it's thick with Portuguese, and they'd do better to leave the city and try their luck with a mattock. Though it's likely that wouldn't get them anywhere, either. Is it the first time you've been to Brazil?"

"Yes."

"What part do you come from?"

"From near Oliveira de Azemeis."

"Never heard of it. I come from Barcelos, near Braga. And it's the second time I've been over, but I don't know whether I'll have time to make good. There's not much hope here, but you get used to it, and then you haven't got the courage to go home with empty hands. I was only back there a fortnight, just to get the homesickness out of my system, and then off again at full speed before they found out I hadn't got a farthing."

"So you didn't manage to turn a penny?"

"What hopes! I spent six years in Rio de Janeiro and almost as many in Argentina. I worked a few months in Montevideo too. I've knocked about and seen things, that I can tell you! And I like moving about. But as for money . . . At the end of all that time I went back to Portugal with only a bit above nothing in my pockets, just because I couldn't rest without going back to see the trees I used to climb as a boy after the nests. And I'd always worked with the idea of going back. There's no false shame in me, so I had a go at everything. I've been shopboy, carter; I always worked like a nigger; and in Buenos Aires I even went down to being a bootblack. Whatever it is, so long as it's work, there's no dishonor, don't you think so?"

"Of course, of course," agreed Manuel da Bouça.

"I learned to read, to see if I couldn't get on better. What I wanted was to be my own boss. If I could have managed that I should have made money. But no such luck. The upshot of it all was that I wore myself out from morning till night, and what for? A few hundred milréis to go back to Portugal and stay a few days. Nothing more. Yes, the first time I came out, Brazil and Argentina were still good. It was the period of the fat kine. If I could have set myself up in something, I could have made good money. But where could I get the capital?"

They were leaning on the veranda, and his compatriot's outlook was so discouraging that Manuel da Bouça felt as though his heart were being squeezed between two millstones. He asked him why, having been so unlucky, and yet having managed to get back to Portugal, he had still wanted to come out to Brazil again.

"Why? Well now, all of us who come all this way over the sea get the idea that the folk at home go on remembering and thinking about us. Then one fine day we manage to scrape together a bit of money to go home. Then it's all wonderful, cordial 'How are you, Mr. So-and-So' all over the place. But what they really want to know is whether you've brought a lot of money back. If you haven't, they begin to whisper about it and some folk even look down their noses at you. There's no dishonor in being poor, but back home those who come back poor from Brazil are always ashamed of it. . . . And another thing that gets us is that we still have a hankering after what we knew when we were nippers. Men and women . . . what a joke! We've gone on daydreaming about Antónia, Maria, Ana, or Josefa, some young wench with whom we had a bit of a flirt, and then you discover that she got married years ago, and she sticks three or four kids in front of you. Everything changes: the old ones pass on, and young ones grow up who don't know us, and you feel a stranger in your own village. So, if you haven't brought money back with you, as soon as you've got the homesickness out of your system you go away again and look for a place where poverty isn't a disgrace. The big mistake is to leave home the first time."

He fell silent. Manuel da Bouça offered him tobacco, and he began to roll a cigarette.

"This is from home," he commented. "There's good tobacco here too, and cheap in comparison." He blew out the smoke and, as his companion was shy and said nothing, he went on: "As for me, if I don't manage something worthwhile this time, I'm not going back. If it's only with a handful of little coins, I'm not going back. It's a long way from home, you think? Well, what about it? You can live anywhere, and I prefer to peg out here rather than have to be ashamed all the time because I didn't go back brash with cash. The homesickness that gets hold of you over here and makes you think your heart'll burst with longing, it soon passes when you get home and see that all's not gold that glitters. Then when you come over here again, you get used to living a long way from home."

This man who had renounced his own country was glad to get it all off his mind after four days' enforced silence, and he suggested that they take a turn in the park till the bell rang to go back to the dormitory. Outside, other residents were walking about too, talking quietly together, denser shadows in the shadow of the night.

"And what are you going to do now?" Manuel da Bouça ventured to ask, still seared by the words he'd just heard.

"I'm going to try the mattock, inland. . . . There's no hope in town work."

Then he was off again in a flow of talk so that his companion couldn't get a word in, telling all about his disappointments and about all the things he'd seen during his life. Discouraging talk it was, spoken with the defiant emphasis of someone defending a personal case, and each word fell like a burning coal on Manuel da Bouça's mind, eagerly open to receive any information about the soil he was now treading.

They separated only in the dormitory, and when the lights went out Manuel da Bouça, with his head under the sheet, began to put a question, in a panic:

Oh, God, shall I be lucky? Shall I be lucky?

Next day his compatriot was called up to the official Employment Bureau, and came back with news.

"I've been taken on with a contract, and it appears they're going to engage a lot more today, too. And it wasn't any too soon. I'm off tomorrow; otherwise I'd be out in the street. Tomorrow makes six days I've been here, and after six days, well, you have to put up with it, but the street door's one of the rules of the house. But it could be worse, couldn't it? After all, it's not bad here. What I don't like is those estate owners who call you gawks and fossils and suchlike, as though you weren't as good as the next man just because you come from places like Portugal, Italy, or Turkey."

"And what's your name?"

"Rufino Macieira."

"Mine's Manuel Joaquim dos Santos. And where are you going to now?"

"Somewhere near Ribeirão Prêto."

"With good wages, of course?"

"Hum! A hundred and fifty milréis a month, and no tips, and you have to look after I don't know how many coffee trees. You can bargain as much as you like, but you can't get more. Well, I'd better go and pack a few things now, because it looks as though I'll have to be moving soon."

Pack a few things . . . And the trunk, the bag? While the other man was moving off, Manuel da Bouça began to wonder where his luggage was. He hadn't thought about it for the last few days. He looked round for an official who could give him information, and came across one who, after setting his mind at rest—it's over there, don't worry—stopped, unfolded a paper, and read out some names, Manuel da Bouça's among them. The men who had been called assembled and went off, hopeful but anxious, to the Employment Bureau.

There they were told that Colonel Alexandre Borba, then present, had come to take on twenty laborers for his fazenda. He was a big broad-shouldered man with a full face, skin yellow with malaria, dressed in a light-colored suit of strong silk, and carrying a good Panama hat by its brim. While the emigrants were coming into the room, he looked them over with the experienced eye of the slave dealer fully accustomed to estimating the strength of each one. And behind him, other figures were waiting, other estate owners waiting their turn to obtain labor.

When the candidates had formed into a group, the official mumbled in Italian (the mother tongue of the majority) the conditions on which Colonel Borba would contract the number of men he required: eight hours' work a day, one hundred and fifty milréis per month, with lodging, but food being at their own expense. On the Santa Efigénia estate, they grew coffee, maize, and other cereals. The colonel didn't mind taking ten men on job work for the coffee plantation: for the care of each thousand trees he would pay two hundred milréis per year. Whichever form they preferred, the contract for the twenty of

them would be for one year. They had only to choose. He
himself, as an official whose duty it was to protect the interests
of the emigrants—and he trusted Colonel Borba would excuse
him, because he meant no offense—was of the opinion that it
would be better to choose the monthly wage. So let them
decide.

The Italians looked at one another perplexed, and Manuel
da Bouça, instinctively grasping the importance of the moment,
stepped forward.

"Would you please repeat what you've just said," he asked,
"so that I can understand? I speak only my own language."

The official smiled.

"The devil! I'd forgotten there was a Portuguese among you."

And he set about explaining the conditions of the contract
while Colonel Borba, his attention drawn to the odd man out,
looked Manuel da Bouça over from top to toe, weighing him
up with an interested eye.

The Italians decided in the affirmative, and the agreement was
concluded with two witnesses to legalize the thing for those
who didn't know how to write. Manuel da Bouça had to accept
too, and with a heavy heart put off for a year the fine things
he had dreamed.

When they went out with their working cards in their pockets,
and the information that they would be leaving at four o'clock
in charge of the steward of Santa Efigénia, he felt a great
emptiness within him. In spite of all the defeatist talk he'd
heard, he had managed to keep up the hope, though he
couldn't say why, that in the end things wouldn't turn out
as bad as they were painted. It had been a vague but comforting
hope. On days of terrible storm when it looked as though not
one blade of the harvest could remain standing, didn't it often
turn out, when you really looked into it, that some measures of
grain were gleaned? But now . . . as things were . . . What
the devil could he do on a hundred and fifty milréis a month?

Depression and the ache of disappointment made him feel

helpless. He felt the need of affection and moral support. Then he thought about writing to his wife, his poor Amélia who was so far away and surely fretting because she'd got no news from him yet. But who'd write it for him? He went to look for Rufino Macieira in one of the inner patios of the hostel. As soon as he found him, Rufino asked about the work.

"Well, did they take you on too?"

"Yes, I've been taken on."

"Where for?"

"I don't know exactly. Santa Efigénia, wherever that is."

"Ah, and how much?"

"A hundred and fifty milréis."

"The same as me. They don't want to give more. Oh, and the boss has decided to stay a bit longer, so we're not leaving till later tonight, after all."

Then Manuel da Bouça explained what he wanted.

"You're just the chap to do me a good turn. Would you write a letter home for me?"

"Why, of course, let's go and see to it."

Rufino knew all parts of the building, so he took his compatriot to a room and, leaving him there, went away and then came back with paper and ink. He sat down at one of the tables.

"Now tell me what you want to say!"

Manuel da Bouça found himself at a loss. The emptiness inside him seemed to spread and spread. His mind went back over all the days that had gone by, traveling back to his departure from home, his love for his wife and daughter, the fairy tales he'd built up about the land of exile; and now his setback weighed on him, cramped him, made him miserable.

"Tell me what to say!" his companion said again.

Manuel da Bouça came closer to the table, fixed his eyes on the white paper, and began to dictate in a faltering voice:

"My dear Amélia, first of all I hope that this letter will find you enjoying the best of health, and our Deolinda too. I am very satisfied. This place is quite different. I've already got work, and, God willing . . ." He went on repeating, God willing . . . God willing . . . but his voice was so low, so slow and faltering that Rufino looked up. Manuel da Bouça was white and his eyes full of tears.

"What's the matter? Don't you feel well?"

"Oh, it's nothing, nothing at all. It'll pass. Please go on writing . . ." And struggling to control his feelings, he stammered out: ". . . God willing, Amélia, I shall get on very well."

12

EFORE you entered the confines of Santa Efigénia, you could see the pretty white chapel perched on some higher ground that justified the name of the fazenda. It looked like some lighthearted child amusing itself by making visitors turn solemn and serious when it pointed its cross at them. It was Colonel Borba's magic charm, and the mouthpiece through which the laborers murmured words of faith to heaven, and supplications to turn away affliction.

Lower down to the left, half hidden by the branches of a peroba tree, rose the reddish-colored roof of the master's house. It was one story only, built a few feet above the ground, with a wide veranda running along its whole length where Colonel Borba liked to lounge in his rocking chair and smoke his cigar as night fell.

Then came the level terrace where, in the old days of slavery, the slaves were allowed to gather together for dancing and other festivities on days when the masters were relaxing after a good dinner. Beyond that was a row of huts that indicated the status of the tenants by their smallness and simplicity. And farther still, on the other side of the jequitiba tree, more than a hundred years old and lifting its verdure high into the sky, lay the coffee plantation itself: first great floors of cement, because Colonel Borba thought that floors of beaten earth never gave proper satisfactory drying; then the tanks where the "cherries" were separated from the "floats" and the number of "sailors" estimated; and last of all, the long rows of valuable shrubs, each of them a bit hunched up, midway between jovial and truculent, and rather proud of its red beads. A great band of territory that seemed interminable—red, fertile, untiring earth, land of blood and gold that awoke each morning in new wealth. It was Colonel Borba's great pride. From his father he had inherited just over two thousand coffee trees that were neglected and in bad condition; and now, just half a dozen years later, there were not less than three hundred thousand shrubs in such fine condition that they made a big impression on the delegate from the institute when he came to study the means of combating the "broca" pest.

Santa Efigénia was the biggest fazenda in the Piracicaba district. It's true, its owner never forgot to hoard his money so as to be able to end his life among jolly wenches in Rio after a turn in Paris, but he never skimped on improvements; he spent good money on purchasing machines to improve the coffee, and fattened a big herd of pigs on the maize grown in the alleys between the coffee shrubs, thanks to intensive cultivation.

And it was these pigs, grunting in the sties and poking their round dark greedy snouts through the planks, that Manuel da Bouça saw when the squad of new laborers passed by and that made him feel sure that he hadn't come to a world completely different from the one he'd been familiar with. Then, soon after, the fowls scratching on the sunny terrace, and the maize patch visible from that point, seemed like old friends greeting him with a familiar smile. All the rest was unfamiliar; each tree, each bird, each plant, the aspect of creatures and things, was new and strange.

With the leisurely gait of people looking round and admiring, the newcomers went up to the steps leading to the veranda of the master's house; and there Manuel da Bouça saw something else that was familiar—the well-groomed horse on which the colonel had ridden from the station to the fazenda. According to the steward's orders, they all assembled round the crupper of the sorrel horse, but several feet back in case the animal should kick out behind, startled by some fly or for any other reason, while the steward went up the steps to the veranda.

The Italians never stopped looking this way and that, taking in the whole landscape, and Manuel da Bouça too, his face dark with unshaved beard, gave full rein to his curiosity. What was going to happen here? In this country, frightening in its vastness, what was their life going to be like? What was the future going to be?

The steward came back followed by a Negro clinking a big bunch of keys. And he led the herd away. Moving off and skirting the terrace, they went round the peroba tree and then along by the low hutments of the Caipira * laborers, here and there catching sight of the bronze bodies of women and children. Halfway along the row of huts the steward halted and ordered the Negro to try the keys in one of the doors. When the door was opened, they could see a square space covered with matting instead of floodboards. It smelled of damp and mold, and at the back two steps led up to another compartment serving as kitchen. The steward looked quickly round the place, then turned to the group and picked out a tenant.

"You, there!"

It was an Italian, a man with a wife and two children, and understanding the gesture rather than the words, he stepped forward. The steward asked his name and made a cross with his pencil in the notebook he had brought. Then he explained that the luggage would arrive later and that Colonel Borba was

* Caipira—countryman, a rustic of southern Brazil.

ready to let all the new people he had taken on have sleeping hammocks and kitchen utensils on credit.

Then, leaving the couple, he went on billeting the others in the next huts, all built on the same plan but differing in size —because a married man always requires more space than two or three unmarried ones. Manuel da Bouça was allotted the last hut but one, and his companion was a Calabrian whose long beard didn't make a good impression on the steward, who believed only in the work of clean, presentable men.

Left alone in the bare huts, and separated by difference of language, the two men awkwardly made their way one behind the other into the kitchen, which, having no outer wall, gave a view over a good part of the fazenda.

They stood looking out absentmindedly for some minutes. Then the Italian took some cigarettes from his pocket, lighted one, and silently offered the packet to Manuel da Bouça, who accepted one and thanked him with a smile. And the two men stood there smoking, leaning one on either side, and looking out over an expanse of land as silent as themselves. But soon the sound of noisy voices came from the next hut, and the Calabrian, stretching his long neck in a hoarse shout, established communications with the neighbors. Then he stepped down from the kitchen over the old tins and other rubbish left by the last tenant, and two compatriots came out and joined him. He didn't want to be impolite to Manuel da Bouça, so he signed to him to come down and join them, and the four men set out on a round of inspection to get an idea of what the new life was going to be. A good way farther on, Manuel da Bouça came to a sudden halt and began to listen in surprise. The three Italians stopped too and, hearing the same thing, gave him a sympathetic smile of fellow feeling. A grasshopper was shrilling nearby, reminding them of their native lands, an unexpected bond across the ocean, and they were touched to the quick.

Night was falling. The sky darkened, the red earth darkened

too, and the coffee trees became a procession of shadows—like close ranks muffled in cloaks lying in ambush against some invisible enemy.

On the higher ground behind the chapel, from the uncleared forest that on windy nights sent mournful music wailing over the fazenda, came a noisy group of men walking toward the four sightseers. When their cheerful "good night" was answered, they stopped and exchanged some awkward remarks. The Italian laborers who had already been there some time shyly fraternized with the newcomers, while the tabaréus,* elbows leaning on the helves of their axes, looked on with sympathetic curiosity.

Then they all moved on again in a single group, the old hands giving explanations to the new, but Manuel da Bouça couldn't understand their gibberish until one of them, who could speak some Portuguese, began to translate for him. And so, glad to escape from his enforced dumbness, he never stopped asking questions till they reached the door of his own hut. But the only encouraging bit of information he got was that another Portuguese worker was living at Santa Efigénia who'd been there for quite some years.

When Manuel da Bouça and his Calabrian mate went into their quarters again, they found their luggage already there, with two hammocks and various kitchen utensils at the back near the steps. They busied themselves over their bags and trunks, not worrying about preparations for an evening meal because it had been said that for this first day Colonel Borba was offering it gratis. Then the Negro who had carried the keys came and showed his white teeth and eyes at the door and asked them to follow him.

In a lean-to at the back of the master's house an old half-breed woman was ladeling out plates of beans from a steaming caldron, and in the dim firelight the plates were passed round to those who had that day set foot in Santa Efigénia for the first time.

* Tabaréus—backwoodsmen.

Soon, nearly all the other laborers had gathered round the place in a friendly way to watch the newcomers, and when the meal was over they went back with them to their quarters to show them how to fix their hammocks and get in without fear of a tumble. They moved from one room to the other, setting things up in the local fashion, and then, when every-thing was shipshape and explanations given how to spend a good night, they stayed on talking.

Counting old hands and new, more than a dozen men had stayed behind in the hut with Manuel da Bouça and the Calabrian, because the neighbors had come in to gossip too. A likable Indian fellow, with a magician's flourish, brought a bottle of rum from inside his shirt as though extracting it from his chest, and the drink passed round till someone held back because of Colonel Borba's dislike for drunken laborers.

"Now, good folk," exclaimed the Indian, "tomorrow's Sunday, and till cock crows on Monday there's time to tap a barrel, let alone just a little nip!"

A phonograph was playing hoarsely nearby, and the shadows of couples dancing could be seen outside—shadows that merged and came and went, contracting and expanding, heads bending and lifting again in weird elasticity.

Then the elderly Portuguese man mentioned by the Italian came to welcome the only compatriot whom fate had brought to these parts in the last five years. He was well turned fifty, with sun-blackened skin and wide wrinkled face; fixed on his mouth, as though between brackets, was an everlasting silly complacent smile.

He was there to do the right thing, he said, because when a man comes for the first time to a place he don't know, it's as though he's walking in the dark. And, having delivered this, he wanted to know where his compatriot came from.

Ossela? Between Oliveira de Azemeis and Cambra? He'd heard tell of such places, but he'd never been there. He came from Freches near Trancoso. And he sat down beside Manuel da

Bouça, while the riffraff went on with their talk, some of them sitting on the bags and trunks and others leaning against the walls.

"Now tell me," he said, "you've been used to land work, haven't you?" And when Manuel da Bouça said yes, he went on, "Because that makes a big difference; when a man gets out here and has to learn first, like I did . . ."

And then his life story began. He'd been at this place going on twelve years, not counting four more spent in Carangola in the State of Minas. It had taken him a long time to get the knack of things, and the natives had snickered at him, because when a man's inexperienced people just can't help grinning. Since then, he'd learned how to work, and now he knew his job as well as any forty-year matuto.* Once, a place had been offered him at a fazenda in Campinas, and he'd been tempted to go, but then just the idea of having to move out from one place and go to another with his wife and swarm of kids made his hair stand on end.

"So you're married are you?"

"Well, no, not married . . . but it amounts to the same thing."

His maternal tongue had become debased; r's were often left out, all syllables accented almost alike, and penultimate stresses carried to the antepenultimate syllable.

"But don't you mean to go back home?"

"Well, yes, I'd like to. That's a thing that sticks like a lump in all our throats. It's just as though the very stones we saw when we were lads keep their hold on our hearts. But how can I go back? A man with wife and seven children, when he earns enough to eat, has to be content with that."

The Indian, now half drunk, got up and proposed a visit to the dance at Fagundes' place, since the phonograph was still playing and inviting to the dance. So the group made for the door.

* Matuto—backwoodsman.

"Shall we go too? And, yes, what's your name?"

"Manuel."

"And mine's Bernardo."

The two men got up and followed the others. Outside, the shadows of the couples dancing were no longer moving about on the ground, but were flickering over the heads of the onlookers crowding round Fagundes' door. There were so many spectators that the latecomers could hardly see what was going on inside.

Manuel da Bouça shook hands with Bernardo (who again said he was only too willing to do anything he could) and then left them. He felt tired out by the events and surprises of the day, and when he got back to the hut he lay down in the hammock, carefully following the recommendations received: first sit down, then lie back, and lift your legs up last of all. When his Calabrian mate came in treading carefully so as not to make a noise, his mind was already in a maze with Bernardo's words dinning in his ears: A man with wife and seven children, when he earns enough to eat, has to be content with that.

And the nasal rusty music of the persistent phonograph went on droning through the tropical night.

At daybreak on Monday morning the column of natives and old hands passed by the living quarters, ax on shoulder, and led the new recruits off for the felling. The work of cutting down trees gave scope for the raw hands, and those who couldn't take the places of the backwoodsmen from Baía in the felling of age-old trees could find plenty to do among the shrubs and lianas.

Colonel Borba's great ambition was to possess five hundred thousand coffee trees, and the land could be obtained only by clearing the wild forest (refuge of Paulist bands in other days) that lay thick behind the chapel. But apart from any other consideration, this clearing was a splendid task to get the new gang used to the ways of the fazenda, so in the morning light, reddish like the soil, there they all were, Manuel da Bouça among them, docilely marching along with a wide-brimmed carnaúba hat on his head.

The forest was awake too, its tangled profusion full of freshness and mystery. The old trees, which were so lofty and austere that they seemed to have been present at the beginning of the world, had such retinues of young trees, shrubs, and plants that if the whole were allowed to grow, well, the land would have to be elastic to make room for it all. Wherever the ax had not yet set its tooth, opening up hatchways through which the sun could kiss the dead foliage lying thick on the ground, the tangle was so dense and rose to such a height that nothing could be seen three feet away. The filtered light passed through all gradations from bright to dark, and some lianas were so green and viscous that they were as startling as snakes. In the reigning solitude, the cry of some bird broke out as sudden as a war cry.

It was all amazing to the new thrashers of the forest, and if their comrades hadn't gone about the day's work with a light heart, they would have kept their eyes open on all sides, on the defensive.

When they reached the clearing that had been opened up the day before, the sun was already lighting great branched candlesticks on the tops of the highest trees. Huge trunks were lying on the ground cut up into three or four lengths, some sweating blood where the saw had passed, others oozing resinous tears that ran slowly down and crystallized on the trodden leaves. The men stowed their simple food in a safe place, and then began the day's work—the old hands casting stealthy glances at the new ones to see the ease or awkwardness with which they were shaping. Ax blows resounded through the forest in a kind of frenzy. Then at about nine o'clock Paixiuma the Indian, his face dripping with sweat, straightened up and gave the first yell of alarm.

"Look out, folks! She's coming!"

The gigantic massive tree was slowly leaning over with dry crackling sounds coming from the great gash. Then, with a sudden crash, an apocalyptic thunderclap, violently smashing the branches of the other trees, with unsuspected strength shattering the crests of smaller trees, in its death dragging everything else down that stood in its path, it fell with a mighty thud. And a new corridor of light was opened up.

With hard eyes and tight-shut mouth the steward closely watched the efforts his men were making, because you can't trust anyone who works under orders. But he was able to find fault with only one of the newcomers for being less handy. All the others, bare to the waist, sweat trickling down, muscles flexing to the movement of the ax as they struck and struck again, were equal to the task. And up to the rest hour, at midday, Manuel da Bouça felt satisfied, because hard work didn't frighten him, and he didn't come out of the trial badly. . . . After all, they did things here the same way as at home. The trees were different, but if you could use your ax to fell pine trees, you could fell any other kind of tree.

But at night, in their quarters again, worn out and backbroken with fatigue, he had to drive himself to get any food ready. While he was moving about, the depression that came over him added to his weariness. In the silent kitchen—with no exchange of conversation because he couldn't understand the Calabrian—two tears rolled from his eyes down into the cooking pot . . . Back at home, Amélia always had his food ready for him, with little acts of kindliness and care for him when he came back from work. Now he had nobody. . . . Now he had nobody. . . .

13

WHEN the time came for gathering the crop. From early dawn Santa Efigénia embarked upon hours of stir and bustle, and the gangs of laborers, some with bags hanging from their chests, others carrying ladders and sheets on their shoulders, made their way to the coffee plantation under the vigilant eye of the steward. The whole year had been passed with this period in view; all hopes had been placed in it, expecting compensation for all the labor and money expended on the care of the shrubs. No effort could be spared now, because time pressed and it was important not to let the coffee get grilled on the tree. The excitement of crop gathering made the whole fazenda pulse with eagerness, even infecting those who wouldn't benefit directly from the yield, whether large or small. Never was there so much singing at Santa Efigénia as during those days when fingers were busy over the branches of the coffee shrubs, stripping the beans into bags carried bandoleer-fashion from the men's shoulders, or onto sheets spread out on the ground. To anyone approaching the plantation at this time, it looked lovelier than ever with its straight lines of green-glistening shrubs covered with red fruits, little oval cherries offering themselves in swift profusion.

The chattering band of gatherers, in their wide-brimmed carnaúba hats, spread themselves out along the alleys, stripping, stripping, filling sieves and hampers in lush plenty of green and red, beans everywhere spilling on the ground from the sheets, to be gleaned and swept up later. The women were out working too, and when a ladder had to be used against some tall shrub to get at the beans, more than one rogue came to try and get a look up their skirts, amid jokes and laughter. The general good humor disappeared only when there was no shade left under the carnaúba, when the fatigue that had been collecting in them all during the day came to a head with the horizontal sun. Then the Indians brought out their most cutting stories about bunglers and fumblers from their wide repertory, to annoy the foreigners and see the last blood that the tropics had not dried up flush in their cheeks. But later on they were all friendly again, and even Manuel da Bouça, who felt the most gibed at, because a lot of these greenhorn stories were aimed at "Galicians," began to think it was droll and all meant in fun. This was the most pleasant time he had yet spent there, and the coffee gatherers, with their nostalgic songs and light wide-brimmed hats moving about among the shrubs along a pleasant slope of land, reminded him of harvesttimes at home—a sad thing to think about now.

One morning, however, he let his companion get up and get the coffee ready without moving to help him. He didn't feel well; a great heaviness numbed his limbs, and his will was as weak as water. When the coffee was steaming in the cups, the Calabrian came up to the hammock with his long beard sweeping his hairy chest, and only his pants differentiating him from Adam.

"Signore Manuel, it's time . . ." he warned in the mixed jargon of a foreigner trying his best to manage.

"I don't feel well. I'll get up a bit later, today."

"You ill? *Ammalato?* Do you want me to tell Signore Capistrano?"

"Oh, no, it's nothing. I'll tell him later, thanks, Senhor Pietro."

The Calabrian drank up his coffee, finished dressing, and went out, because the noise outside showed that the squad was forming.

The years had opened cracks between some of the roof tiles, and a dull light hung in driblets round the cobwebs and rafters, like some dark fluid, then fell on the heavy eyes of Manuel da Bouça when he opened them. The voices of the squad were moving away, the sounds floating back from near the drying floors.

Unable to sleep any more, alone and depressed in the silence of the living quarters, Manuel da Bouça saw everything with a jaundiced eye. He had always found mornings without physical activity irksome and dismal.

He began to think about Janardo—what had become of him now?—and then about Cipriano. Then his restless mind leaped in a wave of homesickness across the ocean to his native village, far away and fascinating; then back again to Santa Efigénia, turning over the same old themes. . . . How could he ever get back to Portugal, when he was earning so little? He'd been there five months now; he hung on to every copper he could possibly keep, but in spite of it they slipped through his fingers like live slippery fish. No matter how he tightened his belt, and spent not a penny more than was necessary on tobacco, the hundred and fifty milréis weren't elastic, and everything left over was all swallowed up in paying off for the hammock and utensils and all the stuff Colonel Borba had sold them for double the price asked anywhere else. He said the men were free to buy wherever they liked; they could go and do their buying in town if they wanted. . . . But that was just tricky talk, because the town was so far away that you had to lose a day to get there, and spent more on the train than you saved on the things you bought. So how could a man save anything? That was why some of the Italians had been there for over ten years, for so long that they talked like natives. . . . But whatever happened, he didn't mean to grow old in Brazil! Why hadn't he gone to North America instead? Zé do Aido had been right, after all! Everywhere people said, and here in Brazil they said it too, that America was the place with money! But how could a man guess that?

He began to wonder whether a quick change in a new direction would be more likely, if it should turn out that he could get the money together to go to the United States. He'd send a letter to Amélia; that's all that was necessary, because when a man had to be so far from home, it was all the same whether it was Brazil or the United States. . . .

The thought of his wife, surging up while he was probing the possibility of a new departure in the conquest of wealth, made him feel more bitter. So far he'd sent her only a few awkward lines of clumsy words, not even a trace of money, however tight he pulled the strings of his purse. What would she think of him? When he'd paid off Colonel Borba, he'd have to scrape up a bit of something to send her. . . . And there you are! A hundred, or at most a hundred and fifty milréis, would be all he'd be able to manage after a year's work. . . .

Now the sun was shining between the tiles, and a yellowish gleam lay across the rafter and dripped a little of its fluid gold, with flies constantly glancing about in it.

The door flew open at a sudden push, and the steward came in.

"Now then, you, what's the matter?"

"I don't rightly know what it is, Senhor Capistrano, but it seems to me I'll be able to get up about midday."

"Well, you know, Colonel Borba don't want idlers on this fazenda. So what's the matter with you?"

"It's just as though I'd had a good thrashing. Every bone aches, and I can't move without feeling it."

"Now that's just nothing at all! I've had that myself often enough, but I've always jumped out of my hammock before sunrise. I think you'd just better get up now, because I don't like having any trouble with Colonel!"

"I'll get up as soon as I can, Senhor Capistrano. I'm not the kind to pretend to be ill just to miss work."

"We'll see about that, we'll see!"

And he went out leaving the door wide open. Manuel da Bouça tried to get up, but he hadn't the strength. His body was weak and full of pains, and he felt his joints whenever he moved. . . . Well, he can't thrash me, and ill like this I don't work! And he stayed where he was. A troublesome ray of light came from the open door, and he covered his face with the flaps of the netting. Another dejected hour passed by, with its round of schemings and tattered illusions. Then he heard a soft voice, a woman's gentle voice.

"You want anything, Senhor Manué?"

He uncovered his face and saw Benvinda standing by his hammock, a mulatress with mild eyes, thick, sensual lips and full-curved body breathing voluptuousness from all its pores.

"Ah, it's you. . . ."

"I heered steward say down at plantation that Senhor Manué was acting sick, but the real trouble was just bone-idleness. So I sneaked off to see whether you needed something, because steward only thinks a man's ill when he got both hoofs in the grave."

"I don't want anything, Senhora Benvinda. It'll soon pass. I'm much obliged all the same, because you're the only one who's bothered about me. But you'd better go back before Senhor Capistrano misses you."

"Well, just let him! But what you got, Senhor Manué?"

"I don't know; I just feel I've got no strength, but it'll pass. In no time at all I'll be on my feet again. Maybe I got too much sun yesterday."

"Yes, that surely it. Yesterday the sun was fit to turn a white man black. What you say to a cup o' nice hot coffee, Senhor Manué?"

"Don't bother. . . . They might miss you. . . ."

"Well, what if they do?"

And, very much at home, as though she were moving about in her own hut, she went to the kitchen, lighted the fire, touched this and that, and then, while the water was boiling, came to the hammock again.

"You not got a temperature, Senhor Manué?"

"I don't think so."

"Let me see, 'cause I just know as much about this as any doc. My dad used to have such fever that his teeth chattered in his head. And I was the one that always knew when it was coming over him."

She took hold of his wrist and stood holding it gently between her hands, feeling his pulse; and her eyes lighted with desire as they looked into his, silently offering herself.

Manuel da Bouça had been feeling this attraction for some time, but to avoid complications he had fought against it, and he was afraid Benvinda might want money. Not that she didn't appeal to him. He'd often wanted her, because she was good to look at and her swaying gait and warm words roused him. But the idea of wasting a copper without its being absolutely necessary had put a check on desire. To counteract the attraction he set his thoughts on his Amélia waiting far away for him to come back; perhaps she was crying because it was such a long time since she'd seen him. So his heart was filled with tenderness for her, and his body had remained passive.

Now Benvinda was attracting his tenderness too, because she had risked the steward's anger to come and see him, ill and lonesome in a place where people thought only of themselves.

Benvinda put his arm back gently inside the netting—no, there's no temperature—and stood there chatting. Listening to her, he began to think over what the native laborers said about her. They were always gossiping about one another, and they said that Benvinda had been in love with the ugliest mulatto in Santa Efigénia; Colonel Borba had dismissed him for a good-for-nothing, and after that she had never looked at another man. At first, Benvinda got annoyed at this talk, but nobody knew whether it was because they called the man ugly or whether there wasn't a jot of truth in the jest. Then she had got used to it, and only shrugged her shoulders and smiled at the jokes.

And now Manuel da Bouça too felt as though he wanted to vex her, as though wounding her would be the best return for the affection she had just shown him.

"Didn't you ever get news of Pernecas?"

Cut short in her talkativeness, Benvinda looked very hurt. "You're not kind!" she said after a pause. "I don't want to hear about that man any more. . . ."

"Oh, no, but if he came back, you'd make it up with him, because when you like someone a lot, you don't forget. . . ."

"He won't never come back," she answered, protesting. "Why should he? And even if he did, you'd see! We'd fallen out before Colonel sent him away. And what you say about liking anyone a lot, well, I never liked him. He was the one always saying he liked me, and I just listened to his wheedling." She paused a moment, and then added, "And now I'm not thinking on any man at all, but if I do, it won't be no smelly nigger."

Troubled by her body with the breasts rounding under the print dress, the look in her eyes, and her full moist lips, Manuel da Bouça felt all the heaviness that had clamped him to his hammock falling away from him, and his old energy came back in a surge of triumph. Benvinda thought it would be just as well to remember the coffee—eh, folk, that water must be boiling its head off!—and she ran into the kitchen.

She came back stirring the spoon in the steaming cup, and when she got to the hammock she tasted it.

"Ugh! What poor coffee you got here! It's just like sweepings! I'm only a woman, but we never drink stuff like this in my hut. I got some coffee that comes from Maratica, and Colonel would give a lot to get the same on this fazenda."

By this time Manuel da Bouça had forgotten all about his good resolutions.

"Can't I come round for a cup?"

But Benvinda pretended to be on the defensive.

"No, I better bring a bit for you here, Senhor Manué."

"But I can't make it good like this!"

"Well, course one can't refuse a cup o' coffee even to a beggar," she answered, giving way with a smile.

"Well then, I'll come round tonight. . . . What time do you go to bed?"

"Oh, dear, I go to bed late."

"Ten o'clock?"

"Closer on eleven."

"Well then, I'll come round at eleven."

"All right."

Then she thought it was time to get back to the plantation so that Senhor Capistrano wouldn't notice, and she went out, closing the door gently behind her, taking all Manuel da Bouça's heaviness away with her. He stretched, carefully lifted his feet out of the hammock, and with one thrust stood up.

Now there were a number of sunrays shining into the dimness of the hut. Outside, in broad daylight, a cock was crowing saucily, but everything else was silent, and it seemed as though the fierce sun had dried up all sound on the plantation. Manuel da Bouça got dressed, stopped a minute in the kitchen to eat what was left from the night before, and then, jumping down from the back of the hut, went off to join the others. Here and there as he went along, to right and left, before and behind, rising from the red earth and vibrating in the air, came the monotonous shrilling of cicadas.

At night the moon opened its eye and gazed at the fazenda

with such softness and delicacy that the whole place stood in a gilded trance as though hypnotized. The branches of the jequitiba with the moonlight shining through them turned into an Oriental fantasy isolated in space. And the coffee shrubs, small dark shapes in the silvery clearness, seemed to be whispering among themselves in a conversation that, though it could not be heard, could be sensed in the mystery of night. The whole of Colonel Borba's veranda lay full in the moonlight, and the shadow thrown by the porch roof was like a dark curtain on the back wall. The shadow of the cross on the roof of the little white church was clearly visible too. And, wherever there was no disturbing breath of humanity, everything was spellbound from the surface of the earth up to the soft skin of the sky. Everything was suspended in a deep lethargy, an enigmatic, imponderable dream.

Leaning against his door, Paxiuma, who had he come across him would have challenged Mané do Riachão himself to a fandango, glanced for a few moments into the moonlit space and then, throwing his cigarette end away and spitting in a squirt, shouted into the hut, "Give me my guitar!"

His wife brought the instrument, and the Indian, tuning up as he went along, walked over to the cement drying-floor and sat down on the edge. Then his voice broke through the silence of the plantation:

> "Little dove, sit down on the stone,
> Little dove, don't go away:
> Because my eyes are not bullets,
> Little dove, to kill you."

It was a nostalgic voice with all the tenderness and fatalism of the deep hinterland in it, and cast a kind of spell:

> "Because my eyes are not bullets,
> Little dove, to kill you."

And the voice went floating slowly, echoing over the landscape lying tense in the moonlight. Then nature's trance relaxed a little, the murmuring among the coffee shrubs was less subdued, and, like a gentle breeze, a soft, warm, sensuous whisper wafted over Santa Efigénia.

Other Indians came out from their quarters and gathered round Paxiuma. Some of the Italians came up too, and Manuel da Bouça because he had a letter in his pocket that he wanted Bernardo to read to him.

Unwearying singer and guitar player, like all his forebears before him, Paxiuma sang out the rallying cry:

"Come up, come up, good folk,
The samba is going to begin. . . .
Just see how lively it'll be,
This warm-blooded samba."

But Bernardo wasn't there. Where the devil had he got to? And looking round again more closely, Manuel da Bouça caught Benvinda's eyes.

He'd just received the letter; it couldn't be from anyone else but Amélia, and in a twinkling it had called up all his tenderness for his absent wife, delivered him from the temptation of the mulatress. . . . No, he wouldn't go round to her hut. What would Amélia think if she knew that while she was waiting over there for him, he was wasting his money with another woman? Because of course she wanted money, of course she did. But now he could watch everything with a quiet mind, thinking of nothing but the letter. To get a letter always made him feel happy. His native village, his own people, his own past, everything that was now so far away and hazed in a mist of longing was brought home to his simple soul in exile, making him more sensitive, more open to feeling and memory. Then sadness followed hard on the heels of this happiness, when he began to think about his inability to fulfill his ambition, and his disappointment at not being able to earn a lot of money quickly in Brazil, as he had thought. . . . But where the devil was Bernardo?

Manuel da Bouça was just on the point of going off to look for him, when he caught sight of him in the distance coming up between two half-breed sons of his. The crowd round Paxiuma was getting bigger. There were coffee beans spread out on the drying-floor, and some of the people pushed them away so as to be able to sit down round the edge; others squatted on the ground, and the youngsters stood with their eyes fixed on the Indian's fingers as he plucked the strings.

Only Benvinda had taken up Paxiuma's successive challenges; they had exchanged three quatrains, and then even she, with a laugh to hide her discomfiture, had given up. And so, unrivaled, the Indian raised his solitary voice and sang a mournful love song in the golden night. The guitar took on a more human tone, moaning softly: first a gentle wail, holding back the tears; then the heart broke, the weeping became more agitated, swelling into louder moans, and the notes from the bass strings were sobs. . . . They all guessed, they all sensed that an unlucky backwoodsman was crying somewhere because he'd loved where he ought not to love. Was he crying in a tapera * where nettles were growing over the ruins of the house where his loved one had lived? Was he crying near the still-saddled horse that had carried her away? They didn't know, but there was crying somewhere, grieving and suffering as when a man grieves and suffers. There was unutterable sadness in the love lament, unbearable fatalism interpreted by the guitar, which suggested humble devotion there in the deep hinterland where souls abandon themselves to pain in single ingenuousness.

And the night was becoming more and more golden! Voice and accompaniment seemed to be an emanation from the very moonlight. Where neither tree shadow nor hill ridge was visible any longer, liquid moonlight could still be seen, nothing but

* Tapera—an abandoned country estate overgrown with weeds.

moonlight probing and enigmatic. The whole place was faced with gold.

And in this fantastic light, Bernardo was straining his eyes —I'm getting old and can't see very well now—at the paper Manuel da Bouça had just handed to him:

"My dear Manuel, I received your letter and hope you are in the best of health; as for me I am going on as God wills. I was very glad you sent word to say that you are all right and that in a few years' time you will come back to Portugal. That is my one consolation, because I've had a lot of worry. Our Deolinda, who was crazy about Afonso, has run away to his house—' "

"What's that? What did you say, Senhor Bernardo?" Manuel da Bouça interrupted, giving a sudden start. "Read that bit again!"

And Bernardo repeated the sentence: "Our Deolinda, who was crazy about Afonso, has run away to his house.' " Then he stopped, hoping to hear what Manuel da Bouça would have to say about it, but he only asked him in a strangled voice to go on reading.

" '. . . It's been a great shame to me, because she says that she did what she's done because we wouldn't let her get married. I shouldn't be so upset about it if it weren't for the annoyance it will cause you, because she's not so badly off. I've cried bitterly and even thought of taking ship and coming to you. . . .' "

"The bitch!" roared Manuel da Bouça. "And my only thought was to earn a marriage portion for her so that she could marry someone better . . . better off than ourselves! Here I've been toiling and moiling and grudging every penny, for this! . . . I didn't come out to Brazil for myself. I could always earn enough to live on. I only wanted more for the girl's sake—"

"I don't know anything about your life," Bernardo broke in, trying to comfort him, "but it seems to me, Sinhô Manuel, that it'd be worse if your daughter had died. . . . Children always cause their parents worry. With bairns come cares. . . ."

"What else does the letter say?" asked Manuel da Bouça, raising his head a little.

" '. . . It seems that they'll get married at Christmas, and that's to give time to hear whether you give your consent or not. . . .'

"You see?" Bernardo commented, "It might be worse!" Then he went on again:

" '. . . Write to me, Manuel, because my heart's as black as night. Tia Joaquina wishes to be remembered to you, and Zefa and—"

"Never!" broke in Manuel da Bouça. "Let her get married, let her do as she likes; she's no daughter of mine any longer! And as for giving my consent—never! If I could only get my hands on him, the low good-for-nothing!"

The night was still warm and clear, the moon now floating in the center of the great dome, and the whole earth seemed to be waiting for a morbid, incestuous kiss. Paxiuma went back to free quatrains:

> "If you got a pretty daughter
> Don't send her coffee-picking;
> Maids become misses
> And misses become women."

Manuel da Bouça turned round with a start, thinking there was some allusion in the quatrain, but then he controlled himself. No, no, they couldn't have heard anything. They were too far away to hear. . . . He got up, took leave of Bernardo, and made for his quarters, downhearted and crushed.

> "Maids become misses
> And misses become women."

As he went slowly along, his shadow moved along too, a patch in the moonlight that contracted here and lengthened there, a thing that, seen in a bad dream, would be frightening.

Near the living quarters Benvinda passed close by him.

"The coffee's on."

He didn't answer. The Indian was still singing, his voice more plaintive and the guitar more nostalgic in the distance. The hut was full of moonlight that shone through the cracks between the roof tiles and through the dividing door from the kitchen. The Calabrian hadn't come in.

Manuel da Bouça threw himself onto his hammock and lay digging his nails into the palms of his hands, brooding over his trouble. . . . Bitch, bitch, triple-dyed bitch! Hadn't it all been meant for her good? He saw her clearly, that evening when she'd asked him to let her get married; he saw her on other evenings, at other times. And the man's face, too, his ugly ferrety face . . . Ah, if he'd only got him there, he'd teach him to seduce other men's daughters!

Pietro, supposing his companion was already asleep, came in on tiptoe, went into the kitchen, and gulped down some water; then, again taking care to make no noise, he stripped and lay down in his hammock.

The Indian had stopped singing, and very soon he passed close by, idly plucking some last muted notes from his guitar. Then everything was quiet. A child's whimper sounded in the distance for a moment, then faded away in the silence. The whole fazenda was still. Only the moonlight went on filtering through the roof.

And I was so fond of her! What will the priest say? And everybody? What talk there must be over there now!

He couldn't sleep. Something had given way inside him and filled him with such despair that he couldn't sleep.

My daughter . . . to go and do a thing like that! Just because I didn't want her to get married to a good-for-nothing!

He began to feel a great need for affection, just to talk to someone to relieve himself, about anything, no matter what. The Calabrian's snores disturbed him more than the annoying regular drip of a leak. He got up slowly and, with the same precautions the other had taken to come in, he went out, to go to the mulatress.

14

Two or three nights a week Manuel da Bouça left the Calabrian by himself and went over to Benvinda's hut—four humble walls, very poor, very unpretentious, but situated in an airy spot on high ground between the chapel and the forest.

Invariably when he got there he saw Benvinda's mother, a very dark Negress, sitting on a mat with her long, almost fleshless legs stretched out with all the bones outlined under the darkness of the skin. Paralyzed, woolly hair turned white, face dried up, toothless mouth, looking like a bit of cast skin sloughed by time, she sat lost in an endless torpor smoking her cane pipe from morning till far into the night. She never looked up at Manuel da Bouça's face. When she saw him come in, her white eyes fixed themselves on his trousers and followed them till they disappeared in Benvinda's room. They both knew that the old woman guessed everything, but the daughter didn't mind, and he, by force of habit, finished up by not minding either.

Benvinda flowed with tenderness and warmth. At first, seeing her so attractive and full of appeal, a provocative mulatress who made the mouths of many a native and foreigner water with desire, Manuel da Bouça thought that the preference she showed for him must have money in view. But time passed, and he became convinced of the contrary. The livelong day she worked as hard as any man to support herself and her mother, but she never asked him for so much as a penny. It was he who, now and again, felt that he'd like to give her a present, and then his hard luck nettled him more than ever, because what he earned was so little that he couldn't even offer himself that pleasure. One day, however, after going through a maze of calculations and breaking the rule to economize to the core that was his guiding aim, he put a note for twenty milréis into her hands to buy herself a dress. But she wouldn't accept it. No, not on any account; he needed it more than she did; he didn't belong to those parts, and life was hard.

Manuel da Bouça felt drawn to her. She was younger than he was—thirty-four against his forty-two—but sometimes she was like a mother to him when she saw him odd-man-out in strange surroundings, poor, simple, not knowing how to read or write, eaten up with the bitterness of not being able to realize his ambition. He didn't want to give way to weakness; after all, the woman's role is to obey. But he felt flattered by the protective tenderness she lavished on him. Only his egotism took fright at the thought of getting caught and having to stay there like Bernardo with a swarm of children, or like the Italians who brought wife and child, or even two children, and then went on adding to the family. Like that, responsibilities increased, but earnings didn't keep pace, and so you could never get away. . . . No, he had nothing against Benvinda; she was a good woman; but Amélia his wedded wife came first with him. It's true, he had no daughter now; but he had Amélia and his home. He must keep free to get away just when he felt like it!

One night when, in his usual easy way, he went into the

hut that stood away from the others, he found Benvinda in tears. He asked her what was the matter, but she wouldn't tell him. It was nothing to do with him, just little personal matters. But he persisted and, still getting no reply, began to fume as in the old days when Amélia disregarded the voice of command.

So Benvinda explained the mystery. For some weeks past the steward had been pestering her with pretty speeches and promises. She kept putting him off, but that armadillo snout wouldn't leave her in peace. Now she knew why he kept on at her; he'd quarreled with his wench, and was looking round for another woman. Even while she'd been on the plantation he'd had more than ten of them, three or four weeks with each one, and then on to the next, because he wanted to try them all. Even if they were maids, he didn't care, and that was why a man from Baía had tried to stick a knife in his guts.

"But he don't get nowhere with me, 'cause I don't like his looks. If I like a man, all right. But if I don't, no, not even if he done me in!"

"Why didn't you tell me about it before?"

"Why? Just 'cause I didn't want to worry you." And she began to cry again.

Manuel da Bouça began to stride angrily from one side of the hut to the other with his hands behind his back, turning over what he'd just heard.

"But if you don't like him, there's no danger," he said at last.

"No danger? You just don't know what a low hound he is. When you don't do what he wants, he gets his knife into you and get you in Colonel's bad books." Then lowering her voice and probing into the real wound, she added, "Colonel told me today that I've got to pay to live in this hut. . . . Steward's put that into his head to get his own back on me."

That made Manuel da Bouça understand why he had found Benvinda in such a state. He felt more and more disturbed, and stopped marching about.

"Why didn't you tell him the truth?"

"What, Colonel? Why, he just do everything Steward want. He know very well that brazen rogue always after the women, but he shuts his eyes. That's 'cause Steward keeps on after everybody and never leaves them idle. And that's just what Colonel wants. If I complained about Steward, I'd be treated worse."

"But if I don't have to pay rent, nor the Italians either, why should you?"

"I'm only a woman, so what can I do against Colonel? If men can't go against him, what can women do? He tell me I don't work hard enough, that I'm real idle and only take up house-room. He said if it weren't for me, he'd put an Italian in here who'd work harder. But tell me, Senhor Manué, don't I work? Don't I work as hard as any caipira?"

Lost in disturbing thoughts Manuel da Bouça didn't reply, so Benvinda went on again.

"If Colonel's daughter was here, I'd ask her to speak to her father for me. She's a nice girl and always ready to help us folk, but she's away in São Paulo."

"But something's got to be done," said Manuel da Bouça just to say something, because he hadn't been able to find any solution in the stupefaction this news had thrown him into.

"If there were only me, I'd know what to do. But there's Mother! Without me, who'd give her food, and who'd look after her?"

The old Negress, sitting on the floor, was staring with white eyes at her daughter and Manuel da Bouça. She didn't move or speak a single word, but she was paying close attention, because the pipe in her sucked-in mouth had gone out.

"How much will you have to pay for the house?"

"I don't know. Colonel didn't say. He only said he'd keep something back. How can he keep something back when I earn so little?"

"We'll have to do something about it, we'll have to do something about it!" Manuel da Bouça went on repeating, as well as other words of encouragement to try to comfort the poor stunned woman; but everything was vague because he hadn't been able to think of anything definite.

He went away about eleven o'clock. And there, outside in the dark night, the uncleared forest, still untouched by ax or flame, whispered sad cadences, his rule to economize to the core and save every penny that came into his hands received its first check, and wavered. . . . Now, if it were a matter of ten milréis a month, he'd like to help Benvinda out, and that'd settle it. But he couldn't because he hadn't got it. What a scoundrel the man was, that was easy to see! And now he could see why Capistrano was always trying to pick a quarrel with him and was so high and mighty! And he'd been thinking all the time that it was because he was Portuguese, and now it turned out to be this. . . .

Manuel da Bouça felt a bitter taste in his mouth. The dislike for the steward that he'd been feeling for months turned into hate. He pictured him there in front of him: tall, lean, colorless, rather lighter in complexion than Benvinda, with hard eyes and dry lips that smiled only when he was with Colonel Borba. Then he imagined himself in a wrestler's clinch with him, revenging the affront and giving him a lesson. Because he really deserved a good lesson. It wasn't decent to treat a poor woman like that. . . .

Then other images rose in his mind: his Amélia, Frágua, Esteves' fields; and with them came the fear of complications. The devil, when a man's least expecting it, he finds he's tangled in troubles!

Then he thought of Benvinda, with deeper hatred for Capistrano, and more affection for her. . . . They could ill spare the ten milréis, he and Amélia, because at the end of six months that already makes sixty; but after all, to help the poor woman . . .

When Manuel da Bouça got back to the hut and groped his way in, the Calabrian was regularly and peacefully snoring.

The next day the whole fazenda was sweating in a violent heat. Great whorls of smoke rose into the sky, and flaky ashes softer than down were falling on every side. They were burning out that part of the forest where they had done the last felling. The fire went slowly eating round the great mutilated stumps dried by the sun; first it licked round the bark, then hardened against the resistance of the dead tree, took the whole of it in its embrace, penetrating slowly, while the creeping flame, fed by the leaves, slipped along with the subtle glide of a snake, nipping the fresh green of the small shrubs spared by the ax. The insatiable devourer was scarcely visible; only the smoke made you suspect its existence, because the blaze moved along the ground and only now and again, when it encountered very dry branches, lifted its quivering vermilion crest. Nevertheless, its destructive action was uninterrupted, and when it came across any sudden check because of cleared ground it crept round the flank and lay siege to the clearing. Then the tall capim grass, creeping plants, thick shrubs, the whole underbush crackled beneath the supple, voracious fiery tongues.

At nightfall, when the squad of laborers with mattocks and big knives went out to isolate the fire, the forest was a huge lidless cinerary urn with tenacious flames issuing from it determined to pulverize the last trunks—femurs and tibias of the mighty corpse in course of cremation. And everything was struck dumb in a muteness that stifled and burned. And there were ashes everywhere, light here and dark there, and a last whorl of smoke rose into the approaching darkness, like the thin smoke trail of a ship seen in the distance.

After the evening meal, Manuel da Bouça skirted the edge of the coffee plantation till he came to Benvinda's hut. He hadn't caught sight of her during the day; and he had avoided encounters with the steward because he was afraid he wouldn't be able to hold himself in if he came face to face with him. So now he was going to see if he couldn't comfort the poor woman by his presence, and find out if there was any news. But

Benvinda didn't seem so upset as she was the night before. When he went in, she was washing the dishes she and her mother had used, and when she had dried her hands she went and sat beside him. As usual the old Negress was close by, sunk in her endless reverie.

Rather pleased with himself because of his decision, Manuel da Bouça had been looking forward to the happiness he would give Benvinda when he told her he'd decided to help her pay for the house until such time as things took a better turn. And now he was almost disappointed to see the calm expression of the mulatress; if she wasn't so upset after all, the sacrifice he'd resolved to make would seem of less consequence.

He was anxious to know what had caused the change, so he asked her briefly what the position was. She hesitated, and then, pressed further, couldn't keep up the pretense of calmness.

"I just didn't want to talk about it any more, Senhor Manué; I didn't want to worry you. . . ." And she told him that the steward had been pestering her again that afternoon with his lust and promises. "He said, if I were willing, he'd get Colonel to forget about the house. . . . So I up and told him that, even if Chico da Barra hadn't managed to rip his guts out, I would if he went on bothering me. And I will do it, too; I will. . . . It'll finish me off, but he won't be able to eat any more manioc, either. . . ."

She turned away from him to hide her face and let her tears flow. And then, for the first time since he'd been going to the house, Manuel da Bouça saw Benvinda's mother shake off her dark hieratic dream to stretch out her wasted arm and touch her daughter's face.

"Don't cry," she murmured. "God don't want to take me, and I'm just a trouble in your life."

And Manuel da Bouça broke in, trying to make his words sound strong, although they stuck in his throat from the emotion he felt.

"Now, now, don't talk like that! That's not the way to set

things right. He can't keep back more than ten milréis for the
hut, and I've decided to give you the money. And if he keeps
more back, then we'll have to see what to do. . . ."

"I don't want you to do that, Senhor Manué," said Benvinda
turning tearful eyes to him. "I'm very grateful, but I don't want
it. You've got a wife, and you don't belong to these parts. You
don't earn much either, and you have to send money home. I
know you are fond of her. . . ."

A new fit of weeping shook her and, troubled at what he
heard, he couldn't think of any way out.

"I'll give you the money," was all he could say. "I'll give
you the money. Now stop crying, it's all settled!" And trying to
see her face, his glance met the white, white eyes of the Negress
fixed on him.

At last Benvinda got up, drying her face and trying to control
herself. Then, standing up and leaning against the wall, she
announced what she had decided to do. She was going to leave.
The fazenda wasn't the only one, and she had health to work.
She'd worked in other places before coming here, and she
wouldn't die of hunger. The pay was bad everywhere, because
they never gave a woman as much as a man, and whenever they
did you a good turn it was with some mean idea in mind. But
she was as strong as any backwoodsman! If they stood with a
foot on her neck to make her do what she didn't want, there'd
be nothing doing! The hardest thing was her mother being
so helpless. . . .

"Don't go away because of the hut," Manuel da Bouça persisted. "I've said I'll give you the money!"

"That's not the reason. I know Colonel wants the hut for
an Italian. He told me so. And even if he didn't want it, and
I paid, Steward would be mad and never leave me alone. He'd
always make trouble and I'd never have any peace. You don't
know the brute, Senhor Manué, but I know how lowdown mean
he is. Even if I stayed, I'd never be happy now."

"But where do you want to go?"

"I don't know. I don't know yet. I'll see. But I'll never stay here. I won't have that mean hound sleeping with me. I even had to spit in his ugly mug today." She stopped, and then went on in another tone, warm with affection: "I'll be real sad at leaving you, Senhor Manué, I was so fond of you. . . . But like that, it'll be better for you too. . . ."

His heart softened as he listened to her, but then his anger came back. What that steward needed was to be thrashed till his bones broke. . . . Thrash him till his bones broke . . . Thrash him till his bones broke . . . Benvinda guessed what was passing through his mind.

"Don't be sad," she said. "Don't feel like that. . . . Don't worry about it."

"If I could only give him a bit of a lesson," said Manuel da Bouça hoarsely.

"Who? Steward? Now don't do that! He's just not worth bothering about. . . . Tell me you won't do that! Now promise me! I'm going away, and you can leave too someday. Don't get into trouble! Promise me!"

He didn't reply. He grew more and more sullen and didn't reply. His hatred for Capistrano wasn't only on account of Benvinda. Right from his first day at Santa Efigénia he'd disliked the steward because of the way he treated natives and foreigners alike, always finding fault with everyone's work, always finding that they didn't sweat enough.

Benvinda felt that what she had already said wasn't enough, so she had to bring out the words that cost her the most pain.

"Remember, you got a wife and she's waiting for you. . . . Promise you'll do as I say. It's a promise, isn't it?"

Her voice shook in the effort to fight back what she really wanted. And Manuel da Bouça promised.

15

CHE official contract came to an end, but Colonel Borba had the announcement given out that the same conditions would hold good for the future. Nevertheless there was a great stir among the last group that had arrived at Santa Efigénia, because someone passing through had said that at Guatapará near Ribeirão Prêto wages were higher and prices of food and drink lower. Guatapará was not like Santa Efigénia, it seemed; it didn't belong to one man, the absolute master of the place, who imposed his inflexible will and everything had to give way to it slavishly. The big fazenda over there was run on progressive lines by a company that paid good wages, and the laborer was treated like a human being. And the standard of living! They had the same advantages as a town. They had everything—cinema, football field, church! And if you didn't want to buy things on the spot, well, there was a special company train you could take gratis to go and get what you wanted in Ribeirão Prêto.

In order to get a job at Guatapará, you had only to send in a note giving age, status, nationality, and domicile; then, as soon as the company had a vacancy, it let you know and even sent money for traveling expenses. Vague rumors about Guatapará had been floating round for quite some time, and then this last bit of real information spurred the ambition of the laborers at Santa Efigénia. And there weren't many Italians who had completed their contract who didn't send off the necessary letter, and Bernardo wrote one for Manuel da Bouça, too, who had no intention of turning his back on any opportunity.

Then more definite facts were set in circulation from the lips of that professional wet blanket the Turkish peddler, who went round selling haberdashery and small articles. At Guatapará, he said, the pay don't go beyond two hundred milréis! So Manuel da Bouça's enthusiasm fell. Two hundred milréis! Whenever would he be able to save anything if he was earning only two hundred milréis a month? It'd take such a deuce of a time that even if you had two lives you'd never get rich. And he'd always thought that you could get rich quick in Brazil, if you were only willing to work! Where was all the money, then? Because he hadn't caught sight of it, either for himself or for the Italians or for the Brazilian laborers who worked from dawn to sunset. What he had actually seen was a lot of poor people with the urge to get on, the same as in Portugal, the same as everywhere. How had Moradais got rich in Brazil? And Sebastião de Sousa, who'd given quite a few contos for Nossa Senhora de La Salette? And the Comendador de Castelõs who'd had a palace built on the top of the Aristal Range from which you could see the sea over toward Torreira, and a school, and a road, and a church? And Colonel Borba? How did they all get rich? When he compared himself with these people, he quite lost heart. Oh, no, you couldn't do it working with a mattock in your hand or picking coffee, as he did!

So he began to weigh the possibilities of the town, vague possibilities that he could only just guess at. The town and its mystery. Its fascination. Thousands of doors that might open on anything . . . No, whatever answer they sent from Guatapará, he wouldn't go. There was no future to that sort of life. The Portuguese didn't get on there. It was plain to see that they didn't go to coffee plantations, not they! Only he and Bernardo—and nobody else. São Paulo, that was where they went. And Santos and Rio de Janeiro, there were lots of Portuguese there, everybody said so.

Then doubts came over him. But what was he going to do in São Paulo? Zé do Aido had done well to go to America! What was he going to do in São Paulo? His hopes fell to the ground, his castles in the air were swept away, and nothing remained. Only the image of Cipriano rose up in his mind, Cipriano and his pessimistic ideas, Cipriano who was almost hateful to him because he'd nipped his dream in the bud. . . . Yes, but I didn't know the ropes then. I can't die of hunger, so I might as well have a go at it. . . .

He began caressing hopes of success again, prosperity, through what work he didn't know, but he sensed it almost as a certainty, a presentiment that success must come to him. Again he went over all the words of admiration he'd heard that day when they had just stood and looked at São Paulo, bustling, dynamic, febrile, lifting into the tropic sky the triumphant song of the sirens of industry. In a city of that size, it wasn't possible that he couldn't find something to do. And what's more, he was ready to turn his hand to anything; nobody knew him there, and all he wanted was to earn well.

Only the thought of Benvinda cast a shadow over the wide prospect his hungry eyes were gazing at. She was going to Guatapará and, although she was of the decided opinion that he ought not to go there because São Paulo was more suitable for a Portuguese, he was sad at the thought of separation. He'd often wished she were less affectionate, so that he could decide things his own way; at other times he swore to himself that he didn't really care for her and that it was only because she was a good woman, and a real good woman she was too, that it all hurt him. He swore it till he believed it himself, but the thought that they were going to part weighed on him. . . . Of course, his only love was for Amélia, that was evident; but there was no harm if a man, wandering over the wide world, had a friend. A man wasn't made of wood; he always needed a woman. And she wasn't just trying to make out of him, oh, no, not at all. . . . Then the picture of Bernardo, tied down with children through an association of that sort, cooled him off considerably. It was the devil, the very devil! He didn't want to get tied down like Bernardo, like the Italians. . . .

When Benvinda was with him he felt better than when he was by himself. She seemed calm and resigned in face of the situation, and whenever he timidly suggested that he should go to Guatapará too, she always opposed it.

"Portuguese don't go to plantations. Their proper place is in shops. You ought to go to the city, and I don't want to bear the blame for spoiling your life. And then you'll soon forget me. Everything passes."

Sometimes when she talked like this he thought she cared less for him than before, and he felt a bit piqued about it. But Benvinda kept up the quiet attitude she had adopted, and if he asked her when she was leaving she gave vague answers. She didn't know what date it would be yet. She was waiting for the people at Guatapará to send for her. He mustn't worry. She'd still be a long time at the fazenda, and it wouldn't matter either, because Steward wasn't running after her any more; he'd managed to get him another woman—Leopoldina.

One night when she was talking like this, Manuel da Bouça said he couldn't believe it. "How can you say that when he's always plaguing me and trying to pick a quarrel?"

Benvinda seemed meeker than usual, and hesitated before replying.

"Oh, that there's just the man's way," she said without conviction, speaking as though making an effort to throw off fatigue.

And soon afterward she talked about going to bed. "It's late, and I'm tired. . . ."

"It's not as late as all that! It's not ten yet," answered Manuel da Bouça, looking at his watch and with his suspicion aroused.

"Ten o'clock? But I'm real sleepy. . . ."

"But I don't usually go till eleven."

"Maybe . . . But today I can't . . ."

"All right, all right," and he got up, displeased. "I don't know what's the matter with you, but you're not the same as before."

"Now don't say that; it isn't true!"

He coldly wished her good night and went out, but he had no sooner reached the door than he heard a sound that made him stop. He went back, found Benvinda stretched on the ground, weeping convulsively, and her helpless mother trying vainly to lift her up.

"Now what the devil's this?"

She went on sobbing. Then she got up, clung to him, and kissed him in a still more violent fit of crying.

"Don't take on, it's just nothing," she said at last. "Go to bed now, and leave me alone . . . leave me alone. . . ."

Manuel da Bouça left her when he saw her eyes were dry again. But doubt began to gnaw at him that the fit of weeping meant there was something on her conscience, and when he got outside the hut he squatted there in the darkness, watching. It might well be that she was deceiving him, because you never could trust women. He could swear she wasn't the same, and she was in such a hurry to get to bed. And she couldn't make him believe that the steward, treacherous as a poisonous snake, had turned into a decent chap overnight! When he went weeding out on the coffee plantation, with the others, it was easy to see what a face Capistrano pulled!

He kept watch for more than an hour, but nothing happened. He waited another hour, and still there was nothing. In all that section of the sleeping fazenda you couldn't hear a thing, however hard you strained your ears, and there was no doubtful shadow moving anywhere. Only the light still showing through the chinks at Benvinda's hut roused his curiosity.

At last the light went out and the hut was plunged in darkness too. He waited some time longer; then he felt cold, sleep took the edge off his suspicion, and he got up. Anyway, if she were deceiving him, it might be better that way. He wouldn't have to mind leaving her then, and perhaps even be longing for her when she wasn't there. . . . Trying to convince himself that he didn't care what Benvinda did, he shrugged, walked to his own hut, and went to bed.

He slept badly, and next morning was wakened early by someone knocking at the door.

"Senhor Manué, Senhor Manué . . ."

The Calabrian woke up too, but as soon as he grasped that it wasn't for him he settled back into his hammock. Manuel da Bouça got up and dressed in a hurry. What could she want at that time in the morning? He went to open the door. Benvinda with a deep sad look in her eyes tried to smile.

"I've come to say goodbye. I'm going now. . . ."

"What's that you say?" he exclaimed, standing rigid in surprise.

"I'm going now. I'm going to Guatapará."

"But what kind of thing's this? You're going away like that, offhand, without letting me know?"

"I didn't want to fret you. I asked folk to keep it a secret. I meant to go off without saying anything to you, but I couldn't." She turned her face away so that he couldn't see her eyes, then went on in a low voice. "Goodbye, and I wish you good luck. . . ."

And she was moving away when, all in a turmoil, he clutched her brusquely by the arm.

"Wait! I'm coming along to help you pack. . . ."

"It's all done. I worked at it last night, and now I'm taking my things away."

She pointed, and Manuel da Bouça saw two half-breeds crossing the terrace with a kind of litter and the old paralyzed Negress, Benvinda's mother, sitting on it. Two other men were following behind with the trunk and poor household stuff that had furnished her hut.

Mechanically Manuel da Bouça set off beside Benvinda, without speaking. There was such a lot he wanted to say, but he couldn't find the words. He wanted to say he was sorry she was going; he wanted to protest, kick up a fuss, hit himself, thrash the steward, anyone or anything, his fate, his lot, the impalpable something that condemned him to misfortune and at the same time rendered him powerless to alter things.

"So it's just like that, just from one day to the next," was all he said.

At the end of the row of living quarters Benvinda stopped and spoke softly, almost in a whisper.

"Don't come any farther. It makes it harder for me."

He clasped her in his arms, scratching her cheeks with his still unshaven chin. "Goodbye! Write to me, Senhor Manué. . . . No, don't write, it'll make me too sad. I hope you'll be happy, and one day maybe we'll meet again."

He watched her walk away behind the men carrying her belongings—the little table, the chair, the zinc bowl, the suitcase, the cooking pots—and the half-breeds carrying the bierlike litter with the old helpless Negress sitting on it in the morning light and the solitude of the path: withered image of ebony, only skin and bones, bones and skin, a body drained dry by lifelong trouble.

When Benvinda had waved to him for the last time and they all disappeared in the distance, Manuel da Bouça turned back still in a daze, as though only just waking from sleep. What a hell of a life, when you're poor!

When he reached the terrace, the Italians and Indian laborers were already there, ready to set off for the weeding of the plantation. Seeing the steward, he went up to him and told him with a scowl that he'd be working only till the following Saturday.

"All right," the other answered between his teeth, "but you ought to have given notice two weeks ago. That's the way to do things properly."

"What's that you say? I don't do things properly?" asked Manuel da Bouça with a snarl.

But the steward only lifted his head up and gave a little smile of contempt. He stood like that a few moments, then turned his back and tranquilly went up the steps leading to Colonel Borba's veranda.

Manuel da Bouça dug his nails into the palms of his hands and bit his lips, fighting down the impulse to go after him and strike him. Then, his blood still boiling, he went to his hut. Pietro had already gone out, but he had left the coffee steaming near the fire and a clean cup on the table, with sugar.

Manuel da Bouça closed the door from the inside, and with a clasp knife began to cut the stitching of his jacket lining, all in a flurry. He took out a small packet of notes and counted them. Two hundred and fifteen milréis . . . Two hundred and fifteen . . . Twenty for traveling and other expenses till he got to São Paulo; that left a hundred and ninety-five for all the rest. Well, he'd landed in Brazil with less than that, so he wouldn't die of hunger. He'd write to Amélia to explain that he wasn't sending the money till he could get a good rate of exchange. She didn't know anything about that sort of thing, and she'd believe it. . . .

By nightfall the news that Manuel da Bouça was leaving had circulated among all the laborers. The Calabrian was the first to say how sorry he was. He'd got used to living with him, he said, and it wouldn't be easy to fall in with another companion as decent as he was. Who knew what kind of a fellow he'd get next! Not that he was staying long himself; as soon as the right answer came from Guatapará, he'd be going himself. He was sorry he couldn't leave right now, but he'd had to send the only money he'd saved to his mother, who was very old and very poor. Then he came to the real point.

"Have you got a job in São Paulo?" he asked.

Manuel da Bouça said no, and so his companion stood silent with his head down, rolling a cigarette. Then Bernardo came up to congratulate him.

"Yes, you're doing quite right! There's no prospects in working on the land. If I hadn't got such a swarm of kids, and were as young as you, I'd break loose too! What I always wanted was to be a merchant, and if I'd been a merchant I'd have made money. But how set about it!"

"But you aren't old yet."

"Aren't I! I'm over sixty, and what's more I'm worn out."

And when he heard that Manuel da Bouça was going on chance, he stayed to give him a piece of advice. If ever he got in difficulties, he must go to the Consulate, because he'd always heard that was the place for Portuguese folk to go when they were down on their luck. There was a League, too, that sent people back to Portugal when they weren't able to work. He was just telling him these things so that he'd know, because of course he'd never need anything of the kind; strong and healthy as he was, he'd soon come across some job or other. And wouldn't he like to be in his shoes!

When Paxiuma jumped down from the wild colt he'd kept leaping under him all morning to break it in, and heard the news, he came up whip in hand, booted and spurred, red kerchief falling from the collar of his jacket and knotted over his collarless shirt.

"That's the devil's own luck!" he exclaimed. "You lucky dog, going to a fine city, with a lot of women and everything a man wants!"

"Have you been already?"

"No, but I've heard tell of it."

And from the Italians he knew less well came words of well-wishing and encouragement. They all hoped he would be happy, and regretted they couldn't do the same. All these tillers of the red soil thought of nothing but their comrade who was going to leave: the natives dreaming about multifarious city life in São Paulo, that lamp of civilization whose light shone right into the interior, fascinating the unsatisfied; the foreigners still ready to believe that the dream gold existed a few miles beyond the place where they happened to be.

An old Piedmontese woman, crazy from affliction and alcohol, who had lived on there at Colonel Borba's expense after her husband had died, came and stood in front of Manuel da Bouça with her tangled hair uncovered and only two teeth left in her wrinkled old face.

"So you're going to São Paulo?" she shouted. "Then be off, look quick about it, make haste! If we'd gone there, we'd be rich today, and he wouldn't have died. Only in São Paulo are there rich Italians! Everybody's rich there. We stayed here twenty years, and then he died. If you'd only seen him, you Portuguese man! You didn't know my Máximo, did you?"

On the Saturday morning when he rolled up his hammock and stowed it into his trunk, Manuel da Bouça felt as gloomy as on the morning when Benvinda went away. He came out of the hut ahead of the other laborers, and stood there outside before the squad formed, looking over the fazenda. It was the last day he'd spend there.

On the nearest shrubs there were filmy spiders' webs with drops of dew caught on them glittering in the sun. The red soil was new and hale in morning freshness. And in the sky not a mist remained, no wisp of cotton wool to absorb night's exhalations; it was all limpid and wide-spreading over limpid wide-spreading earth.

The coffee shrubs were in flower and gave off a sickly scent of jasmine. Speckled with white, they looked like ornamental shrubs in some grand park with white butterflies settled on them. They had come out during the night, and now they were opening their little hearts to the sun. Birds were fluttering about too, some of them coming down with wings flickering and little claws stretched out till they grazed the glistening foliage, only to dart up again when they had caught some invisible insects in their beaks.

In the distance a line of cows and oxen was moving along the ridge of a hill, those at the back struggling to make their way to the front of the shifting frieze with its diaphanous background of blue sky.

This tropical scene gradually faded out and gave place to the picture of his own countryside, his own village tucked away in a corner of Portugal. In a bend of the Caima, mills covered with ivy greedily absorbing the stream that flowed between maize fields. Instead of coffee shrubs, bushes of broom; and the plantation alleys had become rough paths each turn of which held some childhood memory, some adolescent longing: flirtings and first exchange of talk, an attack on Serradais' orchard, playing pushpin with Pisco's son . . . And what had become of *him* now?

The whole valley stretched out, the whole parish with its houses, at that hour of the day plumed with early-morning smoke while the broth was warming up, and farther down the old church with the presbytery near it; but the priest didn't live there any more.

A deep sadness surged up in him, a deep longing to go back, a yearning he had never felt so strongly before. It now seemed to him that Portuguese sunlight was whiter, and he imagined it shining in through doors and windows, streaming over the garden, flowing over the whole village. . . . That day when Amélia was laying the apples out in the loft, what a lot of sun was shining into the house!

The sound of voices near the drying-floor brought him back to earth. The Italians were assembling for work, passing a bottle from hand to hand that each man raised to his lips. Some of them were still yawning, and others came up buttoning their shirts. When he joined the group, they greeted him more warmly than usual, and his own voice was softer on this last day together. And he went off to work, just to give a hand, because he supposed they wouldn't expect any big effort that day, considering that he was leaving.

At four o'clock he straightened up, put his big knife in its sheath, and stood undecided what to do. Then he pulled himself together. He didn't mean to leave without the bit of money still due and so hard to earn, just on account of that scoundrel. So he went up to Capistrano.

"Will you settle the accounts, please, so that I'll have time to catch the train."

"Oh, yes, come along."

Then Manuel da Bouça took off his wide-brimmed carnaúba hat and waved it in the air.

"Goodbye, folks!"

And the whole squad, which was cutting down capim grass in the banana grove, stopped to answer him.

"Addio, addio! Adeus, adeus!"

Words alone weren't enough for the Calabrian, and he ran forward with outstretched arms, and then all the others rushed up to Manuel da Bouça, while the steward waited frigidly some feet away for the embracings and well-wishings to come to an end round the comrade who was leaving.

"Good luck to you! Adeus! Addio!"

From a distance Manuel da Bouça saw Pietro still waving, much affected by his going away. The steward went into Colonel Borba's house, and soon came out again with two notes and a coin in his hand—so many days at so much gives so much, and Colonel isn't at home to say goodbye.

Thinking now about Benvinda, now about those whom he was leaving behind as poor as himself, he went up to his own hut. According to their arrangement, Raimunda was already there waiting for him. He helped her settle the trunk on her head and, as she went out, stood looking at the poor little place he was leaving for good. Then, with a surge of fondness for the Calabrian, he closed the door behind him, flung his bag over his shoulder, and set out on a new chapter in his life.

Part Two

$\mathcal{F}$ROM there you could see the Viaduto do Chá, the entrance to a theater all lighted up, gleaming ribbons of streets and, on the roofs, various publicity signs recommending cigarettes, insurance companies, and remedies for women's illnesses. Higher up, above the crisscross of telephone wires, lay a thin golden haze, a diffused reflection of light crowning the nighttime city.

From down below rose a deep hum, the deep muffled breathing of the city, broken from time to time by the louder hooting of a car or by a bell ringing somewhere at intervals.

In the farther distance were masses of shadow and red knots of light; buildings stood out of the penumbra by a sudden show of doorways in full flare, and in other places long rectangles of illuminated windows glittered, constellating the city night.

"*Diário Popular! Diário Popular!*" a young voice went shouting along the street, resounding above the general noise; and at the same time came the sound of steps on the stairs.

Manuel da Bouça quickly left the window and went toward the passage. . . . No, it wasn't Fernandes yet. They sounded like his steps, but they weren't. There was more than one person there. What the devil was he doing, to be so long?

Then the sound of voices came from the stairs, and Manuel da Bouça felt easier. . . . It is Fernandes after all, but there's someone with him.

So he waited. The two men stopped when they got to the passage, tired from the climb, and he heard Fernandes speaking:

"It's here. There are about twenty of us. These are all rented rooms."

"And do you all work at the same place?"

"Oh, no, we work in different places. Only I and—" Then he caught sight of Manuel da Bouça, and called out, "Senhor Manuel, come here!" Then he went on with what he was saying before. "Only I and this chap work at the same shop."

"Oh!"

"Senhor Manuel, here's a friend from my village who got here today. His name's António da Pita, and as lads we played at tops together. . . . And Senhor Manuel works at the shop with me, and lives here too."

The man who had just arrived had a short moustache, small mouth, and white skin that looked almost damp and milklike, as though he'd spent all his life in a milk-products factory. And he gave a white smile.

"The next room's mine," Fernandes went on. "This one. Come in." He opened the door and they went in, António da Pita carrying an old leather suitcase. "The bed isn't very wide, but it'll do as a makeshift. We shan't fall out."

"Well, a few days pass quickly, but I don't want to put you to inconvenience, Senhor Fernandes."

"It's no inconvenience at all, man! And just call me by my name, like in the old days. Put your things down here, and then we're going out. I want to take you to the movies, to get you used to the life here. And Senhor Manuel's coming too."

"I . . ."

"Once now and again isn't every day!"

"It's because . . ."

"But I'm paying!"

"It isn't that. I wanted to have a word with you. . . ."

Fernandes stopped pressing him.

"António, wait here a minute for me. . . ."

And the two men went out into the corridor.

"It's to read a letter to me," said Manuel da Bouça. "I've been waiting for you something like an hour."

"Yes, I'm later than usual. António came just as I was leaving the shop, and I took him along with me for dinner. Give me the letter."

He ripped open the envelope and went closer to the lamp over the stairs, while Manuel da Bouça listened, leaning against the wall:

" 'My dear Manuel, first of all I hope you are well; as for me, I've been ill for more than two weeks and unable to leave my bed. Our daughter and Zefa da Fonte have looked after me; otherwise I'm sure I should have just died where I was. I didn't let you know before so as not to worry you, and also because I thought from one day to the other it would pass. But yesterday some men came to Bouça from Oliveira, something legal it seems, and then they came to inform me that our strips of land now belong to Carrazedas because you haven't paid what was arranged. Deolinda and Afonso went over to town to talk to the notary and to Dr. Samuel, but they all said there was nothing to be done about it now. You don't know how I have cried from yesterday till now, because I know what a lot you thought of our precious little strips of land.

" 'Write to me, Manuel, because it's a long time since I had a line from you and I don't know what's happening to you over there. Since you went away, I've never known what it is to have an hour of happiness. I'd rather remain poor all my life than go through what I've been through. If you could see me now, you wouldn't know me. Don't forget to write to me, and with a loving kiss from your wife who wishes you the best of health, Amélia.' "

When Fernandes finished reading he saw Manuel da Bouça's face covered with tears, and he put his arm round him to comfort him.

"Don't lose heart, Senhor Manuel! You'll manage to get other strips of land, and your wife'll get better, you'll see!"

"It's a big blow, Senhor Fernandes, a big blow to me! If only I'd never left home!"

Shocked at what he heard, António da Pita pushed his way through the doorway and stood listening to what Manuel da Bouça was saying.

"We all have our sorrows!" said Fernandes. "Now go and get your hat and come along with us to the movies."

"I don't feel like going. . . ."

"Now come along, man. Some amusement's necessary, you know! And grieving doesn't pay one's debts. . . ."

"No, thank you. My precious strips of land. If you only knew, Senhor Fernandes, if you only knew! And the work and trouble I had to get them! And now, from one day to the next, when a man's least prepared for it . . ."

"Now, Senhor Manuel, just you wait here a minute." And leaving him, Fernandes went off along the corridor.

"Have you had bad news from home?" asked António da Pita, coming up.

"They've taken my all! A man works and sweats all his life, and then in the end . . . I did think about it, sometimes, but I never had the money!"

"Can't anything be done about it?"

"What can I do?"

Then Fernandes came back.

"Here's your hat," he broke in. "Now come along with us."

"Don't be annoyed, but I don't feel like it."

"What? Do you think I'd leave you alone after a thing like that? Now then, put on your hat and not another word! When anything like that happens, the best thing is to go out and amuse yourself. So you just come with us to the movies, then go to bed, and tomorrow you won't think any more about it. . . . Death's the only thing that's got no cure! And by the next boat, you'll get a letter to tell you that your wife's as sound as an apple again, you'll see! Lots of things have happened to me, too, but I'm still going strong, and shall keep on carrying on! António, let's go now!"

He went into the room to switch off the light, closed the door, and went off with the other two, *clip clop* down the stairs. Manuel da Bouça could hear a dull buzzing in his ears, and he saw everything vague and misty in front of him.

At the movies his attention wandered from the film and, instead of the people in it, he saw his strips of land with their four furrows, at wheat time, then with stubble, and the green kale dried up in summer. Over toward Ponte Nova was the dark line of pine trees; and down there, at the foot of Felgueira, the old church with its belfry but no bells now; and after that . . . after that . . . Esteves' fields, green, fresh, lying along the Caima, the fields he'd dreamed of getting, the great ambition he'd come to Brazil to attain! Were they still for sale? But however could he get them now? Everything lost, everything! He hadn't managed to do anything up to the present time, and he wasn't managing to do anything now. He just hadn't any luck. . . .

Right in the middle of the hall of a casino full of people gambling, he suddenly saw an iron bedstead, the one he and Amélia used to sleep in, then the whole of the room far away in his native village. Amélia was stretched on the bed, thin, older, ill. Choking with emotion, he could see her quite clearly. She'd been waiting such a long time, and he hadn't sent her anything very much. Just those small sums at Christmas, whenever possible, and God knew what it had cost him to send even that!

The film came to an end, the lights went up, there was a buzz of conversation; then a bell rang and another film began. It was a newsreel, snippets of things from all over the world: an aquarium in London with its fish, its anemones, its strange shellfish—all in slow motion, colorful nightmare creatures that made your flesh creep; then, in France, the unveiling of some monument—behind a marble bust were bare winter trees, rough trunks, and contorted branches visible above a mass of heads and motorcars.

Manuel da Bouça fell back into his own thoughts. For a long time he hadn't seen bare trees. They reminded him of his own village, the bare trees of his own countryside when Felgueira was covered with snow, and the lads set up reed cages to catch birds in the conviction that cold and hunger would drive the poor things into the snare. How long was it since he'd seen a tree like that!

He began to live over past times in that distant corner of the world. The valley moaning on a windy night, with a barn owl screeching in ill omen from the old church tower, and a cart rumbling and creaking in the distance in a most unearthly way. All the houses were lost in shadow, and you'd have to be brave to face a light because only hobgoblins went swinging a lantern zigzag through the dark of the night. When the wind paused in its long-drawn howl, then you could hear water rushing along the gullies, and the muffled murmur of the Caima overflowing its banks, mud and refuse for the whole length of the parish. God in heaven, what would Valseves' marshy fields be like after this! In the desolate night, the rumbling of the cart died away (surely only the devil himself could be out driving on such a night!), the light disappeared over toward Mosteiro, the wind began to howl again—and only the blackness of night remained.

And afterward what comfort in the four logs as they burned on the hearth, and the pitcher of warm wine that you sat drinking slowly!

And in the morning as soon as you opened the window you saw Tia Francisca's roof sheeted with snow, and the trees were bare and white with something of the funny look of puppets about them. The loose soil of the paths had drunk in the snow, and your big boots or clogs went along cracking the icy crust. And the fowls, poor things, looked astounded at the sheet of glass covering the water in the old trough they drank from.

An infinite longing gripped Manuel da Bouça's heart. Each memory of his home village hurt him and roused a deep desire to go back. . . . I'll never see snow again! Never again shall I see a tree without leaves!

A sudden laugh burst out round him, then another and another. The whole audience was laughing. Unnoticed by him, the news had been followed up by a comic film, to close the program. And he sat with his eyes wide open, and with his thick lips apart, watching what the people in the film were doing, but he couldn't see anything to laugh at.

At last the spectators stood up with a rustle and a shuffle, hum of voices and seats shooting back. Fernandes walked out between his two friends, bantering the newcomer.

"Now, António, that's more than you get in Monsão!"

"Yes, rather . . . Only on Sundays there."

Outside, Fernandes stopped a minute to look round the entrance of the theater as though he were expecting someone. Soon, keeping her eyes down, but smiling at him, a dark girl passed by, hair gleaming and thick-set body dressed in a red frock. Fernandes smiled significantly at his companions.

"António, please excuse me. . . . You just go along with Senhor Manuel, and he'll show you the way home. I shan't be long. Sorry, what?"

"Oh, it's quite all right."

He disappeared, pushing his way through the crowd in front of the theater, and the other two set off on their walk home. At first they went along in silence, wondering what they could talk about.

"Have you come out to go into trade?" asked Manuel da Bouça at last.

"I don't know. That's what I'd like, but I don't really know yet. We'll see. I've had some experience in a baker's shop. I was shop assistant in one at Monsão."

"Oh."

"And you, have you been here long?"

"Going on nine years now."

"And aren't you thinking of going back?"

"Yes, I want to, as soon as I can. . . . But you work and work, and as for saving a bit, don't mention it!"

They fell silent, António da Pita waiting for his companion to go on, Manuel da Bouça with the words cut short on his lips, remembering his personal disaster. And so they went walking on. Trolley cars, motorcars passed by, and other people in lively talk. At times their silhouettes were thrown into relief under arc lamps; then they were lost in shadow again. At last António da Pita risked a remark.

"So wages are not high, I understand?"

"It depends. Some people earn a lot, people who're bosses and have got a good business. But people like us . . . Have you got good references or recommendations?"

"I—I've got a letter for a man from Viana. But he's gone to Rio de Janeiro. Then I had Fernandes's address."

"You . . . You're young and have qualifications. . . . You can read, can't you?" Manuel da Bouça asked after some hesitation.

"Yes, I can read."

"Well, it's like this. There are a lot of rich folk here, that's true. And there are a lot of Portuguese here with big businesses. . . . But when you're poor, you stay poor. The same here as everywhere."

"Didn't you manage to get on?"

"I?" Manuel da Bouça gave a bitter smile as though in derision

of himself. He felt the need to open up, to show someone his
state of mind, to justify himself for the loss of his strips of land.
"I? . . . No, I haven't had any luck. And just now I got a
letter—you heard a bit of it, didn't you? My precious strips of
land! And mind, I did all I could to keep them, but I didn't have
any luck! There was nobody to take any interest in me, and when
a poor man has nobody to take an interest in him, what can he
do? When I left the plantations—I spent a year on the coffee
plantations before coming here—in a week I got through the bit
of money I'd managed to save, and then I went about with my
belly empty, with nobody to help me. And it wasn't that I wasn't
willing to work, at just anything. I couldn't find any work. If I
asked anyone what to do and said I was ready for anything,
they told me to go back to land work. As though I hadn't had
enough of that! As though I wasn't plumb sick of it! I swore to
myself that I wouldn't go back to it, not even if I died like a
dog. . . . And why? It's true things are no better in town, but
I didn't come all the way from Portugal to go on living clamped
to a mattock or a scythe. . . . And I'm not the only one who
hasn't had any luck. It's the same with everybody who hasn't got
someone to take an interest in him. Look at Fernandes. He's
been here longer than I have . . . and as for money . . ."

"You both work in the same shop, don't you?"

"We've worked together for three years now."

He fell silent, but Pita was anxious to get his bearings.

"If it isn't rude to ask, how much do you earn?"

"Two hundred milréis. At first I only got a hundred and fifty,
but they gave me a raise last year."

"Two hundred milréis . . . That makes two thousand and
four hundred a year . . ."

"Yes, a single man can manage on that, but don't imagine you
can save anything. When people come here, they think they have
only to spend on board and lodging and can set the rest aside.
Well, let them think it! Does a man only eat and sleep? I earn

what I told you, and I work from morning till night loading bags, cleaning up, setting cases in order, pushing carts along the streets. And if I left the shop tomorrow, there'd be a crowd of people after the job, because times are hard; and even Brazilians among them, because there are Brazilians who need jobs too. . . . Bosses give the preference to foreigners, so those poor devils are left looking for work. . . . I've come to thinking that there's no place in the world good for poor people. So what could I do to save my strips of land? From the time I gave up land work— This is where we live. Go in, please."

They went in and slowly climbed the stairs.

"As I was saying, from the time I left the plantation, I've been holding on, waiting to see if something better wouldn't turn up, some kind of trade in which I could make a bit of money. . . . But only those with money make money. You wait, and hope, and then give up hope. And I don't believe in it any longer. When we first get here and they tell us that all over the world the poor remain poor, we think they're hoaxing us. There's something inside us that thinks, Well, if the others didn't make a success of it, it was because they didn't know how, or because they didn't work hard enough, or because they just weren't lucky. Yes, there are people who aren't lucky. So we go on believing that we must try our hand at this and that, because a poor man who isn't afraid of work must manage to make a good living. Yes, it's like that, and then these fancies all get knocked out of our heads."

He stopped António da Pita at the top of the stairs to make his final point.

"What I want to know is, where is the country where the poor can get rich? Everybody says Brazil is full of wealth, yet even here there are a lot of have-nots, so I don't know what it can be like in other places. . . . Everything's wrong. . . . There's as much poverty as in Portugal. . . . It seems that it's in America where there are not many poor people. I made a mistake when I didn't do the same as a chap from my part of the country—he was thinking of coming with me, and then at the last minute he changed his mind and went to America. And very likely he's doing well now!"

António da Pita found this point of view very depressing, and he tried to react against it by finding that he had greater advantages than Manuel da Bouça had been endowed with.

"Of course, you don't know how to read," he blurted out.

"No, I don't. I began to work from the time I was little, because my father was a poor man too. At school age I was out gathering acorns for the pigs and shoveling up the dung the oxen and horses dropped on the roads. I did try to learn here. But what do you expect! You can't during the day, that's evident; then at night you're too tired, and on Sundays you want to forget your troubles. There are Portuguese chaps who are learning over here, but they're young fellows. Old donkeys can't learn. . . . And even then, that isn't the remedy either; lots of folk can read, and they stay as poor as I am. . . ."

The electric light over the landing shone on the two men and showed up António da Pita's pale face. The slight smile on his lips had faded a bit; he still kept it there from habit, but it had taken on a different expression.

"Go in, go in," Manuel da Bouça advised him. "Go in and lie down, because Fernandes will be late. I'm going to bed too."

"Well, if you think so . . ."

"Of course. Good night!"

"Good night!"

Manuel da Bouça's footsteps died away along the passage, and António da Pita slowly closed the door. The words he had just heard had made an impression on him; they had lodged in his breast in an uncomfortable lump. He put his hat on the bed, opened the window, and leaned out. . . . When we first get here and they tell us that all over the world the poor remain poor, we think they're hoaxing us. . . . Could it be true? Then what about the others, those who had grown rich? And then, he knew how to read and do the four operations of arithmetic. He knew

how to serve at a counter, and he hadn't Manuel da Bouça's
rough appearance. What could a man like that expect? And
then again, he talked that way because he'd lost his strips of
land. . . .

A sudden faith in his own destiny surged up and dispersed
the defeatist fog. It was the same as when he'd been drafted into
the infantry; everybody had said it would be dreadful, and then
it wasn't as bad as all that. A hard life, yes; and not very ap-
petizing food; but that didn't kill you. . . . He had only to
settle down and work and, God willing, in five or six years . . .
With full confidence in himself restored again, António da Pita
left the window and began to undress.

The light from the stairs filtered through the glass of the
transom window and filled the room with dim luster; through
the chinks in the door, it made two yellow lines along the floor-
boards.

2

ANUEL'S constant state of homesickness made him cantankerous, irritable with everything, his surroundings and himself. He was full of resentment against the circumstances he hadn't been able to dominate: he saw "Thou shalt not" on all sides, and he wondered how he had ever been able to believe in making money, buying Esteves' land, and having some return for his labor.

Never before had his mouth uttered so many vindictive words, so many filthy words.

The absence of the miraculous that he'd believed existed in the strange land—in what shape he knew not, but he'd always simply visualized it as gold—made him skeptical. He spent his time making comparisons: So-and-So who'd been there a mort of years, somebody else who'd grown old in exile—and all as poor as himself, except Belarmino, the man he'd got to know after leaving the plantation, who'd managed to lay some savings aside, God alone knew how.

At the shop during the day, when he was working out of sight of the higher employees, he went at the cases in a rage and threw the sacks down roughly, and then Fernandes would whisper, "You have got your dander up today!"

He guessed that António da Pita was living through that first period of confidence that he'd experienced himself, and so couldn't believe the tale of disillusionment. And whenever he got back home at night and found out that the other still hadn't landed a job in spite of all his efforts, he felt an evil kind of satisfaction.

"I told you so! I told you so!" he repeated. "Life don't hold anything for poor people!"

Once, in opposition to this point of view, António da Pita had pointed out that there were a lot of Portuguese who'd made money in Brazil.

"What of it!" Manuel answered angrily. "There are rich people everywhere. Even in my home district there are, and you mustn't think that's a big place like a city. It doesn't reach from here to Braz. . . . But they don't tell us how they made their money. If only they did! . . . You know, it's like what it said in that paper Senhor Fernandes read out the other day: If a man only works, without trading, without inheriting anything, and without profiting from others' toil, then he don't grow rich!"

"That paper Senhor Fernandes read out the other day" was a newspaper full of advanced ideas called *A Plebe*. It circulated through all workshops and was greedily assimilated by all outcasts, and it made a deep impression on Manuel da Bouça when he heard it read out at night. At first, the only thing he didn't agree with was the suppression of property. He didn't see why, having bought land, you couldn't call it your own and leave it to your descendants. But gradually, through the slow infiltration of doubt, he even finished by accepting this theory.

The new indoctrination was effected more particularly by Hermenegildo, the only factory worker living with them in the same building. He was a native of São Paulo, with lanky body, thin dry cheeks, and a loud voice that didn't match the mild luminosity of his eyes. He worked in a metallurgical shop, and at times his doctrines were as burning as the molten metals to which he gave his daily strength. He had infected Fernandes, but when he had tried to familiarize Manuel da Bouça with the new creed, all he had managed was to get the stubborn fellow to reduce the whole thing to a single selfish formula: If I can't be rich, then there's no reason why others should be.

Nevertheless Manuel da Bouça had begun to subscribe his five *tostões* a month for the propagation of those ideas that seemed to explain the reasons for his own failure; he frequented proletarian groups that held militant meetings, and one night he had to go scrambling on all fours over the roofs through the darkness, because the police raided the building and the only way of escape was through the window.

But neither he nor Fernandes spoke of these things in front of António da Pita. He was probably like all the Portuguese who were drawn by the mirage of gold, and might form an unjust opinion of those who championed this defiant gospel. Also, they both thought that time would take charge of convincing him, and Manuel da Bouça even had the impression that it wouldn't take long. António, he had noticed, was already living at Fernandes' expense, because that good chap was always ready to help.

Some weeks went by, and then, one night when Manuel da Bouça was already in bed, Fernandes came in to see him.

"I've just come from the Trade Union," he said in a mysterious voice. "It looks as though it's going to break out. . . ."

"What's going to break out?"

"What I talked to you about the other day. The revolution . . ."

"Ah! Did they say that at the Trade Union?"

"Yes."

"But are they joining in?"

"Unofficially. Garrido says we mustn't join in, because it

isn't our revolution. But the others want to. Hermenegildo's going. . . ."

For a moment the two men were silent in the darkness.

"And you?" Manuel da Bouça asked.

"I . . . I don't know . . . I'll see," stammered Fernandes.

"Well, I shan't! If I ever manage to go back home, I want to get there in good trim."

"But . . ."

"I'm not going, Senhor Fernandes. Shooting's all right when it's only rabbits."

"Well, of course, there's no obligation—"

"Of course there isn't!"

They fell silent again. The dim light from the half-shut window wasn't enough to show up Fernandes' form, and only the red tip of his cigarette was visible.

"Better not say anything to António."

"Of course not."

"There should be more news tomorrow. . . . Good night!" said Fernandes, going out and closing the door quietly.

"Senhor Fernandes! Senhor Fernandes!"

He was already along the passage, but he turned back and came in again.

"Did you call?"

"Didn't the paper say the boat came in today?"

"Today . . . Yes, it did say today!"

"Thanks. It's because of the letter."

And when Fernandes moved off again he began to ask himself the same question he'd been asking all through the last few days: Will she be better?

From the time he'd heard that she was ill, his tenderness for his wife had grown deeper; every hour he felt it, and every minute he had her in mind. In a vague way, too, he felt guilty of some kind of crime, he didn't quite know what, and something like remorse worried him. . . . Poor woman, to have that trouble with Carrazedas, and to be ill on top of it!

Rarely had he waited as anxiously as now for a letter from her, a letter that would bring relief, a letter that seemed as though it would never come. . . . Would she be better? Would she be better now? And he began to picture her again, allowing for the years that had passed, imagining the marks left by the wear and tear of time, in order to see her more clearly. And as always, the thought of his wife was followed by pictures of his birthplace, the longed-for spot so far away and hard to reach.

The village tormented him. Everything he remembered hurt him: people he'd known and the longing to go back and see them; the goat belonging to Tia Rita dos Anjos, that wicked old beast that sometimes went nibbling here and there on his strips of land; great flocks of sheep slowly climbing up the sides of Felgueira, through the chestnut trees. And those days when he went fishing for trout and bass in the Caima, dabbling about with a bag of lime among the muddy pebbles and keeping his eyes well skinned so that the keeper wouldn't catch him at it. The vines in winter, when they dripped tears after the pruning knife; then, come spring they sent out little shy leaves, which later became a cool awning along the walls and terraces for linnets and thrushes to build their nests in. Next the grapes grew and began to take on color and you tried them here and there— this isn't ripe yet, this one ought to be fine quality—till vintage time came round with its ladders and baskets and joking the girls when they showed their knees. And wasn't it a treat to make a bed of green ferns under the branches, with the sun playing in the leaves and shining down to the ground in thin rays full of tiny specks floating up and down and always disappearing as soon as they moved out of the light. Why hadn't he felt this way about it all when he was there, and not only from a distance?—that white white sun making lacework on spring days in the new leaves of vines and oaks, and birds singing in them. . . .

Sometimes he found himself even farther down the great river of memory, as far back as the distant days of childhood: that afternoon when he'd been pedaling on the wooden bike he'd made with Quim's help, and the other lads had run out and barred the way so that he fell off; and that first time he'd known sex, in the ravine at Sobradelo. Was Caroline still going strong in Oporto? What a long time ago it all was! She must be getting on, because she was a strapping wench even then.

He could see the ravine quite clearly: almost completely carpeted with moss it was, and shaded with oaks and willows leaning over the top, some of them with their roots showing through the rim of the ravine; down below, a thin stream of water flowed between soft banks of grass and under beds of watercress; and the stream terminated in a dam near which grew a great mound of brambles where sad-looking bullfinches hopped about from morning till night. Joanina lived close by, and the village said she was always to be had for money, but even when he was a bachelor and ready to run miles after a likely skirt he'd never knocked at her door. The village also said that she was a witch and that the house was bedeviled too, and he didn't want to have anything to do with sorcery. . . . And now he came to think of it . . . Could Joanina still be alive too?

The letter he was waiting for did in fact come the following day. When he left the shop for lunch, he called at the house and found it waiting. Would it say that Amélia was better and in good health again? He grabbed it up and went off to the eating house where he and Fernandes and a crowd of dockhands, great big fellows from Galicia and Minho, usually had their meals. And when he got there he asked his friend to come on one side for a minute. Fernandes had to move the bench and make the others stand up so that he could get away from the table, and then over in a corner outside the general buzz of talk he opened the envelope and began to read:

" 'My dear father . . .' "

" 'My dear' what?"

" 'My dear father . . .' "

Startled, Manuel da Bouça didn't speak for a moment; then he asked Fernandes to go on with the letter:

" 'My dear father, my heart is breaking when I take up the pen to write to you. My dear, dear mother died yesterday and was buried today, after many days of suffering. She talked of you all the time and up to the hour of her death said that her greatest grief was at leaving this world without seeing you again . . .' "

Fernandes stopped reading, feeling that he must do something to help his friend. Manuel da Bouça had turned livid, his eyes were glazed, skin tight-drawn from his nose, and his clenched jaws seemed to be holding in a cry of mad desperation.

"You must be brave, Senhor Manuel! It's something we all have to go through. . . ."

Manuel didn't answer. He fell back against the wall and stood speechless, stricken, tragic. The other men went on talking amid the clatter of dishes, forks scraping on plates, and stale kitchen smell.

"You must be brave! Let's go home; you can't go back to work today."

And Fernandes took hold of his arm to lead him away, when Manuel da Bouça, his chest heaving, gasped out, "My dear wife! I'll never see her again, never again!" And warm tears welled and rolled down his twitching cheeks.

The men near, noticing something unusual, looked round and stopped talking; and António da Pita, who had been watching them both, got up and went over.

"What's the matter? What's happened?"

"Senhor Manuel's wife's dead." And gently, like a brother, Fernandes said again, "Come, let's go home."

With Pita's help, he grasped him by the arm and led him away, helping him along like a drunken man. When they crossed streets, they had to watch out for the traffic, because Manuel da Bouça let himself be led like an automaton, heedless of everything.

"I'll never see her again! I'll never see her again!" he kept repeating over and over again. But at last they got to his room.

"Now, you stay here and don't go out," Fernandes said soothingly. "I'll tell them at the shop what's happened, and when António's finished lunch he'll bring you something to eat. Now don't lose heart. You know, we all have to die some time. . . . And just you lie down; you'll feel better lying down!"

He took his hat and jacket off for him and helped him lie down on the bed. Then, making a sign to Pita to come away too, he went out walking quietly, listening, listening to the sobs that the pillow did not muffle altogether.

Some time went by, and Manuel da Bouça came out of the stupor caused by the bad news. In between mists of tears, he began to balance accounts with the past, and one decision stood out: To stay, stay there in Brazil for always! With his daughter married to a man he didn't like, his wife dead, his strips of land gone—why go back? Just to be laughed at? And what could he go back with? He was poor. . . . And when? No, it wasn't worthwhile!

And that dream of going back in triumph: with his pockets full of money, handfuls of pennies thrown to eager lads who would scamper after them and scramble in the dust of the road to grab the coins; some help for the priest too, because the church was always in need of something; and the purchase of Esteves' land, and good clothes, good hats, and the new two-storied house on the Salgueiros hillside, dominating the valley and shouting its affluence to the whole parish.

Now the dream was gone, and reality would show him only the uncomely features of neighbors always greedy for money, respecting men for their possessions, and not allowing that you could come back from Brazil without wealth. In advance he felt the humiliation he would feel if he went back to the village as poor as he had left it, poorer even because he'd lost the strips of land; proper pride clamored that it was better to be forgotten in a distant land than submit to such vexation. . . . Never would he go back there. Let the girl keep the little house, let her go and live in it if she wanted, because it wasn't likely that she was very well off now she'd married that poor fish Afonso. . . .

So when Pita came in again and held out a parcel, his mind was made up: never would he go back to Portugal.

"Here's something to eat, Senhor Manuel."

"Thanks for bringing it, but I don't feel like it. . . . What time is it?"

"It must be getting on for three."

"Well then, I may as well go to the shop," he said, trying to get up.

"Now don't do that. You aren't up to it, and I'm sure they can manage without you."

"I don't want them to say . . . And anyway I'm not ill. . . ."

He put his jacket on and was picking up his hat.

"At least, take a bite of something," Pita pressed him again.

"No, no thanks. I don't feel like it at all. I couldn't eat; there's a kind of knot in my throat."

"I tell you, you shouldn't go to work, then."

And he went out, followed by Pita, who walked with him as far as the shop. The head clerk also thought that he ought to let him off for that afternoon, but Manuel da Bouça insisted on staying, and took his place near Fernandes, who was packing glazed earthenware into great cases, in nests of crumpled paper, to be sent off into the interior of São Paulo.

Then for the rest of the afternoon while he worked, the thought of his wife never once left his mind, and with the thought of her came the thought of his home village. Now he began to think of it in a different way; there was a kind of pleasure in just thinking about it, but pleasure mixed with bitterness and sadness. Nevertheless it went on attracting and fascinating him over there in the distance, and the decision he'd come to a few hours before began to weaken. . . . He'd like to see the place where they'd buried his Amélia, and buy the grave if possible. He'd like to see . . . He'd like to see it. . . .

Looked at from this new point of view, the death of his wife began to make him consider another course of action. Now he was alone, what if he did go back? What was the use of staying here? Over there, there were still the little house and garden. And if he went out to work for someone else for a few days, he could manage to live. That would be better, that would always be better than this! He wouldn't have to bother about anyone, and he'd be in his own house. He had to die somewhere, and it might as well be there. . . .

The thought of the hundred and twenty milréis he was carrying hidden in the lining of his jacket came into his mind, and he began to calculate how long it would take to save his fare home, and something to buy a new suit and make a bit of a show in the village for the first few days, to hide his poverty. . . . More than a year, getting on for a couple of years, if there were no illness . . .

So he lost heart again. It took too long; the plan became shadowy in his mind and lost its stimulus. If it weren't for the passage, he'd set off right now. . . .

Then his grief at losing Amélia and being left alone in the world brought Benvinda to mind. . . . What had become of her? He'd never had news of her, and so many things had happened since! Such a long time had gone by. . . . After Benvinda, he'd only been with women for money. Now he had nobody, neither here nor there. He had nobody. . . . Yes, if it weren't for the passage, he'd set off. He was getting on for fifty, and beginning to feel played out. Over there, at least he'd be in his own house. And when you're poor, it's hard the world over. . . .

3

*S*UDDENLY, the half-light of the shop was troubled by the echo of a crowd trampling, confused voices, clamor and panic. Pachorrento, the head of the Dispatch Department, went to the door. The noise went on increasing, so the clerks followed him; and last of all, getting over their hesitation, went Fernandes and Manuel da Bouça. In shirt sleeves, the proprietors of the establishment came out onto the balcony over the shop.

Something unusual was happening in the city. People were running in commotion along the wide street. They talked to each other, but didn't stop. Sometimes great stretches of pavement were left empty; then groups came hurrying in from the side streets, stopped a minute to look round on all sides as though they were being pursued, then moved off again in the direction the majority had taken.

All the doors and windows along the shopping street filled up with the bodies and heads of people who wanted to look out:

employers and employees, men and women, some still holding
the papers they had been working on in the offices, and all
pulled up short by the peculiar occurrence that had taken the
whole city by surprise. Such a thing had never happened in São
Paulo before, not even on days when some political demonstra-
tion had taken place. And the people standing in the doorways
questioned those who were pelting by, men bent forward at
a run with their rumps sticking out behind, and clothes rumpled
in the chase.

"What is it? What's the matter?"

"It's the revolution!" someone more polite than the others
answered, panting as he went along.

"What! What revolution?"

"General Isidoro!" Another man just called the name sideways, and went running on.

"The guns are already roaring!" a third man called out of
his own accord from on ahead; and there was vindictive
satisfaction in his voice.

Nothing more.

Suddenly there was a clattering of glass, followed by the
noise of doors banging and objects knocking together—and all
the establishments had closed down. After that, curious faces
showed only at the windows.

The head of the Dispatch Department ordered the light to
be switched on; then, fat and heavy, he made his way up to
the first floor, leaving a trail of pipe smoke up the private stairs.

There was no noise from the street now, and the head partner
of the firm, speaking at the telephone, could be heard quite
clearly: "What's that you say? Then it's serious? All right . . .
All right . . . If they'd only do some work instead of making
trouble! Goodbye!"

Then the head of the Dispatch Department came down again.

"Fasten all the doors carefully, then you can go," he said
briefly.

"What about tomorrow?" one of the clerks asked.

"Tomorrow . . . Just come back when all this has blown over."

And they all hustled into their jackets.

When Manuel da Bouça and Fernandes got outside, the street was deserted. They'd never seen it like that before, not even at dead of night. It was just as though the human race had disappeared; as though the ground had opened, swallowed them up, and closed again.

A light wind was blowing bits of crumpled paper along the pavement, and at the side of the road empty matchboxes, empty cigarette packets, streetcar tickets, bits of string could be seen— all the litter that on other days, under the feet of passersby, didn't attract attention.

The street had the withdrawn silence and desolate stillness of a deserted town. Only now and again did some head lean out prudently. And yet there was a holiday look about the fronts of the buildings: foreign flags had been unfurled on most of them, English and North American, French, Belgian, Spanish, Portuguese, German, Japanese, and a preponderance of Italian. Flutter of color up above, and down below the empty deserted street with bits of paper on the pavement, and Manuel da Bouça and Fernandes making themselves scarce and keeping close to the wall.

"I told you so, Senhor Manuel!"

"Well, and what now?"

"I'm going to the Trade Union."

"Not me. I'm going home. I'm not looking for trouble."

They stopped at Rua 15 de Novembro. There too all the shops were closed, but there were groups of people waiting agog at the corners.

"Well then, so long. I'm off to the Trade Union."

"Think twice, man, what you're letting yourself in for!"

From the distance came a dull rumble, repeated several times in succession.

"They've opened fire," said Fernandes.

The groups of people stood quite still for a moment, then began to disperse quickly.

"It's no good, I'm going."

They separated, and Manuel da Bouça quickened his pace, eager to get home. When he got there, he found the porters and dockhands who lived in the same house in a group discussing events. Each one was giving different details and a different version of what was taking place outside. The only thing they agreed on was that General Isidoro had taken the city by assault and that there were guns and rifles everywhere.

"But who is General Isidoro?"

"I don't know. A military man . . ."

"Oh!"

"The President has already ordered all the troops out."

"But what's the revolution for?"

"Now, what can it be for!"

And for the rest of the day, and while they got a meal together, and during the night when they couldn't sleep, they went on wondering what it was all about, some of them with vague misgivings.

Manuel da Bouça found it difficult to sleep, and woke up about dawn to the thunder of the guns. São Paulo shook with their crashing. Artillery reechoed in the distance, and from time to time the sudden flickering of light through the window was followed by a big explosion. The house shuddered violently. Machine guns, cracking dryly, let fly a long series of points of suspension in the expectation of early morning.

There was the sound of bugles nearby, and on the other side of the wall Matias coughed, so Manuel da Bouça knew he was awake too. He pulled the sheets closer round him and snuggled down to go on enjoying his bed, as he used to back home on stormy nights when the carters passed along the road, humming in a melancholy sort of way. But the noise of steps on the stairs roused him from his selfish pleasure. He recognized Fernandes' way of coming up, and then he heard him knocking quietly on the door for Pita to open it for him. . . . What had been going on outside? Manuel da Bouça couldn't lie still, so he got up, put on his trousers, and went along to see his friend.

Pita, still only half awake, looked startled at what he had seen. Fernandes, dirty and blackened with powder, had come in and put down two rifles and a quantity of cartridges at the foot of the bed.

"Phew! They weigh as heavy as six hundred devils!" was all he said. And when Manuel da Bouça put in an appearance he went on, "Well, Senhor Manuel?"

"We're all right here. And you?"

"All right . . . I've just come in. . . . I haven't closed my eyes all night, but I've given the others something to think about too!"

He began taking crumpled papers from his pockets. Outside, the noise of firing and bugle calls could still be heard, and suddenly a grenade burst close by, shaking the house and shattering windows. Shouts came from all the rooms. Pita, his open shirt showing a very white chest, jumped in his bed; Manuel da Bouça said nothing, but turned pale.

"Now then, my hearties!" Fernandes remarked, "That one only just missed paying a call here. . . ." And he went on emptying his pockets.

"Have you been to the Trade Union?" Manuel da Bouça asked.

"Yes."

"Well, what's happening? And Hermenegildo?"

"He's there. We're all in it, except Alberto, Silvestre, Garrido, and Mascarenhas, who are against. I know it isn't our revolution, but we've got to fight for liberty. We've got to liquidate the federal government, which thinks this is still all scrub. As soon as the revolution's over, and the bigwigs are driven out, the Trade Union will present its demands to help the small people."

"And when will it finish?"

"Who knows! It's only just begun!"

As Manuel da Bouça and Pita wanted more details, he straightened out one of the tracts he'd taken from his pockets and read the incendiary phrases aloud:

" 'The revolutionaries wanted only to put an end to administrative corruption, that swollen microbe that was eating its way through the vital cells of the nation. This vast, fertile, wealthy country was a great corncob into which only a few set their greedy teeth. A group of ambitious men, with their headquarters in the federal capital and vassals in the States, was turning Brazil into a private fief. There was no liberty, because this insatiable phalanx treated the Constitution with the same contempt that the last German emperor had shown for international treaties. When a voice rose in disagreement, then some prison opened its doors. And the people went hungry. The wealth of a great nation had become the privilege of a clique in power that thought only of the people when the election farce had to be staged. The President of the Republic, elected by political groups, outside the popular will, was the chief culprit. Inside the state prisons his agents flogged their adversaries, and in the meantime the exploiters of the people strengthened their rapacious hold.

" 'But now the time to react had come! Outraged by this tyranny, São Paulo had raised the war cry. The time had come to repeat the cry of Don Pedro on the banks of the Ipiranga: Independence or death! Because a people governed in this way had no independence. But the glorious Brazilian Army would know how to do its duty. Politics would be cleaned up. The Constitution respected. Corruption liquidated. The exploiters driven out. In a word, they were going to fight to the death for the cause of the liberty of the people. And this being so the people should take their place in the ranks of the revolutionaries.'

"Well, what've you got to say about that?" Fernandes asked facing his friends, when he'd finished.

Manuel da Bouça began to scratch his leg, and didn't answer

"It sounds just like our monarchists—they scattered no end of papers like that round our parts!" said Pita without enthusiasm.

"And what do you think?" said Manuel da Bouça turning to his companion.

"I?"

"Yes, how are things going?"

"Oh, as to that, they're going to get a thrashing, that's sure. Things are serious. The streets may look empty, but in fact lots of people are out; there are Brazilians, Italians, Spaniards . . . all sorts of them. . . . Because, fighting against the exploiters, we've got nothing to lose, except the casualties; and as things are its just work, work, work all our life long so that they can have everything—fine women, fine automobiles, heaps of money—and nothing for us! This time they're going to get a lesson—oh, yes, they are!" Then he broke off to ask about something to eat. "Haven't you got anything here for a fellow to set his teeth in? The shops are all closed, and I'm as hungry as the devil!"

"Yes, there is something," said Manuel da Bouça. "Matias and Joaquim brought in some beans and tinned meat. That's what saved us."

"Where is it?"

"It ought to be in the bathroom; that's where we put the heater."

"Good, I'll go and see if I can nibble at something and then have a bit of sleep. We've arranged for everyone to be at Luz at midday, to make contact with General Isidoro's troops."

He was making for the passage, but he stopped when he heard the guns roar out again.

"There they are! There they are!" he exclaimed.

"Who?"

"General Isidoro!"

"Senhor Fernandes, have many people been killed?"

"Now that one," he answered, pointing to one of the rifles,

"Well, are you looking? I took that one from a man stretched on the ground in front of the São José Theater. It might come in useful because mine plays tricks at times. . . . And the other man didn't need it anymore. . . ."

While Fernandes was sleeping, Pita came to Manuel da Bouça's room for a talk. Matias and Joaquim came too, and they sat in a circle on the trunk and on the bed, cigarette in mouth, and legs idle on the unexpected holiday. The talk didn't dry up. They told incidents in their lives, and when one stopped another took up the thread, talking about the past. They repeated themselves. Maybe they'd heard the same story already from the man who was speaking. But they listened patiently.

"It once happened to me that . . ."

Now and again, one of them got up and went to look out of the window into the street. It was as empty as the day before. And the guns kept on roaring. Then someone crossed the passage quickly with a heavy tread, and Hermenegildo burst into the room. He was in the same state as Fernandes—dirty, eyes tired with watching, and rifle slung from his shoulder. He nodded to them, then stood for a few seconds looking at his housemates in an attitude of pity.

"That's why we've always been slaves," he said. "Instead of taking your part down in the street, here you are having a pleasant useless chat. . . ."

Nobody answered, and he was moving off to his own room when Manuel da Bouça, vexed at what he'd heard, retorted angrily: "All this has got nothing to do with me! I'm Portuguese."

"Portuguese, nonsense! In this thing there's neither Portuguese nor Brazilians, just men! It's because of that sort of stupidity that we have to live as we do. Whether you're Portuguguese or Italians or Brazilians doesn't matter. What does matter is that you're a proletarian and a man. We're all brothers—and the others aren't. They wear us down to the bone in every part of the world without bothering where we were born. But all you want is to be a bourgeois, like them. . . . Yes, that's what it is, I know. . . . If the revolutionaries win and the Trade Unions pull things our way, then you'll all run up to enjoy the benefits. But now, when we need help, oh, no, it's got nothing to do with you!"

He went off, leaving a silence behind him. Then they heard him bang the door of his own room.

"Well, after all," said Manuel da Bouça at last, "I didn't come to Brazil to look for trouble."

"Neither did I."

"Life's hard enough without that."

"He can talk like that because he's Brazilian and feels at home."

Joaquim made this last remark, and it gave Manuel da Bouça cause for reflection. . . . Yes, but Fernandes was Portuguese, and he was in it.

Hermenegildo had left an uncomfortable feeling behind him, and the men went off one by one till Manuel da Bouça was alone again. Fernandes and Hermenegildo knew more than he did, there was no doubt about that. And if the Italians were joining in too, then they had some reason for it, because people didn't go and risk their skins just for the sake of it. So much wealth, and yet so many poor folk who couldn't live a decent life because they earned too little! All his life, hadn't he knuckled under to all requirements? And all he'd got for his pains was just poverty. And here he was at the present time with his hands still empty. No, some with everything, and others with nothing: it wasn't right. And after all, what had he to lose? His wife was dead, his daughter married, and Carrazedas had taken the strips of land. If the only thing remaining for him was to go back home ashamed of his poverty . . .

He spent the whole morning turning it over and over. If it was for the good of the poor . . . and the only thing left for him was to be ashamed of his poverty back home . . .

About midday, Hermenegildo, his eyes still drawn with sleep, came back with Fernandes.

"You mustn't mind," he said. "I let myself go just now, but I didn't mean to offend. Each man's free to do as he thinks best. . . ."

Manuel da Bouça was lying on his bed, but he sat up when he heard this. He was touched by Hermenegildo's apology, and the decision that had been slowly forming in his mind suddenly crystallized.

"I'm coming too," he said.

4

"HERE, lads, this way! This way! They'll have to come this way!" And the mulatto scaled the wall with his right arm stretched out firmly grasping his rifle. The band of rebel civilians and soldiers behind him scrambled over the solid enclosure in an instant, and jumped down inside.

Inside the park in flower, the rebels halted, uncertain what to do. The wall was too high to serve as a parapet, and they couldn't use the railed portion because then the body would be exposed.

"Over there!" one of them shouted. And all of them with the same thought ran for the birdhouses, pulled them apart, and with the pieces built a rough platform.

Inside the mansion, from behind the walls of the balcony, the frightened face of a man showed from time to time as he watched the vandalism without protest. And the sound of rifle fire came cracking nearer and nearer in loud bursts.

"Quick! Quick! They're getting nearer!"

Other combatants came up. They swept round the ground floor of the mansion and took possession of the garage, carrying off tins and boxes, turning plant pots upside down, laying hands on anything on which they could stand behind the wall. Others, lighter in weight, climbed the trees and perched in the forks, hidden among the foliage.

Suddenly the park fell silent as the noise came nearer. For a minute, a minute and a half, breathing was stifled and movement suspended. Then, coming into the main road from the nearest side street, a platoon of legalist troops emerged, and the sham silence of the park was broken. A shot rang out, then another and another; the whole wall became a many-mouthed gun firing without pause and without order. Two soldiers fell on the spot; a third, in the act of falling, desperately grasped at his comrade's arm to get him to drag him away. Taken unawares, the platoon broke ranks and ran for shelter into the public garden on the other side of the road. Hiding behind benches and shrubs, they answered the fire, but the enemy was out of sight and bullets were wasted in the air or uselessly ripped pockets in the wall.

Inside the park, the first exhilaration evaporated and was followed by discouragement. As though imitating them, the legalist troops were hidden too, and the revolutionaries were firing haphazard into the garden. Some changed their position, trying to get at the adversary from a corner of the park, till just about dusk the firing seemed to be petering out for lack of a mark, when the disagreeable warning was shouted from the top of a tree: "Run! Run! They're here!"

The revolutionaries saw soldiers lined along the railed side of the park with rifles pointing inside. In a sudden panic at the surprise attack, they took shelter behind the nearest tree trunk or made their way lizardlike through alleys and arbors. In the early dusk of the park, they became shadows making off with the light leaps of wild things. And the legalist troops sometimes interrupted their volleys to take single aim at figures looking for shelter. Soon afterward the park was in the hands of the besiegers.

Then at last Manuel da Bouça came across a mark for his gun—a weedy kind of man in uniform who was standing still in the distance, also with a rifle in his hand. Wondering whether he should or whether he shouldn't, because he hadn't much liking for that kind of thing, heaven knows, he stood prudently behind a thick trunk, squinting along the smooth barrel. Then the man who was offering his breast in that imprudent way turned sideways like someone listening to a voice speaking some way off. And he looked such a poor sort of chap, as unaware and crazy-careless as a blind-born rabbit, that Manuel da Bouça hadn't the heart to shoot him. He let his finger have its way and—*poom!*—fired into the invulnerable sky.

"How's it going?" asked Hermenegildo, who then passed along the grove.

Manuel da Bouça felt ashamed of his weakness.

"I've given them something, I can tell you!" he answered, stretching the truth. "And you?" But he didn't hear the reply, because a loud shout came from not far away.

"Let's make for that point there, because we'll catch them off their guard!"

This suggestion found supporters who crept stealthily to the wall and climbed over where some trees formed a dark fringe of cover.

"Some stay here and keep them occupied while we go round by the street."

The last sunlight had not moved a millimeter up the tips of the trees when the soldiers were attacked on open ground from the flank. They went to pieces, and the rebels who had stayed behind could fire on them at will. The only thing left was flight, and the soldiers disappeared down the road, hotly pursued, leaving a comrade fallen against the railing with one arm hanging like a limp puppet. Then the last defenders of the park ran for the wall to join their companions in pursuit.

Manuel da Bouça had taken only a few steps forward when he stumbled on a dead man stretched on the dark fallen leaves, blood streaming from his mouth. . . . Where the devil had he seen the chap before? Somewhere here . . . Perhaps one of the big stores? . . . He bent down to have a closer look. Yes, he'd seen him somewhere before the revolution, for sure. The face was long, dark, and bony, with great nostrils, and skin stamped with pockmarks. The eyes were open and glazed, staring up at the branches of the tree.

Manuel da Bouça moved on a few steps, then came back, drawn by curiosity. Who could it be? He stood looking at the dead man, racking his brains to remember. Then he saw that there was some jewelry on the body: two rings on the left hand, one almost hidden by the blood that had run down the fingers, and a chain on his waistcoat. Who could it be? He'd seen that face somewhere. . . . He moved on again, thinking it over, his feet rustling in the leaves, rifle on shoulder as though on the march. Near the wall he stopped again. Vague thoughts and possibilities, shreds of plans were stirring in his mind, stirring slowly like clouds hiding the sun yet not completely dulling its brightness. And mixed up with it all, now fading away, now lighting up, was the picture of his home village. Its scenery, its fields and inhabitants, all its appeal. It appeared and disappeared among the mists, but left a great weight of longing behind. . . . Who could the man be? Not very poor, evidently, since he'd got two good rings and a chain. . . . He looked around cautiously. There was nobody about. All the revolutionaries had scaled the wall, and now the firing was sounding from a distance. The park was quiet, yielding itself in lassitude to twilight as though nothing were happening, as though nothing had happened there.

Manuel da Bouça went on seeing clear pictures of his home village, far away in some lost corner of Portugal. And still two years before he could get back! Next he thought of the shop, his room, the head of the Dispatch Department, bags and cases

—his everyday life. At the end of two years' work, he'd go back with empty hands, because there wouldn't be much left over from the money he'd saved by the time he'd paid his fare and other expenses.

The thought of going back in the near future was growing clearer, stimulating his mind. It became a fire inside him, flaming and burning. . . . Why stay here any longer? Just to go on working with no prospects for the future? And if he took the things, who'd be any the wiser?

He went back to the place where the dead man was. Darkness had enfolded it, making the form look bigger, taking the color from the blood that had run from the mouth down the shoulder. Who'd be any the wiser? He imagined his departure from Santos, going on board, then back in his own village, the end of the life he was living. . . . It don't matter to him; he's dead. Then again, somebody else might take them. And so he went on trying to clear a way through his scruples. . . . It don't matter to him; he's dead.

He was still doubtful about it, so he pulled himself together and moved on again. Then suddenly he turned, and in a quick impulse ran back to the corpse, knelt down, closed his eyes, grabbed the hands, let them fall when he felt the slimy blood. He braced himself again and nervously set about his task, quickly stripping off the rings and pulling out a watch that came along with the chain. Blindly he pushed everything into his pocket, and stood up. Once on his feet, he opened his eyes and saw the teeth of the dead man gleaming white in the darkness. Then he stepped out, and at once had the feeling that the corpse was getting up and following him, so he broke into a run across the park and didn't stop to take breath till he found himself on the other side of the wall, out in the deserted road.

There was no sound of firing to remind him of the revolution, and he began to walk homeward, in a daze, just setting one foot in front of the other. He was already on the path through the public garden, where dark gravel picked out fanciful arabesques on the white, when he heard the clatter of a troop of cavalry in the neighborhood. With pounding heart he leaped quickly behind a bench, but the troop passed some way off and he didn't even see them. Then the thudding of the hooves died away in the distance.

Then only did he think of the revolution and his companions-in-arms. And when he felt the rifle on his shoulder, with its barrel almost grazing his neck as he bent forward, he quietly drew it off and laid it on the grass. Then he left his hiding-place and quickly crossed the garden.

Shooting burst out again on the left toward Higienópolis, but it didn't rouse him anymore. He had completely changed; his one fear now was that he might be taken for a revolutionary and not get safe and sound home. Straining his ears to catch the slightest sound of danger, carefully scrutinizing the streets, he slipped along near the walls and sometimes flattened himself against doors. He dared to breathe freely only when he found himself on his own stairs. Then he heard the firing become more violent and spread over the whole city; when night fell the guns began to roar again, and he fell to wondering about the fate of Fernandes and Hermenegildo. What had become of them?

Up in the rooms, his housemates were surprised at his appearance. They gathered round to ask what had happened, and he carefully toned down his activity in the revolt. Yes, he'd been out there a bit, but just to see what was going on, because he wasn't either on one side or the other. And as soon as things got serious, he came away, not because he was afraid, but because he hadn't come to Brazil to get mixed up in revolutions.

While he was talking, out of the corner of his eye he watched Zé de Freitas' expression, because that chap seemed the least reliable of all those present.

"And the President, has he hopped it?" asked Joaquim.

"I don't know."

"They say he's run away and that the rebels are already in the Campos Elísios."

"I don't know."

"And over at Mooca?"

"Mooca?"

"The people opposite said everything was smashed to bits."

He shrugged his shoulders: he didn't know. And—excuse me I'll be back in a minute—he went off to the bathroom, where he took his hands from his pockets and quickly washed the bloodstains from them. Then he remembered his bragging. Why the devil had he said that to Hermenegildo? And it wasn't true. . . . He hadn't killed anyone. He'd only fired a shot into the air! And now, if what he'd said got round, it might drag him into trouble. . . .

Then came monotony, day after day of rifle fire and the continual roar of guns. At first people kept out of the streets; then they got used to it and nipped from one pavement to the other to go to a friend's house for a chat, or to the grocer's where the hospitable door was always ready to open and close again.

But Manuel da Bouça didn't go out, because he was afraid suspicion might fall on him. He was afraid the legalists might win and find out that he'd carried a rifle in the rebel ranks. For him, life had become once more something to be treated with care, and he wondered how he had ever come to jeopardize it by deciding to fight against people who had never done him any harm.

This period of waiting, and the uncertainty in which he lived, and the uncertainty that hung over the city got on his nerves. And at nights he could get himself off to sleep only by counting the times he'd already, in imagination, been over the scene of the future sale of the jewelry, and his return to Portugal.

The news that came in gave no indication of what the

following day might bring. Some people came along saying that the rebels were already victorious, that Bernardes had been driven from his position, that within a few hours the guns would stop pounding factories and mansions and begin firing salutes to the new régime. But others were skeptical; they talked of heroic sacrifices on the part of the rebels, yes, really heroic sacrifices, but they were ending in bloody defeat. What was true (and the newspapers were publishing pictures that everybody could corroborate) was that the Central Market had been burned down; the reservoir on the Avenida Tiradentes had been damaged by a grenade and was spurting more water than a whale; certain streets, like the Rua Tabatinguera, Almeida Lima, and Conselheiro Furtado, had been wrecked along great stretches; big buildings were cracked and riddled with shrapnel; a number of districts were scarred with ruins; and the whole city was full of wounds and deep breaches. The number of killed and wounded nobody knew, for the struggle had been savage, but there was no available space left either in cemetery or hospital.

And beyond that, who could know?

Manuel da Bouça spent the day listening for the footsteps of Fernandes or Hermenegildo, the only hope of reaching some certainty through the lurid mists. They hadn't put in an appearance since the beginning, and António da Pita, seeing himself left without shelter, had already wondered aloud whether Fernandes might not be dead.

They gave no sign of life, but on the other hand, the corpse that Manuel da Bouça had robbed in the park at dusk was always coming into his mind. In vain he reasoned with himself: Well, he didn't need them anymore; he didn't need them anymore! . . . In vain, because the memory of this act embittered all his hours.

The possibility of going to hell had always been something as remote to him as the possibility of getting the winning number on the lottery tickets he bought at the fair. He'd never seen

Satan except painted in the flames pictured at wayside shrines, under the feet of an angry archangel. These pictures were small and faded, so they left no great impression on him of the torments of punishment. He was afraid of the fiend who walks freely on lonely roads at dead of night with his retinue of witches and dogs following behind him, and who dazzles benighted Christians till they become so blind that they step over precipices thinking they're treading firm ground. But he'd never thought that he'd meet him in hell, because he'd never supposed he was so evil as to merit such torments. At present, however, he didn't see the satanic fires as he had seen them till then; now they had grown big and twined round his body, licking round it, roasting it as though he'd been basted with oil.

So he felt as though he wanted to get rid of the rings and the chain without delay, because money would be less likely to remind him of his moment of sacrilege than the jewelry itself. But neither Ferandes nor Hermenegildo had come back, so that he could find out whether he could go out at last, without fear of bullet or prison.

Then one night when everybody had given up expecting it, Fernandes returned home, thin, pale, dirty, hollow-eyed, and as jumpy as though his own shadow were after him. And he didn't come back to tell his expectant companions the flowery details of great deeds that had been accomplished. He came back talking in a low voice, just hinting at things, and began bundling up clothes and articles on his bed. He was clearing out; there was no hope.

"Isn't Hermenegildo coming?" asked Manuel da Bouça.

"He's sleeping over there. . . ."

"Over there?"

And from Fernandes' expression, they knew what he meant. "When did it happen?"

"He was killed yesterday. . . ."

They all stood silent, and Fernandes went on tying string

round one of the bundles he'd got together. Manuel da Bouça felt cut up about it. . . . Poor chap! Now he wouldn't be able to tell what he'd heard, but it was a pity he was dead. There was no getting away from it; he was a good sort of fellow. He had that loud voice and manners, but he was a good fellow. . . .

"But, Senhor Fernandes, where do you mean to go?" Pita asked, worried.

"I don't know. I'm going off with some friends. I don't know where to."

"Maybe nobody saw you. And nobody here's going to talk. . . ."

"Maybe nobody saw—hum!"

There was no sound of guns now; rifle fire had ceased too, and the streets were full of an uneasy silence. A car, hooting in the distance, seemed to be moving in a dead city. Fernandes had finished bundling up his clothes.

"Now lads, and you António, please keep my trunk here till I can send for it. . . . And, oh, yes . . . António, I'm sorry I can't do any more for you now. You were relying on me, and now I . . . Come, let's say goodbye." They clasped each other, and then Fernandes added: "You can use anything I've left behind. And let's see, perhaps Senhor Joaquim can give you a helping hand. But he's poor too, poor chap! Anyway, goodbye!"

And he was going to shake hands with his friends, when Manuel da Bouça nudged him.

"Just a word or two . . ." And he led him out into the passage till he thought they were out of hearing. "And what about me, Senhor Fernandes? Are they going to put everyone in the lockup?"

"It looks like it. But you . . ."

"Well, I joined in, you know."

"Yes, but I didn't see you afterward!"

"I was only there that afternoon, but I'm afraid they'll accuse me."

"Maybe not, since it was only the one afternoon."

"And what if I went along with you? Is it far?"

"I don't know. I'm going with some friends, with Godinho . . ."

"That chap from Santos?"

"Yes."

"Then let me come too, Senhor Fernandes."

"There's no time."

"I can get all my belongings into one bag. Please let me come. I joined you, not for long, it's true, but I did go, and if anyone knows about it . . ."

He was so insistent that Fernandes gave way.

"All right, but get your things ready in no time; keep mine too, and take everything down to the door. I'll go and talk to Godinho about it, and I'll be back for you in a minute. But don't let the others come down with you; we don't want to attract attention."

Manuel da Bouça hurried into his room, and Fernandes went to say goodbye to his friends.

"So long, old man! No, don't come down, it might get us into a mess."

"Goodbye, Fernandes." And from the landing António da Pita, moved by the leave-taking, watched his one prop going away, his one hope, one of the frail reasons that had decided him to quit his village and go and try his luck in Brazil.

Manuel da Bouça came up carrying a bag and with Fernandes' bundles under his arms. The others were astounded.

"Are you going too?"

"What, Senhor Manuel too?"

"Yes, I'm going. I went out that one afternoon to see what was going on. . . . It did no harm to anybody, and it don't weigh on my conscience. But perhaps it's best to go. . . ."

"Well now, Senhor Manuel!"

"Now that's the last thing I expected!"

However, he didn't let their exclamations stop him, and gripping the bag more firmly under his arm so that it wouldn't fall, he said goodbye.

"Good luck, men. So long, because we'll surely be seeing each other again one of these days."

And amid the silence of the men who were quite taken aback at this turn, he went down the stairs at a quick pace. On the second flight the shadow of man and bag flickered a minute on the wall, distorted and disfigured, and then disappeared.

When he got to the bottom a car stopped at the door; Fernandes got out and called from the darkness in a low voice, "Senhor Manuel!"

"Here I am."

"Come on; let's be off."

5

$\mathcal{G}$ODINHO, a native of Santos, was a talkative chap, and each morning when he came to the room where they slept he always brought alarming news. The victors didn't know how to be generous in their triumph, and were meting out vindictive punishment to the defeated. There was not an inch of empty space left in the prisons of São Paulo and Rio; men were crowded into filthy cells, and floggings were a daily commonplace. The police, subservient to victorious despotism, tortured the prisoners to make them denounce their companions. It was said that they had attempted to assassinate Maurício de Lacerda, and that José Oiticica was already on his way to exile. Vessels were being loaded up with prisoners from Rio de Janeiro to be sent to the Island of Rasa e Oyapock, over the way from the convict settlements of Cayenne. Other vessels were firing up to set out for Santos and fetch other loads of prisoners from there. The government was determined to maintain itself in power by violence, and in spite of their love of liberty, the

Brazilian people had to put up with it. There was talk about shootings that were being carried out at night, just like the old days when people were shot for high treason in barrack yards. Men were picked up on any slight suspicion, for personal revenge, and through denunciation, and once in prison there was no appeal against arbitrariness, because the victors were afraid of their own shadows. After the flash in the pan of liberating revolution, tyranny and vindictiveness reigned supreme. And there was no protest, could be no protest, because any gesture of disagreement brought risk to life itself, and the press was completely muzzled.

"General Isidoro did quite right to skip off with his men! At least the police were left gaping there!" exclaimed Godinho, his thoughts taking a more optimistic turn after getting the bad news off his chest. "But it'll all pass, and they won't be basking in the sun for long. Either I'm very much mistaken or the President won't keep his seat very long. The Brazilian people won't submit to anyone who makes a mock of liberty. And what's more, you can't play with hunger! I can remember what I went through when I was over there with you. And if it hadn't been for my brother—God give him health!—when he fell ill and made it up with me so that I'd come here and keep an eye on his business, I'd still be eating the same devil's bread. I swear that if I'd still been in São Paulo I'd have joined in, and that's flat! Even as it was, I went over to see how things were going on, and when I met Senhor Fernandes I felt ready for anything. If the revolution hadn't come to an end that day, I don't know where I'd be now. Everybody said: 'Now don't you go to São Paulo; things are looking ugly, and they won't let anyone pass. . . .' But I went and got through somehow, because there's no rifle that'll make me turn back!"

Godinho, with his spate of words and cult for the tragic-heroic, made the room throb with disquiet, but Fernandes, who knew him well from the time when they had worked together, listened without comment. Manuel da Bouça felt more disturbed, and wouldn't let him go down to the hardware shop below without asking some questions to set his mind at rest.

"And here? Have they picked up many people? Can I go out today? Will they know we were in the revolution?"

Godinho reassured him, and only then did he feel settled enough to light up the cigarette stub that had been sticking on his lower lip while he was listening to the tale of government repression.

Since being in Santos, he'd been out twice: once to sell the jewelry and once to go to the consulate. And even then, he hadn't been able to take one step in peace, what with imagining that every passerby was a policeman and feeling every moment as though he were being followed.

He'd already asked himself once or twice whether it wouldn't have been better if he'd stayed in São Paulo, as though it all had nothing to do with him, and then when it blew over get on with his own business and leave quietly. But the thought of Freitas with his shifty little laugh and sticking up for the government convinced him that he'd acted for the best. And through it all he'd taken good care to keep Godinho up to his promise to look after the passage and the passport.

"Well, have you been able to attend to things?"

"Yes, it's all done! You're to leave on the *Andes,* and tomorrow you'll have to come with me to get your ticket."

"Will they suspect anything?"

"Of course not, not they! If anything unexpected happened, I'd just shove you into a car and take you to the Portuguese Consulate. They couldn't touch you there. But there won't be any trouble; you were in it only one afternoon, and wouldn't be noticed among so many people. . . . But I couldn't say the same for Senhor Fernandes. Someone might get hold of him in no time. . . ."

Manuel da Bouça cheered up at times, but usually he was worrying about whether they wouldn't be suspicious, whether they wouldn't catch him when he went to buy the ticket, or

even when he was going on board. This possibility filled him
with alarm; minutes dragged like hours and brought a load of
qualms and sinking feelings. What if they took him on the eve
of departure! Just when he was on the point of going back to
his village and realizing his dearest hope!

"Senhor Fernandes, do you think that tailor whom Godinho
sent here was all square?"

"Of course; otherwise Godinho wouldn't have sent him."

Then in silence they both sank back into their private obsession, because on his side Fernandes was cogitating about his own
uncertain future, and the vague possibility of perhaps moving
over to Porto Alegre, where one of Godinho's friends could help
him, when the victors grew tired of their triumph and things
settled down again.

But one night, when they were already in bed and the light
out, Fernandes couldn't keep it back any longer.

"Now, you're the lucky one!"

"Me? Why?"

"Wouldn't I just like to be going back with you!"

"But I'm going back with nothing; I'm going back just as I
came . . . with empty hands!"

"But you're going! Whereas me, what's in front of me? Some
day there'll be fewer people left to lay their hands on; then
they'll think of me."

"Maybe not."

"Well, and if they don't, what's in front of me at Porto Alegre?
Just work for others, always work till you drop with age like a
donkey that can't work any more. I'm already fifty-three, you
know."

"And I'm getting on that way."

"But you're going off!" Then he lowered his voice, and said
with heartache and longing: "Senhor Manuel, I wish I could
go back. I often think about it. When I first came out here, my
aim was to stay for four or five years, and then go back. But it's
getting on for twenty years now! And if I went back to my

village, I shouldn't recognize it, and nobody would remember me. My mother's dead, and friends have forgotten all about me. Even then, I'd like to go back. It's always a good thing for a man to see the place where he was born. The times I think about most are when I was little. I can remember it all as though it were today. If I went back, I'd go and see all the places where I used to play. . . . But I'll never be able to go back; that's sure."

It was the first time Manuel da Bouça had ever heard Fernandes complain, and he tried to cheer him up.

"Who knows, perhaps you will."

"Well, how? By working for others? You had the pluck to do the necessary. . . ."

"Me?"

"Yes, by saving, and stripping it from the body to pay your passage."

"You're right, it took some doing!" And the picture of the corpse with its white teeth and bloodstained hands rose in his mind and plagued him. "Yes, it took some doing!" he said again with feeling, as though he wanted to impress the words on his friend's memory.

When Godinho came that morning, Manuel da Bouça was up and waiting for him, with his hat already on, and dressed in the new suit that, spick and span, made his body look straighter.

"Well, shall we get going?"

"And the trunk?"

"It's already there, don't you worry. You'll find it when you get on board."

Manuel da Bouça gave a smile of unspeakable relief. Freed from the fear in which he'd been living, a feeling of satisfaction swept over him. He wasn't afraid anymore. It didn't seem possible that they'd come and catch him now, with ticket and passport in his pocket, and on the point of going on board. Fernandes jumped out of bed with his shirt unbuttoned.

"I can't go with you to the boat, you know, I'm sorry."

"I know it isn't possible."

"I hope you'll have a good crossing, and that you'll be happy. If there's anything that I can do someday, write to me care of Godinho, and he'll send the letter on to me."

"Thank you, Senhor Fernandes. And if you want anything from over there, just say . . ."

"No, no, thanks. If I could only go back too!" And for the first time since he'd reached manhood, tears came into his eyes.

"Goodbye!"

"Goodbye! I hope you have a good journey!"

On the stairs a thought struck Manuel da Bouça, and he stopped.

"I've just thought, Senhor Godinho, did you find anything out about Cipriano, the chap I was telling you about?"

"Oh, yes, I heard something, but it might just as well be nothing. I went to the grocery, and they told me he'd left years ago. He got a job in a bar, and then folks lost sight of him. Nobody had any news of him after that. Perhaps he went off to Rio or São Paulo."

"What a pity! I'd liked to have seen him!"

Then they moved on down the stairs, Manuel da Bouça taking care not to let his new suit brush against the wall. But out in the street, the old anxiety came over him again. Wouldn't people be suspicious? Wouldn't someone recognize him who'd seen him in the revolution? They came to a turning, and he pulled up short.

"Don't let's go that way; there are a lot of people."

"Well, the more, the better; you're less noticeable like that."

So, on Godinho's right, he walked on toward the dock, heart thumping and missing beats, and eyes on the pavement so that nobody could get a good look at his face.

The quay was in full sunlight—great sheets of white cut up here and there by the dark shadows of cranes and ships. They had to wait a short time, but it seemed interminable to Manuel da Bouça. Another ship had docked near the *Andes,* and from it a straggling procession of emigrants was coming ashore, Italians, Spaniards, Portuguese—the usual bunch, the usual scene. The same kind of women in peasant dress, the same babies and young children upset by the crossing, the same men looking forward with ambition—and all in needy, seedy promiscuity. They came stumbling along the gangway, carrying bags and bundles.

Others like them had disembarked the day before. For tens of years the same scene had been repeated time after time—an endless procession of hungry people Europe had spawned but didn't feed, except at those times when there was a shortage of flesh for cannon fodder. And the groups coming ashore always had a gloomy look. However bright and colorful the dresses of the woman, the whole thing always exuded a wretched atmosphere of want and depression.

And off they went, legs a bit unsteady on treading firm ground again after so many days at sea; off they went, following an instinct, a naïve idea, and trusting in they knew not what—lives deflected from their natural course, smitten with the desire to make money, and ready for any vicissitude because their home place was not their own and didn't even give them enough bread.

Seeing them, Manuel da Bouça's mind went back to the day of his own landing and all the illusions he'd brought with him, illusions these people were bringing too. . . . And what had become of Janardo? What had become of Cipriano? And to think that if Cipriano hadn't written back to the village to say he was earning good money, he, Manuel da Bouça, wouldn't have crossed the ocean relying on him. Ah, well . . .

"Now's the moment!" said Godinho, tapping him on the shoulder, and then giving him a friendly clasp. "I hope you have a good journey!"

"And don't forget, remember me to Fernandes," answered Manuel da Bouça. He went quickly up the gangway of the

Andes, stopped at the top to show his ticket, then walked along to the third-class deck, Godinho keeping up with him along the quay.

"Now you can talk about the revolution, because they can't go and look for you there!" said Godinho, and Manuel da Bouça, leaning over the ship's side, felt safe. He felt so relieved to be out of the uncertainty that Godinho reminded him of, that he could only smile, smile stupidly, almost happy.

Godinho couldn't wait any longer; he was needed in the shop, so he again wished him a fine crossing and good luck, and said that if he ever wanted anything, well, he knew where to write. Then off he went, waving for the last time from the corner of a warehouse.

Now that he was alone, Manuel da Bouça turned to look at the deck, which was a muddle of passengers, crew, and winches working noisily. He had the sudden feeling that the whole thing was very familiar, as though years and years had not passed by since his first crossing. The same smell, the same open holds, the same sheets of iron painted red and black, the same tarpaulins, and almost the same faces.

And he stood thinking over that first crossing: his ambition to get on, the disdain with which he'd listened to that offer of a job on the land at two hundred milréis a month. He saw it all as clearly as though it were only yesterday, from the moment he went ashore with Janardo, quite certain that he could earn more than they had said on board, up to the moment when Cipriano had told him the truth, up to his acceptance of the job he'd refused some hours earlier, up to his realization of the poor man's real position.

His happiness vanished and, turning back to the quayside, he looked pityingly at the last emigrants going ashore, stumbling miserably along with their women and children. Poor devils, they thought they could make money out there, if they were only willing to work. He'd thought that too, but he'd seen through it later. Hermenegildo and Fernandes had been right when they told him that a man never got rich through work alone. If it weren't true, why he'd be as rich as rich could be. Then again, those who were rich wouldn't let everybody else grow rich, because evidently there wouldn't be anyone left to do the dirty work. . . . America must be the spot where a poor man could get on in the world. But in other places, not a bit of it. He'd always worked like a nigger; he'd been as niggardly as a Jew both in Portugal and Brazil, and what had he got out of it? This new suit, the trunk down there under deck, the bit of money in his pocket—and even then it was all due to the rings he'd stolen from a dead man. . . .

The emigrants were already passing out of sight behind the roomy warehouses. Only dockhands remained on the quay, people coming on board the *Andes,* and bags and boxes. But soon a young mulatress passed along the jetty, walking with a sway of the hips, and she made him think of another woman. He was going away now, and it was all so long ago, and he'd heard nothing about her since, but he felt a wave of tenderness for her. What had become of Benvinda?

Manuel da Bouça felt even more downcast. The happiness he'd imagined he'd feel, when looking forward to the hour of departure, had vanished. And now that he was on the point of leaving it, he found that the land of exile was binding him with a gentle melancholy, like a yearning he would come to feel in the future—a yearning for the land, and the people who lived in it: Benvinda, Fernandes, Hermenegildo who was dead, Matias and Pietro, and even for the bad times. . . .

Then he suddenly thought about his berth and his trunk, and he went off, ticket in hand, asking the way now and again, along the dim corridors of the third class.

And everything was still familiar: the half-light of the aisles where the bunks were, the sticky dampness of the floor, on all sides shadowy forms wrapped in blankets, a prey to seasickness; the foul smell of the human stable. His bunk was under that of a man who was lying down, dirty, and so transparent he was certainly consumptive. Dissatisfied with this, Manuel da Bouça went back on deck. The *Andes* was getting under way with a bustle of sailors, hawsers, voices shouting orders up forward.

There were many people going back, some along the sides of the ship, some sitting lost in their own thoughts near the air vents, shuffling their feet on coils of rope. They came from Montevideo and Buenos Aires—Spaniards mostly, with a sprinkling of Italians. Years ago they had landed in Argentina and Uruguay, the very image of those who had just landed at Santos: healthy, full of illusions and the urge to get on. They had dreamed of conquering a fortune with the strength of their arms and the sweat of their brows. They had labored day and night, cleared the land and cultivated it, lived on distant ranches out on the pampas; they had pushed their way up the Paraná, given their bodies to the insects and fevers of the Gran Chaco in an anonymous, uninterrupted struggle for gold—and always in their minds the dream of buying a bit of land in their native village and building a new house near the old one where they were born. They forgot themselves in grueling labor, and the day they woke up again to the fact of their own existence, they discovered that they were as wretched as the day they landed. More wretched, because their illusions had been stripped away. They were ill, drained dry, old; and all they had left was to beg death to put off the day. Many were being repatriated by their consuls; others had scraped together the small savings of all their years of exile to get a stall for a couple of weeks in the oceangoing stable. There they were on their way back, hundreds of them.

There were a few in the first class, too, who were going back successful, but you could count them on less than ten fingers.

The *Andes* was working its way farther and farther from the quayside, under the radiant blinding sun of tropical midday. Manuel da Bouça could see the roofs of the city: low and almost all of the same height, they stretched out level as far as the foot of Monte Serrate; then they became higher and more imposing as far as the José Menino beach; and from there they dwindled away, becoming scattered and humble, along the bay of São Vicente.

He kept his eyes fixed on the scenery, but he felt more and more downhearted, lost in his own disaster, and uninterested. . . . Now he knew what life was like for poor people who had no luck. Now he knew all about it. . . .

And the *Andes* crossed the bar with the cargo of exhausted, almost moribund human flesh that America was handing back to Europe—people the world didn't seem to want; and they trailed from one hemisphere to the other, despised and rejected by their fellow men.

6

Coming ashore, Lisbon and memories of the first time he'd seen it, getting into the train, the masculine strength of the language as spoken in its land of origin, running into the tunnel—everything, everything was beginning to pall, to dwindle in significance in face of his overruling desire: To get home!

Near Santarém he caught sight of a long row of motionless shadows in gentle moonlit slope. Olive trees! It was years and years since he'd seen any! And they seemed to have a soul. As he sped by, they seemed to be whispering memories of the past. Now he was really back in his homeland. That gate glimpsed in passing, a little white house, an old mill with its four wings, a tumbledown wall—lovely, lovely!

In the morning, the pinewoods of Ovar came forward to meet and greet him. They reminded him of his childhood and filled him with a feeling of contentment, and as each pine raced quickly away toward the rear of the train it took a wave of familiar tenderness with it resuscitated from the past.

At Espinho, he changed into that old birdcage of a train that served the Vale do Vouga—a simple likable toy train that trilled childishly when it approached stations. Then they would set off again. And everything seemed like a dream he might be dreaming in his room of exile far away on the other side of the Atlantic.

To the right the noble outline of the castle of Feira stood out in relief. Farther on they came to São João de Madeira. Then, with his heart beating and eyes hungry for what would come next, away they went again, and he was more and more feverish and anxious to arrive.

At last—his own country town! Just the same as when he left . . . No, there was a wide new avenue leading away from the station. Passengers were already climbing into the bus. He got in too, but there was no one he knew, however hard he looked. How glad he would have been if he could have stretched out his arms with an exclamation and put them round friendly shoulders!

The bus set off noisily through the center of the small town, stopped at the door of the post office, then went on again.

"Stop, stop here!" Manuel da Bouça called out.

They were in the main square, and the ticket collector looked round in surprise.

"I want to get out here. And please leave my trunk at Senhor Tavares' shop, at Salgueiros. How much is it?"

"Three milréis."

He paid and got out, sensing the displeasure of the other passengers, who were annoyed by the delay.

The bus went off again, and he stood in the middle of the square, having a good look round to see where he was.

No, it wasn't possible. He couldn't go back home as he had set out, in that old bus; of course he couldn't! What a sorry figure he'd cut, and what would people say?

He got his bearings and set off again; then in the main street he stopped, perplexed. . . . The devil, I could have sworn Carrelhas' place was just here!

There was a draper's shop close by, and inside a tall youth was leaning over the counter, watching him. Still perplexed, Manuel da Bouça went in, but only to receive bad news.

"Senhor Carrelhas is dead," answered the shop assistant. "But you'll be able to get a car at the Grillo, just next door."

He thanked him and went out shaking his head over the dead man. . . . Poor old Carrelhas! Poor old chap! But after all, he was getting on in years.

At the garage, they fixed the price—thirty escudos, dearer than in Brazil—and Manuel da Bouça got in.

The car set off, turning round by the prison and racing all out toward Cidacos, leaving a clear picture of Nunes' Agency and bearded faces of prisoners fixed in his mind's eye, though he caught only a fleeting glimpse in passing. But he soon forgot them when he saw the new green trees growing on the slope of La Salette.

Then came the forest of Covo, with some great bare stretches in it, and, in a curve bordered by olive trees, the Palace of the Counts, with the siren from the glass factory sounding away behind it.

He leaned forward and ordered the driver, "Speed up a bit!" then sat back again so as not to miss anything of interest to his homesick eyes. He wanted to see everything, and as they went along he was thinking of times past: that afternoon, that morning, that Sunday at the fair, and walking along the road and passing pine trees, cork trees, and oaks. When they were coasting down to Vermoim, a hen flew in a flutter from under the wheels of the car; and then, as soon as well-known houses came into sight, he felt that he wanted to savor his joy at seeing it all again and take it in slowly.

"Now you can slow down," he leaned forward and told the driver.

A deep nervous thrill filled his being, brought tears to his eyes and made him weep for joy. . . . Vermoim! Vermoim! Was the fountain still down there? And the fields? Such lovely fields! He felt he could hug all the country people he saw in their cottage gardens, on the road, and among the maize patches. He wanted to hug them all, even the mild donkey grazing slowly and peacefully by the side of the road. The fountain was still there.

"Very slow now, please!"

And there the fountain was, very old, its half-moon wall cracked and worn, but with its trickle of water still singing as in the old days, and its garland of ivy always green.

The car began to climb up to Sobradelo, and he could just catch sight of Teixeira's house, and Aninhas'; then they went round two more bends, and they were in Salgueiros.

Manuel da Bouça's heart was thumping violently, and he was trembling as much as that night when he'd asked Amélia if they could call the banns. From there, you could get a glimpse of Frágua, and Bouça, his own dear place. . . . But he couldn't see his own house. Where was it? Looking anxiously round, he forgot all about the car, and jumped when it came to a stop.

"Isn't it there?" the driver asked.

"Yes, this is the place."

And he turned round to look for it again. Why, there it was. The trees had grown taller, and almost hid it. And the walls didn't show up in the distance, because no one had taken the trouble to keep them whitewashed, and so they'd turned a dull dark color.

People were beginning to gather at the door of Tavares' shop, and he got out of the car, rather stiff, and uncertain what attitude to adopt, one impulse urging him to timidity and another to arrogance. He didn't recognize any of the people who'd come to look. Who could they be? Then they drew aside to make way for him, and he went into the shop and up to the counter and asked for Tavares.

From the dark back-shop an old man with a white beard came forward slowly, staring fixedly with shortsighted eyes.

"Now, God bless you, and come out and shake hands!" said Manuel da Bouça.

The old man went on staring, still puzzled.

"It's easy to see you don't recognize me! It's Manuel da Bouça . . ."

"Ah, I was just thinking it was you, but it's so unexpected I couldn't believe it!" The old man lifted up the flap of the counter and came out to clasp the newcomer in his arms. "Now, who'd believe it! Who'd believe it! How could anyone be expecting it! So that trunk's yours, is it?

"Yes, it's mine."

"Martins left it here without saying who'd sent it, but I saw at a glance it belonged to a 'Brazilian.' We haven't the money to buy trunks like that here!"

Manuel da Bouça gave a smile, feeling pleased, almost superior.

"It's your Deolinda who's going to be glad," the old man went on. "Does she know?"

"No."

"Ah, you wanted to give her a surprise! Good idea, good idea!" The onlookers from the door were now standing around Manuel da Bouça, and he gave a glance of inquiry to Tavares, who explained who they were. "Why, they're my children, and the farrier's children."

"What?" Then, waking up to the facts, "And I didn't recognize them! How they've grown! But the years have gone by, and they were only little when I went away. But I'm beginning to remember now. This is Palmira. . . ."

"No, it's Rosa."

"Yes, that's it. This is Rosa, and that's Palmira."

"Now you've got it right."

His trunk was placed in the car and, after a little more talk, he left them. The car set off to take the road to Frágua but, a little beyond the bend, he ordered it to stop, amazed at what he saw. Just in the very place he'd dreamed about, blatant, dominating the whole valley with its wide balconies, stood a luxurious villa. . . . Who'd hit on his idea, just the thing he'd meant to do with the money made in Brazil?

The more he thought about it, the more he was amazed as he stared at the ostentatious building with a garden one side, and a wide garage door at the end. Whose was it? It went one better than the house he'd planned for himself, because he'd never dreamed of a car, and the land used for the garden would have yielded more as a kitchen garden.

"Whose is it?" he asked, turning to the driver.

"I don't know. I haven't been in Oliveira very long—I used to work in Oporto, and I've been this way only once or twice."

So Manuel da Bouça went on turning it over in his mind. Whose could it be? Whose could it be? And right there . . . But there was nothing he could do about it.

"Let's move on."

Farther along, another innovation attracted his attention. Negrais' field had been turned into a football ground, and the lads were letting off steam in a practice game. How changed everything was! Going to Brazil, it was as though a man died and came to life again a long time afterward.

Then he caught sight of a familiar pine tree in the distance; he'd often climbed it as a boy to get the pine kernels, but he'd always overlooked it when calling up scenes of his native village. Now he felt a rush of happy emotion because it still existed.

In the up and down of the road an old woman stepped aside and close up to the bank, to let the car pass. Manuel da Bouça recognized her.

"Tia Rita dos Anjos! Tia Rita!" he shouted, and again ordered the car to stop. "Well, how are you?"

"God bless you, Senhor Manuel! How glad I am to see you! It's years since you went away, but it seems like only yesterday!"

"Well, at any rate, we old ones do recognize each other!"

"And I was only dreaming about you the other week."

Tia Rita spoke in a respectful tone of voice, and looked him over with sharp eyes, with a villager's inquisitiveness. And when he moved on again, she curtsied and wished him well, eager to get into the good books of the new lord of the land.

Then at last—"Here it is; stop here!"—they drew up by the Bouça gate, and the repatriate stood up in the car to have a good look at everything. This was his life, his past, his house, his cottage garden, his old cherry tree. The old cherry tree was still there, and the fig tree too! He smiled at them as though the very trees and stones could respond and be stirred with the same emotion that throbbed in his mind, in his bowels, in his whole body. For some moments he stood like that, unable to believe it was real, fearing the whole thing might vanish, fade away, and leave a greater longing behind, as had so often happened in Brazil.

The driver began to fidget in the car, and brought him down to earth, so he got out, pushed the gate open, and went up to the door, and knocked. But there was no answer. There was nothing but silence inside and out, nothing but peace round creatures and things. For a moment he stood looking at the closed door. It's true, he hadn't let the girl know. . . . Then he turned to the driver.

"Get the trunk out and put it inside the gate."

Afterward he came out slowly, opened his wallet, and paid; and, for a short time, the purring of the motor disturbed the silence of his homecoming, till at last he saw the vehicle disappear round the bend in the road. And he stood alone with his "Brazilian's" trunk in front of the deserted house, where the tenderness of other days no longer existed, where the love of his life had died during his absence. Nettles had sprung up; the ened; the walls were stained with dark patches, testifying to paint had scaled off the door, leaving the wood bare and black-neglect. Everything, the cabbage patch, the outer wall, the vines, breathed desolation and told of the man who had gone away, and of Amélia who had died.

The silence was unbroken. At that time of day, the people of Figueira were out in the fields, and Manuel da Bouça could see only one human being—a dirty slobbering child sitting in a cottage garden in the attitude of an Oriental priest.

The all-pervading loneliness saddened him, the look of the empty house, the closed door that appeared to have no connection with him, seemed to be choking him, bringing tears to his eyes till he found he was crying. My dear wife! My dear wife! The image of the dead woman appeared before his eyes, inextricably twined in his past life, and called up deep longing, deep grief for vanished days that would never return. . . . He must go to the cemetery to see where the poor woman was; and if he could, he must buy the grave so that nobody else would be buried in it.

A whistling in the distance made him go to the gate, and, wiping his eyes, he looked along the road. A boy was coming along on his way back from school with a book under his arm and his hands in his pockets. When he saw Manuel da Bouça he didn't know the face, because he was only eight or nine years old, and he stopped whistling and looked shyly down at the ground.

"Here, my lad, would you like to earn ten tostões?"

"Yes, I would."

"Do you know where Deolinda lives?"

"Yes I do."

"Where is it?"

"Down on the bank."

"Well, you just run along then, and ask her to bring the key and come quick because her dad's there. Do you know Deolinda?"

"Yes, I know her."

"Good. Here you are, and when you come back I'll give you the other five tostões, so be quick about it!"

Alone again, he began to walk up and down in front of his closed, neglected house. The sun was shining on part of the garden and along the road—it attracted his attention, and he stood enjoying it, satisfying the hunger he'd had for it, white like this, mild, soft. The parish from Salgueiros to Frágua, from

Santo António to Mosteiro, lay in a green shell shape between the mountain slopes, and he let his eyes linger on it. The mild sun was shining on it all, so white, and he'd longed for it so while he was in Brazil!

Suddenly he was struck again by the new mansion that had been built up there by the roadside, in the very place where he'd dreamed of building something of the same sort. Who owned it? It must belong to some rich "Brazilian," because only rich "Brazilians" had money like that to spend. But if it was a "Brazilian," then it must be someone who'd left later than himself, because he hadn't heard of anyone who'd left before him. And how had he managed to make money? How had he grown rich?

He felt hostility welling up against the unknown owner of the house—the unknown man who had succeeded where he had failed, who had taken his place, who had got there first. Who could it be? With money having lost its value, work like that couldn't have cost a penny less than a hundred contos. . . . And he could never have made that sum, even if he'd stayed all his life in Brazil.

Depressed and humiliated, he turned away from the mansion and began to calculate what work he would have to put into the garden to get it back into its old condition, and how many days' work he'd have to do outside to earn his daily bread. He thought about it without enthusiasm, almost with dismay, as though the damage done exceeded his strength to repair it.

He'd made it up with Deolinda, because as soon as he set his eyes on her he felt so glad that he forgave her everything. But during the evening meal he couldn't restrain his curiosity any longer.

"Tell me," he asked her, "who owns that new house up at Salgueiros?"

"The new house? It belongs to Nunes."

"Nunes?"

"Yes, Nunes who has the agency. The man who got your passage and passport for you."

"Oh!" And on the heels of surprise came vague suppositions, doubts, suspicions. "So it belongs to Nunes. He must be rich, then?"

"Yes, very! Everybody began to want to go away, and it was more than he could do to keep up with it. He had his agencies in Cambra and Oliveira, and he used to send a clerk out here to find out who was thinking of going to Brazil or America. The whisper went round that he was shady and that he even had to go to prison because he sent some men off from Castelões without the proper papers. First they were to get into Spain, and then on to America, but the whole thing was found out. Then people said he'd given bribes to get out of prison, but whether that's true or not I don't know. What I do know is that he wasn't there long, because a week after I heard all about it I saw him go by in his car, toward Cambra."

"And has he had the house long?"

"Getting on for three years now. He spends the summer there, shooting on Felgueira and fishing in the river. He always brings a lot of servants, car and everything. It's said that he's got the biggest fortune made in these parts in recent times. . . . And nothing will get it out of my head that he worked things with Carrazedas to get hold of poor men's land."

"What? What's that you say?"

"Well, everybody's hinting that's the trick. Didn't you see what happened to our strips of land?"

Someone knocked at the door, because when the neighbors came in from the fields and heard the news they came round to welcome Manuel da Bouça home. There was Fernandinha with her sons, Tia Ambrosia, Soão do Serralho, and others in the background, half hidden in the darkness. There were congratulations from this one, words of welcome from the other, and Manuel da Bouça smiled and thanked them pleasantly. They stayed to talk a bit, respectful and unassuming, with a question here and a question there, and from time to time a quick reference in passing to the fortune he must have made. So Manuel da Bouça felt flattered, and hadn't the courage to give the facts.

"Well, it isn't as much as all that. . . . Not so very much . . . You do the best you can. . . ."

To tell the plain truth would spoil the triumph of the moment, bring an awkward silence into the cordial atmosphere, make him feel small and shamefaced. A sudden cowardice made him cling to the prevarication when he saw the covetous eyes of his neighbors, old acquaintances who would despise him if they knew the truth. Not finding any excuse to justify his poverty without going down in the consideration he had hankered after, he couldn't bring himself to be honest about it; he was being flattered and made much of, just as he had dreamed he would be if he came back rich, and he let it appear that fortune had smiled on him in Brazil and that blessed was the life of the fighter returning home.

When the visitors thought it fitting to take respectful leave, he went with them to the door, answering requests for loans with encouraging murmurs. He almost believed he was rich, and could hardly credit the reality that he was poor.

When the last neighbor had passed through the gate, Manuel da Bouça's eyes fell on a long row of lighted windows opening on the night over toward Salgueiros; he didn't remember having seen them in the old days; they certainly weren't there before he left.

"What a flood of light!"

"That's from Nunes' house," Deolinda explained behind him.

"Oh!"

"He had an electric cable brought from the mines at Nogueira do Cravo. It's the only house in the district with electric light. People say there's just everything imaginable in that house."

Nettled, Manuel da Bouça went in and closed the door so as not to see the light streaming over the valley from Nunes' residence, annihilating the darkness and suggesting wealth and power where only humility had existed before.

He looked at his own house full of cobwebs, and in the dim glimmer of the oil lamp wavering over the old worm-eaten lumber, it looked more wretched, more poor and empty than when he had left it and gone away in search of gold.

7

ARLY next morning, as soon as the sun glinted through the roof tiles, he began to turn in his bed, unwilling to lie there any longer, eager to go out and see his native place.

"Deolinda . . . Deolinda!"

"Yes, Dad?"

"Have you got any coffee?"

"No, but I can go and buy some at Salgueiros if you like."

"That'll take too long. Anything hot will do."

"Well, there's a bowl of soup left from yesterday. Will that do?"

"Soup . . . Yes, that'll do."

He heard his daughter jump out of bed in the next room, then go along to the kitchen. He got up too and began to put his clothes on, his heart heavy with memories of Amélia, memories that were more poignant in that room where they had slept together for so many years, in the bed that had seemed big and desolate during the night he'd just spent in it.

When he'd finished the soup Deolinda gave him—he'd got used to coffee and this was the devil of a change!—he went out, and his eyes were immediately struck by the freshness and greenness of the country morning. But a sudden thought made him turn back.

"Look now, can you remember Zé do Aido? Has he come back from America yet?"

"Of course I can remember him! Yes, he's come back."

"Well . . ." But he hadn't the courage to go on.

"What were you going to say, Dad?"

"Oh, nothing. He lives in Castelões, doesn't he?"

"No, not now; he's gone to live with his brother-in-law in Baralhas."

"Oh."

Then he set off again at a slow pace, making for Santo António to see his wife's grave. He tried to lose himself in the well-known scenes, remembering the longing he'd felt when he used to imagine it all, over there in Brazil; but now that he was back, the fields and trees didn't bring the satisfaction he'd expected. The thought of Zé do Aido dominated everything. Very likely he'd made money. Very likely he'd got a big new house like the one Nunes had built. What a fool he'd been not to go to America too! If only he'd guessed that Brazil wasn't the place and that you couldn't get on there.

Halfway along the road the desire to make sure whether Zé do Aido had been successful or not became stronger than his tenderness for the dead woman and, giving up the idea of going to see Amélia's grave that morning, he turned off toward Baralhas.

If only he'd guessed! America was the place where a man could no doubt make his way! He noticed that people working in the fields stretched up when he went by, and looked upon him as a conqueror, a fortunate being, a "Brazilian" possessing wealth and property, because the news of his return had certainly flashed through the whole neighborhood. And so his poverty weighed on him the more, and dashed his spirits, while at the same time the thought of Zé do Aido stood out more strongly in his mind.

When he caught a glimpse of Baralhas through a tunnel of cork trees, his eyes glanced over the line of unpretentious houses, expecting to see a big new smart building prominent among them. But to his surprise, the hamlet didn't seem to have lost its old humility during his absence. It was just the same jumble of little rustic houses, some white, and others the color of yellow earth because there'd been no money left over for whitewashing. And all of them aligned along the road that covered them with dust each summer. Well, then, he must have had his house built in Castelões.

At the first wineshop he saw—it was Marcelino's, he remembered—he went in to ask the way.

"Zé do Aido? Why, he's almost next door. He's at the cobbler's, the third door along."

There was an old acquaintance from Lordelo there, so Manuel da Bouça ordered wine and drank too, but nervously and in a hurry because all he could think about was the friend who'd gone to America. At last he went out accompanied by Marcelino and Fausto.

"This is it," they said, a few steps farther on.

But Manuel da Bouça could hardly believe his eyes. He thought there must be some mistake, and turned round to the men behind him, then looked inside the place again. At last, as surprised as though he'd seen someone fall down from the sun onto the earth, he recognized Zé do Aido in one of the two men sitting there on cobbler's stools, hammering away at leather.

"But . . . but . . ."

Then Zé do Aido recognized him and got up to welcome him and clasp him in his arms.

"Senhor Manuel! God bless you, man! I've only just heard you'd come back, and didn't I feel that I'd like to come along and shake hands!"

He found a box among the lasts, tools, and old shoes and offered it to Manuel da Bouça, while Marcelino went away again because of the shop, and Fausto stood propping up the doorpost.

"This is my brother-in-law," Zé do Aido went on. "He was in Oporto a long time; then he came and set up here in Baralhas. . . . And this is Senhor Manuel da Bouça, from Ossela, who went off to Brazil years ago. . . . Ten years, isn't it?"

"Yes, almost. Nine years and a bit. And how long did you stay over there?"

"Seven years."

"Less than me. And . . . how are things? What's it like over there?" He wanted to go straight to the point, straight to the thing that interested him, but he made a roundabout approach because he had to hide his own position.

"Over there it's . . ." Zé do Aido sat down and began to talk of this and that, gripping the hide and the hammer out of habit. And he chatted on about America, asked questions about Brazil, and went on talking circumspectly about the whole thing till Manuel da Bouça thought the proper time had come to cast the hook.

"And what kind of luck did you have?"

"Luck? Now don't talk to me about luck!" answered Zé do Aido ironically. "It was something that just never came off!"

And because Manuel da Bouça insisted, he told the story of his adventure with Anacleto and Rosalino.

Nunes had offered to get them into America if they paid five contos each. That was quite a figure, but there were a lot of difficulties to be got over first, and once over there the money you made would soon cover expenses and leave a nice bit over. So he and Anacleto and Rosalino had accepted; they sold what they had and handed over the fifteen contos. After that, there would be no more bother, Nunes had said, because he'd arrange everything: papers, passage, everything! And when the time came to leave, he'd let them know.

Then one afternoon Serafim from the agency at Cambra had

sent for them and said, Tomorrow's the day! He'd even gone with them himself as far as Valença, where they'd spent a whole day, with Serafim always talking in a low voice and asking them not to tell anyone that they were going to Spain. In the evening a man they didn't know came in and looked at them a minute, and then went out again to talk to Serafim. After midnight, when they'd already gone to bed at the inn, the same man came back and told them to follow him and not to talk in loud voices. Then Serafim left them, guaranteeing that everything would be all right and that they needn't worry.

They went along for a long time in the dark till they came to the banks of a river, which they crossed, and when they reached the other side another man met them, took them to a car, and told them to get in. Next morning they came to a town, Vigo, as they found out later. They spent the day there in a courtyard, and at night, again cautiously so that no one should see them, they were taken on board a big sailing vessel called the *Aïda*. They were put in a hold where several Spaniards were already lying hidden, and they weren't allowed to go on deck till anchor was weighed. And when this did take place, they were already yellow from the foul smell of the hiding-place.

The wind swelled the sails for more than a month before they saw land ahead, and Rosalino was nothing but skin and bones because he threw up everything he ate.

At last, when stomach and guts had got to the end of their tether, they reached Boston. It was nighttime. The captain ordered all the *Aïda*'s lights to be put out, and they cast anchor a good way from the town. Then a ship's boat was got ready in which he, with Anacleto and four Spaniards, took their places. The sailors rowed noiselessly so as not to attract attention, and then when they reached a dark point on the shore the master, who'd come with them, looked perplexed and began to mutter to himself: "The devil! This is the place all right, but why isn't there someone there?" He spent some minutes scrutinizing the darkness; then he came back and said, "Wait here, we'll be back again soon." And off he went with the sailors back to the *Aïda* to fetch the other emigrants.

They waited there a long time, not knowing what to do, and then a shaft of light swept over the darkness of the sea and they saw the ship's boat, full of men, breasting the waves. A tug was hurrying toward it, keeping it full in the light. Then they saw three of their comrades jump overboard. Later they heard that one of them was Rosalino, and he'd been drowned because he was a poor swimmer.

They were watching the tug creeping close up to the ship's boat when a dark shape rose up near them, asked if they'd come from the *Aïda*, and told them to follow him.

They were in such a daze that they just followed him. Their savior was a Spaniard. He hid them during the time that the authorities were examining the case of the *Aïda* and of the crew and passengers who'd been taken, and after that he told them to look out for themselves, because he'd been tricked by the ship's captain too.

Yes, in America there was certainly a lot of money, but it stayed in the hands of those who had it!

"Just like Brazil!" said Manuel da Bouça with feeling.

"What?"

"I mean to say there's a lot of money there, but not just anyone can make it," he said, correcting his slip.

And Zé do Aido went on with his tale. He'd spent days and days—just he and Anacleto, because he didn't get on with the others—without work and hungry, and they couldn't make any complaint about it either; otherwise when you were least expecting it you might get put in prison, because over there in America vagabondage just wasn't allowed. Yes, they had come across quite a lot of Portuguese who were earning good dollars, but they had to spend it all because the cost of living was high and they paid out just as much as they made. At last he'd found work too, and had spent some years toiling and moiling away, till sickness overtook him and the consul had to repatriate him because it looked as though his case was quite hopeless, and with all his efforts he hadn't been able to save a ha'penny to get a blind beggar to play.

"But doesn't anyone get rich there?" asked Manuel da Bouça in surprise.

"As for that, yes, but it seems it was in the old days. Anyway, rich folk there are. But then, there are rich folk everywhere. Even here, and not so far away either. What I'd like would be for there not to be any poor."

"That's just it, that's what I say!"

Zé do Aido's bad luck didn't weigh on Manuel da Bouça; he felt better about it than when he's been imagining the other man had made money. Nevertheless, his own defeat chafed him more than ever, not only in face of his friend who simply admitted his setback, but in face of all the other people he knew who welcomed him as a conqueror. For a moment he saw himself with his wallet full, with a lot of jewelry, a lot of money, smiling about his wealth in front of Zé do Aido who had given ear to others and changed his mind about going to Brazil. But, poor as he was, and with the true state of affairs weighing on him heavily, he struggled to keep his end up.

"Well, you see, in Brazil, when a man's got the knack, he can still get on and make a future for himself. I hadn't realized things were so bad in America."

"You made a nice little sum, I suppose? I've heard some whispers about it."

Manuel da Bouça didn't undeceive him.

"Oh, one does one's best, one does the best one can. . . ." he said, looking modest. Then he got up and in the grand manner drew two cigars from his pocket and offered them. "These come from Brazil. When you've smoked one, you just die for more!" He stopped near the door and went back to the story he'd just heard. "So it's all over with Rosalino, poor chap! But what about Anacleto?"

"Oh, he came back a year before me, and he didn't bring a

farthing either. You're the only one who's had any luck. He stayed over here a few months, and then went off to Africa. He's over there somewhere now, but I haven't heard anything of him for some time. . . . We made a big mistake when we didn't go along with you."

"Well, here's the best of luck to you!" said Manuel da Bouça, stretching out his hand. "I'm very sorry about Rosalino. He was an odd character, but he wasn't a bad chap. . . . So, goodbye till next time. And if you want anything, you know, I'm over there at Frágua."

And he went out holding himself straight and stepping along with a firm tread, showing off his new suit and looking important. But as soon as he left the hamlet and turned into the lonely bypath that cut off the bend in the road, he relaxed. You're the only one who's had any luck. . . . He went on a bit farther, but the words still rang in his ears. . . . You're the only one who's had any luck!

Making his way along the track through the pinewood he felt more and more downhearted and depressed. What a hell of a life! If it wasn't in America, then where was the place where the poor could get on and lift up their heads?

When he got home, he found a rosy little round-faced boy who went and clung to Deolinda's skirts at the approach of the stranger. He was four or five lively years old, so that even those walls that breathed neglect seemed to brighten up.

"Hello there!"

"Now then, run along and give a kiss to your granddad," said Deolinda.

"Eh? What's that?"

"It's my son . . . your grandson."

"And you didn't tell me about it!"

"I didn't know how you'd feel."

The boy came nearer and stood on tiptoe to reach Manuel da Bouça's face.

"Well, what's my little man's name?"

"Manuel," answered the lad, "like my granddad."

"Oh, and who told you that?"

"My mom told me."

Manuel da Bouça picked him up and kissed him tenderly. And all through the midday meal with the boy opposite him—he ought to sit at table, you know, to learn how to be a man—his eyes kept wandering over the little rose-white body of his grandson, and he was filled with an emotion he had never felt before.

When he went out again he wanted to take the boy with him, but Deolinda wouldn't let him.

"No, he'd better stay here. He's been sneezing a bit, and perhaps the sun wouldn't do him any good."

Manuel da Bouça had to give way to this maternal precaution, and he set off alone on his walk to Mosteiro, to see it again and satisfy his longing. When he got near his old strips of land, he felt so depressed that he turned away, afraid that someone might see him there and read the truth in his face. The day before, to mask his failure and explain the loss of his precious strips of land, he had put a lie in circulation to the effect that he'd forgotten the arrangement made with Carrazedas and that a letter from his dear Amélia had come too late.

He was sure people had believed it, and now he felt ashamed to be there, only two steps away from the land that had been his, the land he'd lost in a deluded effort to acquire more. It was being well looked after; it was fresh and bright-looking, the cabbage very green and the maize very forward, as though water got there by itself. It was a bitter pill for him to swallow; he turned away, went down to the bank of the Caima, and crossed the bridge.

On the other side he began to look around again, letting his eyes feast on the fields stretching from Cimo de Vila to Gândara, from Gândara to the lower slopes of Felgueira—maize crops as far as the eye could see, and foliage everywhere. And everywhere there were human forms bending down in the eternal ritual of labor; everywhere there were toiling arms stretching down to the soil, and throats singing nostalgic songs.

The afternoon reminded him of another afternoon long ago, that afternoon when he'd deplored the fact that these people didn't rebel against the humble daily round, didn't break the bonds that bound them to their native soil and valiantly set out to conquer wealth in other worlds. It was almost as though they hadn't moved since he'd last seen them all those years ago. There was the same expenditure of strength, the same limited round, the same struggle for daily bread. But he didn't look down on them now, as he had done in the past—all those sweating bodies that cast moving shadows on fields bathed in sunlight. As he felt the shame of his defeat growing deeper and keener, he almost envied them.

He began to weigh the possibilities of taking to his mattock again, looking after his garden, and working outside for someone else. But he couldn't see himself very clearly living the kind of life he'd lived before; going out early to Marques' fields, or someone else's fields, seemed almost impossible, and then work, work, with a drop of wine in the afternoon, and then the walk home at night with his fellow-laborers, talking along the road. He felt something inside him that he couldn't explain even to himself, something that cut him off from the land; something that had made its way into his being while he was over there, turning him into a different man from what he was before he went to Brazil. He didn't feel at home among these native scenes; he seemed to be looking at everything with the eyes of someone who hadn't come to stay, who isn't able to stay, and the hankering after his former life was therefore more intense—that former life that would never come back. . . .

He wandered on as far as Mosteiro, with Esteves' fields always in sight, the land he'd dreamed of buying, and he'd gone away to Brazil to do it—four or five years he'd allowed to make enough money, and then the return with prosperity and wealth. . . . What a delusion it had all been! And who owned them now?

Did they still belong to Esteves? They were as well cared for as his own strips of land, so they certainly belonged to someone who made the most of them; they must yield baskets and barns full of produce. . . .

Even when he had his back turned to them, the fields attracted him like a magnet, and in the cool softness of evening they were the source of bitter disappointment, vexation, and darkness of spirit.

He didn't call on the priest because, as things were, he couldn't put two words together with any ease; nor had he got any money to give for charity or church repairs; so it was better not to set foot there.

He turned homeward feeling that there was no place for him in the village, and he avoided people so that they shouldn't see his face. When he stepped over the threshold of his own house, there was one question he wanted to settle.

"Tell me," he said to his daughter, "that land that belonged to Esteves, is it still his?"

"Oh, no. It isn't his any longer. Why, are you still thinking of buying it?"

"Well, perhaps . . ." And he turned his face away so that his daughter couldn't see it.

"No, it doesn't belong to him any longer. António Pisco bought it."

"What, that chap from Ponte Nova?"

"Yes, that's him."

"But did he manage to get out to Brazil?"

"No, he didn't."

"Well, you remember, he was thinking of going with me."

"Yes, he was thinking about it; but later on, I don't know what happened, he decided to stay here."

"And how did he get the money?"

"A cousin of his who lives in Ul lent him some contos, and then he began trading in livestock. He goes round the fairs buying and selling, and as he's got the gift of the gab he manages to get on. We've had a bone to pick with him because he cheated us over some goats we bought. And he had trouble with a Cambra man, too, the other day, about an old horse."

"And the land?"

"Oh, he made an arrangement with Esteves about that, and paid bit by bit. He seems to be well on his feet now."

"But does he look after it himself?"

"Not he! There's more profit in trade, so he's always moving from place to place. He's got hired men there to look after it."

Night was coming on. Manuel da Bouça let himself drop down onto the bench to turn this news over in his mind. So Pisco too . . . In the dusk of twlight and his own spirit, his grandson was the one ray of light shining through the gloom. He set him on his knees and began to work his legs to imitate the trot of a patient horse. . . . Eh, eh, eh!

"When do you want me to eat?" he said to his daughter a bit later.

"It's ready now; I've only got to put it on the table."

The kitchen looked just the same as in the old days: the same cooking pots, the same plates, odds and ends of furniture, soot, and the water jar—the same hearth. And yet there was the feeling that time had gone by, that loneliness had gained a footing there; there was something empty about it, a sad emptiness that neither he nor his daughter nor his grandson could fill.

About eight o'clock, as on the evening before, friends and neighbors came in again. They talked over a glass of wine, told him about the properties he ought to buy, said he ought to have a woman in the house to look after him because Deolinda had her own affairs to attend to—and when they went away he was sick of telling lies and hiding his real position.

Deolinda had stayed in the kitchen washing the pots and plates, and as soon as she saw he was alone again she came up more shy than usual.

"I'd like to ask you something, Dad."

"Well, what is it?"

"It's—it's—You won't be angry, will you?"

"Why?" She still hesitated, so he went on, "Now then, out with it, what is it?"

"It's Afonso. . . . He'd like to see you. . . . He'd like to come and pay his respects."

Once or twice he'd thought about his son-in-law, but now the idea of meeting him like that without previous preparation took him unawares and made him frown.

"Can he come in, Dad?"

"Of course," he agreed, curtly.

Deolinda went to the kitchen door.

"Come on, come along in!" she shouted into the darkness.

Afonso came in showing proper deference; he was holding his hat awkwardly in his fingers, and looked doubtful of his reception.

"God bless you, sir! Was your journey all right?"

"Yes, thank you." And Manuel da Bouça stoutly held out his hand.

The man he now saw in front of him wiped out the bad impression left by the youth he had known, and warm sympathy welled up in him. His son-in-law bore marks of the passage of time too. He'd lost the old happy-go-lucky look, and now had the appearance and manners of a man with responsibilities. And when the little boy saw his father, he ran up and clung around his legs, laughing and prattling.

"Sit down," said Manuel da Bouça.

"With your permission . . ."

They couldn't find much to say. They were shy and on their best behavior, and the proper talk didn't come easily, but though speech was backward, friendliness was in the air. Manuel da Bouça offered a cigarette, and that eased the situation. Time, however, was getting on, and Afonso got up to go.

"Well, I'd better be getting along now."

"If you'd like to stay we could put a mattress down somewhere. It'd be better than going off at night along those roads."

"That's true, but there's nobody at home, and though we haven't got much . . ."

"Well then, come back tomorrow. You must be missing Deolinda a lot, aren't you?"

"No, no! I'm getting along all right. The boy was the difficulty, but now he's here." Then he turned to his son. "Do you like your granddad?"

"Yes, I like him."

So Afonso went off loaded with recommendations from Deolinda: not to forget to keep an eye on the fowls, because foxes were out on the Macinhata mountains; and not to forget to give the meal swill to the pig; and to watch the water from the dam, so that the maize wouldn't get washed away; and this and that and the other—all the final rush of words of the careful housewife.

When at last his "Good night, wife!" sounded in the distance and Deolinda closed the door, Manuel da Bouça turned to his daughter.

"And how are you getting on with him?"

"We're managing all right."

"And does he treat you well?"

"That he does! There aren't many like him in this parish, I can tell you. A hard worker, fond of his home, and he doesn't spend his time in the wineshop—there aren't many who can boast of that!"

"And what about making a living?" asked Manuel da Bouça, striding from side to side of the kitchen.

"We can't complain, thank God. There are others worse off than us."

"But his bit of land . . ."

"Oh, we're renting more, too. Last year we sold fifty measures of maize and a pipe of wine. This year, if there's no mishap, we'll be able to sell a pipe and a half. And we sell rabbits and poultry at the Nove market, too, when convenient. We work hard, and we can't save anything, that's a fact; but we don't owe

anything to anybody, either! No, we can't complain of our lot—
I hope the devil isn't listening!"

When he heard this, Manuel da Bouça thought about how
he'd opposed the marriage; he remembered his dreams of wealth,
the flight of fancy in which he'd acquired a marriage portion for
his daughter—all as empty as smoke, without substance, a mocking illusion. A sudden pang of anguish took him by the throat
and choked him. . . . After all he, the man who'd cherished a
wider ambition, and gone out after it across God's earth, who'd
ventured all and sacrificed himself, was in the end the most luck-
less, the most miserable of them all!

8

THE decision was so firm and free from any contrary considerations that it seemed as though he'd made his mind up long ago. During the night he'd tried to fight it down; the bolster had made his cheeks burn and the folds of the sheets had been like torturing ropes around him. But it was all useless. He couldn't find anything the matter with it; rather, from all points of view, it had shown itself to be the only real remedy for the evil. So his mind was made up. He would go! That very day he would set off for Lisbon. He would go away before an inadvertent word or gesture revealed his true position. Nobody knew him in Lisbon, and if he starved there, if the truth came to light there, what did it matter? What did it matter when nobody knew who he was, whence he came, nor whither he was going? It was here in his birthplace that he wouldn't be able to live without humiliation, without hearing whisperings behind his back when he went by, without giving up his self-respect. And, more than anything, he hadn't the courage to face friends and acquaintances—those who made much of him, thinking him a man of property—once they knew the truth.

The thought that the bowings and scrapings and good opinions of those who today took him for a rich man would turn to coldness and contempt, that they'd even regret they'd been so deferential when the news of his bad luck in Brazil began to be whispered through the village, spreading like a train of burning gunpowder from the cottage gardens to the pumps and from the wineshops to the church: that thought daunted him more than the poverty itself.

The possibility that Lisbon might bring him days of hunger and bitterness seemed easier to face than having to bear, here in his own village, the vexation of not being rich—here, where it never entered anyone's head that you could come back from Brazil as poor as when you went.

When the shafts of morning light made their way through the chinks in the roof tiles, he had already weighed up all the possibilities of earning a living in town, and—keeping clear of other people from this district settled in Lisbon, because they mustn't know anything about him, so that they couldn't spread talk all round the place—all he had left was self-reliance, hope for some unexpected turn of luck, and the urge for adventure that, years ago, had already propelled him to the other side of the Atlantic. Even so, he preferred to batter himself against the doorless wall of the future; anything was better than exposing his defeat here.

His birthplace didn't grip him any more. The homesickness he'd felt over there, his early life that had seemed so pleasing when he used to think about it in Brazil, seemed to have lost their fascination. He was even surprised that he'd wanted Esteves' fields so persistently; now, if he had the money, he wouldn't use it to buy those fields, he'd spend it on something else, on shaping another sort of life—a way of living that appealed to him, vaguely, under the flashy tinsel of the city.

"Deolinda, will the meal be long?"

"It'll take a bit longer, but if you'd like a bite of something to be going on with—"

"No, it doesn't matter. I'll take a walk up to Santo António, and while I'm away you can get the trunk ready; it's better not to leave everything till the last minute."

"You're still set on going, Dad?"

"Oh, yes."

"You could stay a few more days, couldn't you?"

"What for?"

"To have a rest, and see all your friends. Like this, you haven't had any rest at all."

"Well, well, the village is all right when you're not used to towns. And anyway, in Lisbon I'm not far away, and whenever I feel like it I can come and see you." Buttoning up his jacket, he looked across at her. "Now, don't cry, girl! Lisbon isn't Brazil!"

"I thought you'd come back to live with us, Dad."

"Perhaps someday . . . who knows?"

He put his hat on, stroked his grandson's cheeks, and went out, his heart softening at the thought that he was at last going to see Amélia's grave, and blaming himself because he hadn't been before.

He walked slowly along the rough road that wound up and down, up and down, from Frágua to Santo António. He felt sad, almost as sad as that day he'd set out for Brazil—how many years ago.

Two Australian mimosa trees stood in front of the cemetery, casting deep shadows. He couldn't remember them. They weren't there when he left. And inside, there were cypresses too that he couldn't remember having seen before, and some new graves.

A different feeling came over him now. He stretched his arm out with reverence, and something like apprehension, as though he'd come to steal, and pushed the barred gate open.

There was no one inside. White roses, whiter than anywhere else, myrtle, rosemary, cypresses; and he remembered an All Souls' Day with candle wax dripping and spreading on the soil and seizing it in a cuttlefish shape. At the far end were half-a-dozen burial vaults, closed with gratings through which one could see niches, and a lamp burning in one of them.

Which was her grave?

He went round the box hedge, to the left, remembering Deolinda's instructions: It's the one with a black cross and white lettering, near the tallest cypress.

He found it easily in the humble section of poor plain graves. His Amélia's was the most recent. Within sight, there was no other grave on which the grass was so thin as on the one surmounted by the black cross with rough white lettering.

He knelt down, joined his hands, and prayed. He prayed for a long time, but at last his mind wandered from the words his lips were murmuring and was entirely given up in longing to the image and memory of the dead woman. His grief grew deeper. He lost himself in the past. The thought of his youth came back as clear and insistent as though it had been lived but yesterday. Nights of desire and pursuit of adventure when he'd gone forth, stick in hand, after some skirt—ready to contend with anything that wasn't a ghost from the other world. A carefree time with no thought of trouble, a time when the least rebuff drew him miles and miles. Then he'd begun to talk to Amélia, and they'd taken to each other wonderfully, because she was a nice serious girl, and even the priest had heard all about her good points.

He knew other young men were hanging round her, some of them with means, but she wouldn't listen to any of them; and he couldn't contain himself for joy, because it proved she liked him for himself. The day the banns were called he'd been drunk without having taken a single glass.

And they'd thought of nothing but their future life together—we've got to get our linen together, our barn, our salting room, you'll see! And when finally they had got married, they'd felt such thankful satisfaction each time they brought some new chattel home. So happy he'd been! . . . My dear wife, my dear wife, and I'll never see you again!

Then came the birth of Deolinda, and that had been another great joy for both of them. They hadn't talked about it much, but neither of them thought of anything but the child. If she stirred in the cradle at night, as soon as ear caught the sound, the child didn't go unheeded, because Amélia was all attention. And the days when he'd gone out to work for other people had seemed as though they'd never end, because his one thought was to get home again and be happy with the child. . . . Oh, happy times! There had been worries, because everybody has worries, but the big trouble had come along only when he got it into his head to go to Brazil. . . . And what remained of it all now but a tumble-down little house he hadn't the heart to live in, and a patch of ground, with the spot where his Amélia was buried, his dear Amélia whom he'd never see again!

Slow and warm the tears rolled down his face and fell on the grave, and the soil drank them up. And he stood up with one last wish in his heart: to buy the grave so as not to lose his Amélia's remains, so that nobody else could be buried there. But a painful thought made him take out his wallet, and count the notes it still contained. He counted them over once, twice, three times. . . . Then he stopped to calculate, and then again he went back to counting, separating the notes and setting them aside for strictly essential needs. No, he couldn't make it do. In the past, a grave used to cost ten milréis; now it must cost about two hundred. He couldn't make it do.

And with the wallet still open in his trembling hands, he looked at the grave and murmured: "Amélia, I worked so many years, so many years, and I haven't been able to get enough money to buy your grave, not even by robbing a dead man!"

After the despair he'd felt at the cemetery, Manuel da Bouça couldn't bring himself to spend the bit of money left over on hiring a car to take him back to town, as he had intended. To waste money after giving up the patch of earth where Amélia lay

seemed sacrilege, an action that could be followed only by remorse.

So in the evening, just as he had done nine years ago, sad at
heart he slowly went up the hill from Frágua to Salgueiros, walking behind old Rosa, the odd-job woman who was carrying his
luggage.

He had kept the news of his departure from neighbors and
friends, so as to avoid gossip and explanations—because when a
man's straightforward at bottom he doesn't like calling black
white, and he's always afraid that a friend will stamp the truth
on his face.

And just as he had nine years ago, he forbade Deolinda to go
with him to the highway, because he didn't want any tears and
he didn't want to attract the attention of the people who were
working near the road. . . . If they got to know everything once
he was in Lisbon—because these folks have got a setter's scent
for nosing out other people's lives—it would upset him; yes, it
would upset him, but he'd have to put up with it. But while he
was still here, oh, no! Deolinda would be the first to suspect
something, because a man with money would never give as little
as he'd given to his grandson to buy lollipops—but no harm could
come from her. Whereas the others . . .

At Salgueiros he wanted to avoid attracting the attention of
people at Taveres' shop, and he asked old Rosa to walk toward
Pontão. But she was surprised at such a strange request. She said
the bus would stop in that place only if there were a few people
on it and plenty of seats, whereas it had to stop at Tavares' shop
to take the mail, even if it were full.

"Well, it doesn't matter."

So they came to a halt just outside the village, and he stood
looking back at his poor little house there in the distance, the
fertile land he'd dreamed of buying, the place where he'd been
born, which was losing him now . . . for ever. No bond remained, because the man who had gone away had got used to
another environment, and the fertile plots of land roused no real

love in the heart of the man who'd come back. He wouldn't feel homesick now; if he could take away his grandson's prattle in his mind, and ensure perpetual possession of Amélia's grave, then going away wouldn't trouble him—even though it were for the last time.

From that spot he could see Nunes' mansion, too; it was visible from all over the parish, visible from all round. He took a stealthy look at it, so that old Rosa wouldn't notice. Then he saw someone he knew coming up the road. It was Lopes of Sandiãis, and he'd already caught sight of him and was smiling some way away. . . . The devil take him! Now he couldn't avoid a talk, and he was on the point of letting himself be led off to Tavares' shop so as not to arouse any suspicion by a refusal, when he heard the rumble of the bus. He breathed freely again. The bus stopped and he climbed up— Goodbye, Senhor Lopes, I'll be seeing you again one of these days!—and handed down a few coins to old Rosa, with his heart darker than night itself. But he wasn't carrying inside him that anxiety to come back, as he had nine years ago, when he set out for Brazil. All he wanted now was to hide his wretchedness in Lisbon. His only wish was for people to forget him, for ever, and never think about him again.

The bus passed in front of Nunes' mansion, and the road was full of the heavy scent of Nunes' roses; then it stopped near Tavares' door to take in the mailbag, and he had to put a different face on and call out that perhaps he'd be back soon; he was going to spend a few days in Lisbon, and then he'd either settle down there, or come back, according to what he decided.

The bus set off again, and he was free of the necessity to tell lies. He let his eyes wander over the parish in a last farewell, and he felt a strong impulse to cry—to cry for his wasted life, the past that would never come back, the illusions he had shed one after the other all along the difficult road. He was keenly aware of the irrevocable, of time lost, the years that had drained him, aging him while he'd been running after a will-o'-the-wisp. He stifled the sobs in his throat so that no one would notice, so that no one would know.

The bus hurried on, carrying him to where he'd be forgotten, carrying him away from his life as a tiller of the soil, to hand him over, crushed and unprotected, to another life that still lay hidden.

Everything went by rapidly: houses, trees and roads, everything blurred, effaced, in the mildness of the country evening. Only Nunes' big house stood out, haughty, blatant, arrogant— Nunes who had grown rich without going to any of the Americas, who had grown rich battening on those who sold their all to go and who had to stay over there, delivered up to the accidents of fate, or who had come back poor, disillusioned, and worn out, like Manuel da Bouça!

PUBLISHER'S NOTE ON THE AUTHOR

Ferreira de Castro was born in a rural, parochial section of north-ern Portugal on May 24, 1898, into a life of privation and adventure worthy of a fictional hero. His family was impover-ished, his schooling negligible; but at the age of twelve his unrequited passion for a girl of sixteen provoked him into an act of courage meant to establish his manhood: leaving his small village, he set out alone for Brazil to try his fortunes, as many of his countrymen had already done. He crossed the Atlantic in a miserable ship, and on landing in Pará, was at once sent into the heart of the Amazon jungle and set to work in the supply office of the rubber-plantation workers. His chief concern at the time was to earn a bare living. But the jungle life became an anguished and obsessive experience, and from it, years later, grew some of his greatest novels.

Ferreira de Castro's first novel was not great, but he wrote it when he was fourteen. His ambitions were beginning to take exciting forms. By the time he escaped from the jungle into Pará, staving off starvation by whatever means he could, he believed he had a mission to fulfill. And just as he was turning eighteen his dream came true: he had begun writing for the small local papers, and his first novel was published.

He had come by this time to take an intense interest in the great problems of humanity, whose general condition he per-ceived from the misery and poverty of his own. It was partly this vision of universal suffering that led him to return to Portugal after the First World War, and to begin a new career in Lisbon as a journalist and novelist. But in Lisbon he was unknown, and though he placed occasional articles and short stories with news-papers and magazines, he spent much of his time in the street and out of work—as it were in ferment, reading voraciously and indiscriminately—while he sought means to keep from starving.

In those years he succeeded in publishing several short stories and two novels, but it was not until 1928 that *Emigrantes* appeared—according to Jaime Brasil, in *Books Abroad*, "chronologically the first literary work with a social and human significance to appear in the Portuguese language." This novel, and another, *A Selva*, published in 1930 when Ferreira de Castro was thirty-two years old, and translated into nearly every principal language, made him famous first in Portugal, where their success was enormous, and eventually throughout the world.

After that he was to be reckoned as among the greatest writers of the epoch, and with each new work his reputation steadily mounted. His struggle has always been against the universal injustices in man's social condition, but unlike most of his literary compatriots, he has never assumed the facile posture of a propagandist. All his work shows the extraordinary power of imagination and psychological penetration, the independence and pure poetical fervor of a great literary master.

Though since his early success Ferreira de Castro has traveled a great deal, he has also written prodigiously, and now, according to Mr. Brasil, "he is at the height of his creative power—Writing in a language which lacked literary prestige beyond the frontiers of his own country, he has succeeded in making the literature of Portugal internationally known, discussed, and admired."

Of *Emigrants*, the author has written:

"The problem of emigration is not a problem of itself, but the consequence of one much greater and more profound. It would be a mistake to attribute to Brazil, which is one of the most generous countries in the world, or to some other American countries, the specific responsibilities for the disasters that befall the emigrants by virtue of their ambitions. In truth, most of the emigrants are not prepared for the struggles they will encounter, and are among the poor and ignorant which Europe transports daily. No, the real problem is different, it is universal. These men embark on their adventures because they are hungry and because they are convinced that, in this world, only those who have money have the means and the right to enjoy life.

"In some cases, they are duped by their own countrymen, who exploit them for profit, and persuade them, in their naïveté, that even such as they are—primitive, ill-bred, ignorant—they will find, in some distant country of the planet, fabulous riches."